2025 ANTHOLOGY

Editors & Staff

Independently published by *Driftwood Press*
in the United States of America.

Fonts: Sifonn, Josefin Sans, Agency FB, Bembo MT Pro, & Merriweather

Published in March 25th, 2025
ISBN-13: 978-1-949065-36-7
Please visit our website at www.driftwoodpress.com
or email us at editor@driftwoodpress.net.

Table of Contents

OF COURSE, OBVIOUSLY, OVERWHELMINGLY

Charlie Watts

SATURDAY NIGHT

The boys, Jimmy and Lou and Speed and Duncan, are up in the barn, in the empty hay loft, smoking weed and drinking the same bottle of skank wine they'd hidden there last Saturday. They are talking about boobs and butts and seeing how it feels to flex their tiny boy muscles. They are trying to figure out what they like and why God made everything so complicated. They all talk at once, but none of them name that scratchy kernel at the back of their throats because, of course, obviously, overwhelmingly, it is different for each of them. Duncan will not tell about what he'd seen his uncle doing, last month, down near the pump house. Lou thinks if he asks about what that feeling is he gets when he climbs the knotted rope in gym class, the others will beat him. Speed wants to know if the other mothers sit the way his does on the couch, watching TV while the house boils around her with animals and babies. And then Jimmy. He's the only one who knows for sure he's going to die. Soon. He might tell them. Leukemia, boys, straight up deadly. Or he might save it, present it to them at the last minute like a birthday cake coming around the corner from the kitchen, his mother holding the platter and singing the song even though she is crying, and his cousin screaming about the sparklers spraying cinders on the cat.

The girls, girls not connected to those boys except for Cindy, who is Jimmy's cousin and who thinks Jimmy's a jerk because of the way he talks over the teacher during health class, are in the Rec. Room at the library. Mr. Desant, the interim librarian who does not have a Library Sciences degree but who has passed all the CORI checks, has offered to keep the building open on Saturday nights, mostly because that's when he does his downloading. Cindy is the one who invited the others—Lisa, also a cousin, Davone, and Nosh—to join her so they can practice their monologues for Debate Team. And, of course, they are not doing that. They are talking about the troubling case of Bettina and what is the right thing to say about the fact that she truly and fully smells like a just-emptied pickle jar. Perhaps it's the family's choice of laundry soaps? Perhaps it's a medical condition? Nosh has read about one that involves the degradation of sensitive areas of the body. *You know, Cindy, bathing suit areas*, Lisa explains. Davone does not trust Mr. Desant, so she stays near the door, biting the go-to spot on the inside of her cheek. Lisa thinks they should, in fact, involve an adult. But not her mother because—as these girls have experienced first-hand—Lisa's Mom would tell them to stop being crazy bitches and get on with their schoolwork. *It all seems so avoidable*, Cindy offers. Then she thinks to herself, I really am more mature than these other girls. Nosh points out that Bettina never joins any club, never contributes to pre-game bake sales, never speaks in class, and never lends her conditioner after P.E. So, basically, fudge her. Davone jumps when Mr. Desant opens the door and says, *girls, what's up? How are those speeches coming?* He smooths his Stars & Stripes tie between two fingers and Cindy bursts out laughing. She says, *Mr. Desant, did you know there was once a flood that washed away this whole town?* Lisa goes to the chalkboard and draws a huge, yellow heart. Mr. Desant leaves.

The men, Rudy, Mac, Clem, and Duane, sit in Clem's pick-up at the far edge of the hay field, out of reach of the headlights on the highway. Rudy and Mac are in the back, petting their rifles the way you would an impatient cat sitting on your lap. Clem, in the driver's seat next to his brother, Duane, is Jimmy's stepfather and he, obviously, is not talking about the leukemia. Clem grips the spotlight handle, knowing that if any kind of deer comes up out of the woods, all he'd have to do is flip the switch and that would be that. It's not hunting season but all of them except Mac have empty freezers and being hungry isn't a great hobby. Duane goes to pull out a cigarette, but Clem swats the pack out of his hand and says, *are you serious*? Rudy stands, handing his rifle to Mac, then jumps out of the truck bed and moves toward the tree line. *Christ*, Clem says, *do you seriously want to be out here all fuckin night long?* Mac laughs but Clem is serious. He punches the dashboard, just above the radio. Rudy shrugs, turns, then takes a piss. *The thing is*, Duane begins, *Linda says she's giving it another month, two max, and then if she don't like what she sees, she's goin'*. Clem squeezes harder on the spotlight handle. *Well, make it right*, he says, knowing that for sure this won't happen and then Linda, Duane's sassy-ass wife, is going to dump him and everyone will be sad. Mac grinds the back of his head slowly against the truck cab. He's been in love with Linda since 10th grade. Rudy takes his rifle back and sits down in the grass, wedging in against the rear tire. *That's not a great angle*, Clem says. Rudy raises the rifle and puts his eyeball against the scope and says, *whatever*, just as the buck breaks into the open and Clem zaps him with the spotlight. The animal stands his ground, glass-eyed. The veins across his chest stand up as thick as licorice whips. The men stop breathing, each in their own way working through the slaughter-math. Rudy pulls the trigger and there's a huge pothole of sound and smoke and absolutely no deer on the ground.

The women, Ginny, who is Mac's girlfriend, and Catherine, who is LeeAnne's co-worker and has only one eye, are standing in LeeAnne's back yard. They're waiting for Bobbi, LeeAnne's sister, who was supposed to be there at 6:30. But now it's almost 8:00 and they've already finished all the Diet Pepsi. *Shit*, LeeAnne says, we're going to start without her because she wants the whole thing over and done with before Clem gets home from his late shift at The Home Depot. He says they fine you a quarter if you don't say The. The women go out into the yard where LeeAnne has made a pile of all her mother's mu-mus and sweaters and brightly colored pajama pants. *It looks like a Christmas tree*, Ginny says. LeeAnne hasn't smiled in a long time and it feels strange. Catherine is still not sure this is legal. She's been scrolling on her phone through the town website. *Never mind with that,* LeeAnne says, taking up the gas can. *Do a circle around! Make stripes! Throw in the can!* The women have ideas. *Shut the fuck up*, LeeAnne says, just as Bobbi arrives, tick-tocking into the yard like she's on a catwalk. *Woman, where the hell have you been?,* LeeAnne asks, tossing the empty can toward the swing set and fishing in her jeans pocket for matches. *Car crapped out. Had to hitch*, Bobbi says, taking hugs from Ginny and Catherine who, honestly, do not know why they are there but are stoked to be part of something. LeeAnne glares at her sister. *Light that fucker up*, Bobbi tells her and they all whoop and shriek as LeeAnne strikes the match and fires it toward the pile. At first, it's a disappointing flicker in the dim light, much like their mother. Just not that interested in itself. Then, bam, it's all on fire, a huge cone of crazy colored polyester vapors that warms their faces. Catherine and Ginny jump away but LeeAnne and Bobbi hold hands, super-tight, staring at the fire and, overwhelmingly, LeeAnne wishes her mother could feel every lick of those flames instead of already being dead, laid out in her Special Size coffin at the funeral parlor with turquoise eye shadow as thick as window putty.

MONDAY MORNING

Duane wakes up with his hands pinned under his butt. He can smell jalapeño dip on his mustache. The ceiling stain where the hip roof is leaking has gotten bigger. Now it looks like a bobcat in flight. Linda asks if he has anything to say. She's facing the wall. Duane can tell from the flickers that she's looking at her phone. He feels light-headed and clenches his muscles. *Anything you want to offer?* What she's asked him, what she wants, is for him to have integration between his aspirations and his actions. Worse, she needs him to have words for all this that he can say with confidence instead of just cramping up and hammering his fists against his own belly. *You never liked this house, did you?*, he asks, and of course he knows that she knows this is a dodge. *I don't care about this house one way or the other*, she says, sitting up now and fluffing out her hair with her fingertips. It is such a beautiful thing—her arms, her elbows, the side of her breast, the little round bone on her wrist—that Duane wants to cry. But that, too, is heading in the wrong direction even though Duane sees his suffering as the best thing he can offer. *I told Clem*, he says, now sitting upright and pinching his nose. *You don't think your brother has enough on his plate? Jesus, Duane, you are not this stupid.* He presses his teeth together as she gets up and walks around the end of the bed in her briefs. *Clem told me to make it right*, he says, but she continues into the bathroom without reply. Duane decides in this exact moment that he's going to quit his job at the refinery, get the band back together, and really and truly make a go at it. Cut a demo. Play out wherever they can. Run hard and fast and make just enough noise to quiet the goddamn devil banging around in his head telling him that there is no possible way for him to be worthy of the space he consumes in the world. He punches his thighs, quietly. It's going to be a big week.

Jimmy gets up early and goes into the bathroom so he can look in the mirror. He thinks that the harder he stares at himself, the more impossible it will be to die. On this day he decides to shave off his hair because they had said, well, radiation. Clem, who plays the role of his father but who is not the original one who got his mother pregnant, keeps his hair cue-ball short, so what's the big deal? Jimmy finds the trimmer in the drawer and sets it up with the zero blade. He'd watched his mom do it to him when everyone got lice in middle school. All the boys pretended it was just a cool pre-summer haircut. The machine is heavier than he'd imagined, and the blade shoe feels cold on his temple. He hears his mother yell for him, telling him to let the dog out, but he digs in, watching his blond hair fall away from his scalp and drop into the sink, light and disorganized. The first pass looks like an accident, like when the dog, Dipsie, swallowed Clem's electric tester and they had to do surgery. Jimmy stops when he's got his hair half off. Pretty good. Only a few strays and one hot spot. Now he hears Clem coming up the stairs, calling for him, swearing at the dog. He plunges quickly in on the other side. Without the distraction of hair, he can see the blank moon-shape of his face and he thinks, wow, what is the point of me? He switches the razor off and stands back, making a quarter-turn just as Clem slaps the bathroom door and it comes open enough for Dipsie to squirm in and see what smells like but definitely does not look like her boy Jimmy. She starts whimpering, wheezing, and then Clem, obviously, says, *oh my Christ*, and calls for LeeAnne while he kicks the dog back out of the room and goes to Jimmy, taking the razor out of his hand as if it was a loaded pistol, his mouth open but no words happening until LeeAnne steps into the small, humid space and starts laugh-crying, saying, *what the fuck, Jimmy. You jumped the gun. They never said it was definitely going to fall out.*

LeeAnne, who is still not awake, really, even after the zap of Jimmy butching off his hair, gets in her car and prays the battery isn't dead again. She turns the key and the motor responds. For once. *It's a Nova*, Clem keeps saying. *Do you know what that means in Spanish?* Clem has been taking Jimmy to school in his truck ever since the cancer. Jimmy says they listen to country music and Clem makes fart jokes. Jesus, LeeAnne thinks, what would it be like to have a mind that's satisfied by such simple things? Because, overwhelmingly, her mind is Vitamixing everything about her mother's funeral—not counting her Mom's weird cousin who is literally a trapeze artist and has six kids that he brings to every event, they probably won't even fill the first two pews—to the zit she's got on her thigh to the fuck-wad at the bank who said he would approve the re-fi on their house if she would show him some *special consideration*. Jesus, if she'd only recorded it. Then there's the thing on the news about some part of the planet melting into the sea and ruining everything and the fact, the apparently irreversible fact, that the one good and true thing in her life, the most complex and most miraculous, the thing she made, her baby boy, has been handed the shortest fucking stick of all. She gets to the hospital, parks nose out so it's not so hard to get a jump, and goes to Level B-2, Medical Records, where she works. One-eyed Catherine has made her a K-cup of hot chocolate and already fired up the computers. Catherine, LeeAnne thinks, is one of those women who was beamed in from the 50s. She wears dresses and presses her hands between her thighs when she's happy. LeeAnne loathes her and depends completely on her to pull them through the brain-poppingly boring job of turning paper records into well-behaved computer files. Several times a day, a doctor or a patient has a full melt-down in the earbud of her headset and she would very, very much like to tell them—as a helpful point of contrast—about the many-layered cake of misery that represents her life.

Cindy smacks her alarm, drops her feet to the floor, and sees the tube-top she doesn't want to wear to school. She doesn't like the mono-boob look, but it was the one request Davone made at the library: that they all wear the same thing so that no single one of them would be *vulnerable* at the assembly. Lisa had explained what vulnerability meant. Cindy wonders why people always think she doesn't understand. Walking to school, she crosses 3rd Street and sees a glimpse of herself in the still-dark Rexall Drug Store windows, her face and hair overlayed in the reflection onto a sexy zombie nurse Halloween costume. Because her mother Bobbi is a nurse, Cindy herself does not want to be one. Everything about it sounds mean. At 2nd Street she comes to the corner with four churches. The Lutheran cathedral, where she's standing, is her favorite. Even though she doesn't go to any church, now, Cindy wants to be a minister. She sees it as putting on a kick-ass play. Every week! With people singing and costumes and speeches and then, at the end, she'd get to stand on the front steps and the people coming out of the building would shake her hand. Touch her shoulder. She's not worried about the God part, because she knows nobody knows. For her, God is like when you tie a floating birthday balloon to the back of your bike and go for a ride down by the river. You can't watch it, but you know it's right there with you. Blowing around. Seeing everything. At 1st Street she goes left toward her school. A big red pick-up lumbers by and she knows it's her cousin. Rude Jimmy. She watches as the truck pulls into the school and Jimmy drops out of the cab. Only he doesn't have any hair. His head is as white as a hardboiled egg and he's holding his books at his side in a weirdly gentle way. The pick-up roars away but Jimmy stands still on the sidewalk and raises his hand to acknowledge her, which is not something he would do, Cindy thinks, and it is of course, at that exact moment, that they both know something is fully and completely broken.

THURSDAY EVENING

Cindy does not like Thursdays, even though it's close to the weekend when she can be the way she wants to be and make plans. The normal problems with Thursdays include Lisa's mom Linda being the one who picks them up from Debate Team. Linda likes to ask them intrusive questions about their periods and drugs. She says the word bitch a lot, as if that would make them happy. Maybe it does. The other ding on Thursday is that her dad has a late shift, so Cindy gets dropped at the hospital with her mom. She has to stay in the cafeteria until nine. Her mom's friends come by and drop off free puddings and packages of graham crackers, both of which make her feel bloated. This particular Thursday is extra-dark because now everyone knows about Jimmy's leukemia, and they are talking about it like it's a thing he went and did. Linda says, *you must be so worried, Cindy-girl, is there anything I can do?* They are looking at each other in the rearview mirror. Linda's eyelashes are so long that strands of her real hair keep getting caught in them and she has to blink to free them up. Obviously, Cindy does not know how she feels about her cousin being scheduled to die. Everyone is going to die. But she can't say that. On Monday, outside school, Jimmy had said, *hey, I have cancer.* She didn't say anything then, either, but she did put her hand on his shoulder and use him as a crutch while they walked up the school steps. He felt softer than she'd always imagined. At the hospital, the nurses use tougher words, like *sucks* and *blows* and *fuckin' tragedy*. Her mom gets hung up with patients until 10:30 and then storms into the cafeteria with all her bags and a huge container of ice coffee. She sits down next to Cindy. There's a spot of blood on the sleeve of her scrubs. It looks like a red beetle.

LeeAnne hates bills, especially the reds and purples of *overdue*. She has them fanned out on the kitchen table, trying to measure the depth of the hole they are in. Clem has brought her a beer, and even a Drinks On Me coaster, but he's not going to engage. They've got his $849/week from *The* Home Depot and her $754/week from the hospital, and it sounds like a lot, but without her mother's $2,138/month in Social Security, they've cratered from comfortable saving-for-a-pontoon-boat to "are we going to have to Airbnb the garage?" Plus, LeeAnne realizes as she sucks on her beer and looks into the living room where Jimmy has his hands laced over the top of his new-bald head, watching a baseball game with Clem who is explaining about how they wash AstroTurf, that there will be the bills for her mother's funeral and then, *hopefully,* the tidal wave of Jimmy's medical bills. Now she is crying because it's not even clear they will get a chance to bankrupt themselves on keeping Jimmy alive. The doctors haven't said. They don't know. Nobody knows. LeeAnne wants to know. She wants a lot of things she can't have. Her mother used to give her the Jesus-has-a-plan speech, peppered overwhelmingly with recriminations about how if she, LeeAnne, had only done this or that along the way, had only made a few different choices, had only hung out at different, better bars, that plan would have been a damn sight sweeter, *you hear what I'm sayin?* LeeAnne realizes she's panting, her heart pounding from the conjuring of her mother. Dead-eyed, gum-snapping Eileen. LeeAnne wants to let her go, back-fill the past with a fairy tale about small town living and simple virtues. Jump into gratitude journaling and guided meditation. But, honestly, without her mother to push against, she's just not that motivated. Clem comes in for another beer and says, *you got it figured* and she says, *fuck no*, but she reaches out for his thick hand anyway because at least Clem is a steady thing and she likes the feel of his whiskers on her neck.

Jimmy does not like walking the dog with his mother, but the baseball game is over and Dipsie is sitting by the door, already yipping. He hooks her with the leash while his mom waits on the sidewalk. She lights a cigarette. They walk. Jimmy waits for the questions, assuming they'll be about school, but she doesn't say anything. At the first corner he looks over and sees tears on her cheeks even though she's trying to hide it with the cigarette. *Mom?* Then she laughs and tells about how her friend at work, Catherine, finally dropped the f-bomb on one of the doctors. *It's okay, Mom*, Jimmy says, because, really, he doesn't feel that scared and the only thing that's going on in his body is that when he takes a deep breath, it feels like he's missing a step on the stairs. Dipsie stops to leave a steamer under someone's rhododendron. They walk on. Now LeeAnne asks about Christmas, which is not a thing LeeAnne does, but she wants to know if there's anything special he wants. She bites her lip and fires the cigarette butt into the middle of the street. Jimmy watches the comet-trail of sparks and says that it would be awfully great to have a bigger mini-bike. Like a 120cc instead of the 90 he's got. *Oh-but*, she says, thinking, of course, of the fact that he won't be able to ride it until spring when who knows whether he'll even be able to drink a smoothie, never mind rip it up at the quarry with Lou and Speed and Duncan. Jimmy remembers that his grandmother's funeral is in two days and his cheeks turn red. Dipsie pulls harder on the leash, knowing they've turned the third corner and next comes home. His mother is staring ahead, hard, like she's trying to see through the dusk into a different day. *Mom?* LeeAnne says, *that's good dear, we'll do that.* Jimmy claws his brain for more words but comes up only with the thought that tonight, instead of aiming at the chickens in Mrs. Parker's back yard with his BB gun from his bedroom window, it might be a good idea to write something down for his mom to read. After.

Duane hates practicing his solos in the garage. It's so high school and he is fully thirty-nine-years-old, married sixteen years, a father. He adjusts his butt on the shop stool and begins his progressions without the amp turned on. He can hear his knuckles snapping. It's bad. Sloppy. His fingertips are soft, missing their marks. But he keeps going, closing his eyes and overwriting his own sound with the music in his head. The door to the house opens and there stands Lisa. *Oh,* she says. *No worries. You need a soda?*, Duane asks, smiling. *Yeah*, she says, but there's something more. She gets her soda and sits on the old couch that smells like motor oil and wet dog. Duane is working out a riff, building off an old standard, staying with the blues scales for now and sucking his lip in over his bottom teeth as he looks at his leggy daughter sitting side-saddle on the couch and picking at her toes. He can imagine her off the rails at twenty, lonely at a big party. Or large-and-in-charge at forty, single mom, setting aside money, taking her own daughter to concerts. *What?*, Lisa asks, now looking up into his stare. *Sorry, I was just*, Duane says. He looks back down, working his fingers over the strings, trying to remember it all. The one big show they played was up at the college. They were called DogFace and Linda was their trombone player. She wore tight black pants and six-inch heels and was the best of all of them. *Have you talked to Jimmy?*, he asks, trying not to sound like he's singing. *At school. He said he doesn't feel crappy. He shaved his head*, Lisa says, taking a guzzle from her Pepsi. *Shit*, Duane says. *Dad? Is everything okay?* Duane nods at her and says, *what do you mean*, but, obviously, he knows exactly what she means and it's at that moment that his fingers remember how to do this, how to get to where they need to be even before he asks them to go there. *I just*, Lisa says, standing. *Yeah*, Duane says, nodding. *It sounds good, Dad. I like that one.* And then she leaves the garage and Duane takes a huge breath and flicks on the amp.

SATURDAY AFTERNOON

LeeAnne is fanning herself with the program even though she's freezing. Minister Shelly is doing the review of her mother's life, trying to make it sound like there were things other than her death that were graceful. Her sister Bobbi, sitting to her left, keeps blowing her nose. There's a song. There's a prayer. There's a guy no one knows who tells an awkward story without an ending about going to a drive-in movie with Eileen. No one mentions their dad in any way. Finally, Jimmy goes up to read the poem that LeeAnne has asked him to read, the Irish blessing. Overwhelmingly, when she sees her doomed boy standing there in his too-long suit, his bald head looking blue in the altar lights, her body goes to steel. Bobbi's whispering, *take a breath*, and Jimmy is reading badly, and Clem is humming, a clown-level smile on his basic, good-guy face. Someone puts a hand on her shoulder, the back of her neck really, and she turns, missing the end of Jimmy's reading. It's her brother-in-law Duane handing her a hard candy. His soon-to-be-ex-wife, Linda, is smirking. LeeAnne turns back forward and watches Jimmy return to the pew, head down, arms swinging ape-style. He's wearing sneakers because they forgot to get good shoes. Bobbi is now fully crying. There's another song, so they have to stand and getting up feels to LeeAnne like she's lifting a house. But once she's up, knees locked, hymnal racked against her gut, she begins casting the spell that will forever bind her dead mother in a perpetual flaming bardo of having to watch, having to float around in the whatever and witness every single fucking intractable thread of trauma she had put into motion. Eyes open, Eileen, this is your life. Over and over and over. And when the song ends and it's quiet and everyone can hear LeeAnne laughing, she realizes that Clem and Jimmy have switched and it's Jimmy holding her hand now, patting it because what else is he going to do.

Duane is having another iced tea even though he's not thirsty. Linda has already left the reception, telling him that LeeAnne was giving her the evil eye and when he said, *maybe she's just sad about her mom dying and her kid having cancer*, Linda flashed her atomic melt-down face, took his keys, and said, *find your own fucking ride home.* Clem comes over with a beer and says, *we gonna get a deer tonight?* And the thing is, Duane doesn't even want that. He just feels tired. So tired it's like he's stoned. Clem moves on without getting an answer. Duane sees LeeAnne sitting alone at one of the round tables, eating a piece of sheet cake with her fingers. He goes over with his tea and beer and asks if he can sit with her. When she laughs, bits of the cake spray across the white tablecloth. *Jesus*, she says. He sits down. *Jimmy did good*, he says. *He did*, LeeAnne says, finishing with the cake and wiping her whole face with a paper napkin. She leans back in the folding chair and crosses both her legs and arms. Duane thinks they are both looking across the room at his daughter, Lisa, who appears to be arranging the younger kids into a game configuration. *There's trouble*, Duane says. LeeAnne says, *what,* and Duane realizes she's not looking at the same thing. She's not looking at anything. *I mean*, she says, sitting forward and setting her head down on the table, *where is it written that we have to like our parents? Honor and obey. Check. But that's different*. Duane is so startled by all this that he puts his hand on the middle of her back and of course he says, *Linda hates me*. LeeAnne replies, *everybody knows that, Duane, and it's okay.* Then she turns her head the other way. He leaves his hand on her back because it feels real and important. He drinks his beer. Jimmy has joined the game Lisa organized. It looks like Simon Says, but the little kids don't understand what they're supposed to do. Mostly, they're just flopping around on the floor, taking turns touching Jimmy's bald head.

Cindy is standing with Nosh and Davone, reassuring them about their dresses even though, really, she couldn't care less. What she's focused on, obviously, is Minister Shelly and the magic of how she moves around the room in her robe. As easy as a bag caught in the wind. She does two-handed handshakes, Cindy observes, always the quick catch and release. *We're getting a puppy today*, Nosh reports, causing an eruption of excitement from Davone that allows Cindy to bolt—*cool, cool, so cool, be right back*. She has spotted something that Minister Shelly has missed: her aunt LeeAnne has her head down—her whole head down—on a table in the corner and the only one with her is Uncle Duane. He's a sad sack, not qualified for this, Cindy thinks. Striding toward the table, she ignores her own mother who wants her to help change out the chicken cacciatore pans. That is a good question, Cindy notes: why isn't her mother, who also lost her mom, as upset as Aunt LeeAnne? Maybe it's a nurse thing. Cindy arrives at the table and scoots a chair up next to her aunt. Uncle Duane acknowledges her by taking his hairy hand off Aunt LeeAnne's back. Gross, Cindy thinks. *Tell me about it, Aunt LeeAnne*, Cindy says. She focuses in on her black patent leather shoes to keep her head from spinning. *What? Oh, hello, honey*, LeeAnne says, now sitting upright. *I'm sorry about Grammie Eileen. I didn't*—but LeeAnne cuts her off. *Child, don't you worry. No one knew Grammie Eileen. Not even me and your mother.* Uncle Duane stands up. *You ladies want anything to drink?* He scoops together the empty glasses and bottles on the table and presses them against his shirt. *Not me*, LeeAnne says. Cindy says, *thank you, Uncle Duane. Can you get me a coffee? Two sugars?* And with this, LeeAnne starts laughing, hard, then crying. She tucks her face in against Cindy's fresh-clean neck. To Cindy, it feels like standing in the lake when the minnows come and peck at your dead skin cells. Tap, tap, tap. She smiles.

Jimmy is outside with Lou and Speed, even though he'd rather be inside, sitting at a table and watching the way people don't really talk *to* each other. Lou is explaining about the new trucks he got for his longboard. Clem hustles by, carrying two huge bags of reception trash like punks he's throwing in jail. When he gets to the dumpster, he launches them both up into the air with a whoop and a kick of his left heel. *Is that your dad?*, Speed asks, squirming. *He's not a regular dad, is he?*, Lou says. Jimmy shrugs and follows Clem back into the parish hall to get another soda. His shirt is untucked from the game, earlier, with the rug rats. He rubs his head, wondering if all their sticky cake-hands have left marks. Weird smokey line drawings like the cave paintings they're learning about in history class. The cancer has lowered Jimmy's resistance to learning. Without so much time ahead of him, it's easier to handle the here-and-now. He sees his mother sitting at a table next to his cousin Cindy, who's tapping her shoes together in a way that Jimmy likes. He goes over and sits with them. *Oh baby, come sit next to me*, his mother says. His uncle Duane arrives with a coffee, which he hands to Cindy. He's spilled a lot into the saucer, but Cindy looks up at him, takes the coffee, and says, *why thank you* and Jimmy feels like maybe he's in a movie and everything he can see around the room—Minister Shelly belly-laughing with three old guys, Speed and Lou blocking the exit doors like bouncers, Clem fishing recyclables out of the trash cans, Lisa leading the little kids through the crowd Willie Wonka-style—was thought up by some director sitting in a sky crane. He's got a megaphone. Quiet on set, roll camera, action. And then, cut. End of scene. That's a wrap. His mother takes his hand under the table and squeezes it in the way she does. Cindy smiles at him, sipping her coffee. Duane leans way back in his chair and says, *boy oh boy*. And Jimmy decides, of course, obviously, overwhelmingly, to close his eyes and see what will happen.

HOW IT SOUNDS IN THE AIR

A Conversation with Charlie Watts

James McNulty: Welcome to the pages of *Driftwood*, Charlie! We're always thrilled to publish a new stream of consciousness narrative—my personal favorite writing style. That said, *stream of consciousness* is a wide & flexible descriptor. How would you describe the style of writing in "Of Course"?

Charlie Watts: Thank you! I'm grateful for the chance to land in the *Driftwood* pages. In truth, for this story, I began with a set of rather restrictive (and somewhat arbitrary) structural "rules" that were helpful to me in getting going. These included writing one paragraph per page, not adding line breaks for dialogue, organizing the order of scenes by shared characteristics, etc. For me, especially when I'm having one of those "terror of the blank pages" days, having an almost physical scaffolding for the writing can be extremely helpful. Later in the process, I usually abandon all that. Or, as in this case, I end up trying to make it part of the story. But then, within that structure and within each scene, I tried to deliver a moment-to-moment stream of consciousness experience for the reader. Maybe the best way to describe the writing style of this story comes from Jimmy himself, in the end, when he talks about a camera filming from a boom crane—able to sweep over all the various things that are happening for the characters (both externally and internally). This is definitely my preferred mode of writing, having read way too much Faulkner (and early Cormac McCarthy) when I was in high school and college! It's perhaps also a reflection of the way I experience things in my head—a bit of a running river (sometimes exceeding its banks) rather than an orderly progression.

JM: Speaking of the rules you initially set for yourself, we did have some discussion during revisions about whether to utilize italics for dialogue in a story that holds such dense formatting. Please talk about the consideration that went into how to weigh and measure the stream of consciousness, and how you landed on the form you did.

CW: Yes, I really appreciate the back-and-forth we had on this—and I'm glad we landed where we did (e.g., using italics to signal dialogue). A few of my colleagues who read an earlier draft had similar input and suggested that I was asking an awful lot of folks to keep up with the toggle between narration and dialogue without giving any signals. I think what led me to offer the story, originally, without any of that type of support, is that I love wrestling with rhythm in my prose. As my friends know, after studying fiction in college and grad school, I had a long "break" of working as a communications consultant, helping to raise our three kids, and generally just being over-extended. A friend brought me back to the writing table by convincing me to do a poetry workshop (led by the poet, Catherine Morroco). The inherent ask of poetry for *compression* and constant attention to rhythm and pace turned out to be hugely compelling for me. (The shorter length of my poems was also a better fit for my available writing time!) As I've moved back toward short stories (and longer work) I think I've retained that interest in—and enjoyment of—careful consideration of not only what a sentence says, but also how it sounds in the air and, ultimately, what the visual snapshot is that any given scene or simile leaves behind in your mind.

This particular story operates under more structural "rules" than most of my writing, however. As mentioned, the techniques in this one began as crutches to get me started, but then took on a life of their own. I began to get interested in trying to say/show something about how groups of people exist—especially when they are in groups that might look homogeneous from the outside (e.g., "boys" or "girls," "men" or "women"), but that are likely anything but when you peel down a layer or two. By isolating these groups very specifically at the start of the story, I think it created some natural energy/ momentum toward then showing them alone, or in different combinations. By the end—in the context of LeeAnne's mother's funeral & reception—it's more about the collective experience and how people can be so utterly hit-or-miss when it comes to understanding, seeing, and caring for one another.

JM: I love that section toward the end—where the dialogue and pacing all seem to break down a little bit in accordance with the grief felt and the low-key chaos of the scene. I was also interested—within that section—in the *expectations of grief.* The grief felt for the mother who has passed isn't conventional and expected. Can you speak to this at all—the differences in how we each grieve?

CW: To me, grief is like an element—fire, water, earth, air, and grief. Perhaps some of that comes from living with a hospice chaplain (my wife, Holly) who has taught me a great deal about the ways in which grief manifests. And, significantly, the ways in which different cultures *expect* grief to manifest. That's extremely compelling to me—exploring the moments when characters somehow violate these spoken and assumed norms. LeeAnne's bitter fury about her mother shows itself in different ways. She's eager to have the backyard bonfire of all her mother's crap, but, equally, she wants the funeral to be well-attended and the readings to be right. Contradictions like these are, obviously, fertile ground for fiction (and life, I guess). I also believe that managing grief often requires more capacity than may be available in one human being. However, as I was trying to depict at the end of the story, I think there are times when grief can be managed *collectively*, bringing people together in ways that can be surprisingly graceful. Or, sadly, as I think is especially apparent on the world stage these days, in a way that intensifies suffering.

JM: With such an emotional premise at the forefront of the story, how did you steer away from being sentimental? How did you conceive of the narrative surrounding this premise?

CW: The core emotional premise comes from a real-life experience I had with a 3rd grade classmate who died, rather rapidly, from leukemia. The whole class went to his viewing. Always a very skinny kid, the cancer drugs had made him puffy. I think it was the first dead person that most of us had ever seen. While it wasn't particularly on my mind when I started writing the story, it got there fast as I tried to imagine what the secret anxiety or fear or "unspeakable" experience was that each of those young boys might have been carrying. Jimmy's was the heaviest, of course, so that shaped the rest of the story.

My father, who was an English teacher for much of his career, always said the most difficult things to write well were the non-dramatic moments. The mundane trip to the market. The afternoon of waiting. Not the earthquake or the epic battle scene. That was good coaching for me (although I have to admit that roughly 100% of my high school and college stories were heavy on the blood and guts...). Now, when I know I'm touching on something big/heavy like a terminal illness or a miscarriage or anything that explodes, I remember his observation and try to ground the moment in two ways: one is by being as specific as possible in the details and really call on all the senses to make *this* particular childhood death story its own thing; the other is by trying not to miss the paradoxes and crazy contrasts that, for my money, allow readers to appreciate the *humor* that is abundant in our life experience. Jimmy cutting off his hair too soon and making the dog cry. Duane and his ever-present awkwardness. We're all big weirdos (a phrase I'm stealing from my wife) and I think presenting that side of things keeps stories away from being too sweet or sticky-sentimental.

JM: This is all great advice: specificity & paradoxes. I particularly like the latter because I'm far more familiar with the former. While the specificity gives the story its own uniqueness, the conflicting tones, the paradoxes you describe, keep the reader on their toes, yeah? I think of Bong Joon-ho, a popular filmmaker well known for balancing multiple, oft conflicting tones; in *The Host*, for instance, a funeral scene is played for humor, despite the film generally being an action movie. So your tip here to avoid sentimentality and cliché is effectively: keep the reader on their toes and keep the scenes & characters pin-point specific. I think these tips show in your writing here, and they're working out very well for you.

There's so much wonderful, intimate specificity on display here, but admittedly there isn't a streamlined, conventional plot to follow. The narrative is contained to four days & quietly delves into—with understated precision—the lives affected by Jimmy's diagnosis. In writing such a realized, grounded story, how do you keep a reader's attention without conventional plotting?

CW: It's interesting—plotting feels like my kryptonite. I enjoy reading mysteries/thrillers, but I can't even imagine what it would be like to map out the detailed structure of a piece of that nature! I do follow the old adage that each scene/section, in some way, needs to develop or deepen or at least relate to the previous ground of the story, so I find myself frequently saying, *okay, this happened, so what happened next and why?* With so many different characters in this story, I actually made up a set of note cards that included the character's name and their relationship to all the other characters. I put those on a bulletin board and drew lines that traced the strongest connections. Then I did the same exercise for each paragraph (which, in this story, are each discrete scenes). It all made for a pretty big mess... but, I think it also allowed me to visualize (and keep track of!) where I wanted to go.

Talking about plots brings to mind the tricky issue of *endings.* While I'm certainly partial to what I understand as Chekov's notion that story endings are less about transformation and more about things returning to the way they were before, I do feel like a satisfying story delivers at least some sense of *movement* within a character (or characters). For me, most often, that movement relates to accepting that one has very little control over what happens in life. So the movement for Jimmy (at least in part) is that he comes to a place where he can genuinely *accept* that all he can do is wait and see. The struggle between striving to make the world cooperate and at least accepting, if not fully embracing, *emergence* (which I think of as the unknowably complex and spontaneous process by which experience arises) seems to be part of most everything I write!

JM: Your description in that first paragraph—did this process occur before or after drafting? What did outlining look like for this project—pre-drafting?

CW: For me, outlining generally comes mid- or post-drafting and is usually an effort to try to understand if the scenes and characters and writing style have any chance of holding together as something compelling. A close writing friend and I often used to debate about this question of *where do you start?* Is it the concept (I want to illustrate a train-wreck of a funeral)? Is it the character (I want to profile a guy who can't get out of his own way)? Is it the style (I want to write big long paragraphs with no line breaks for dialogue)? Whichever place I start—and I've probably done all of these—two things are critical for me. First, I have to be genuinely engaged/excited by what I'm seeing on the page. That may seem hugely obvious, but even if I don't know what I'm doing or whether it's going to work (because I usually don't!), I need to have that blind enthusiasm in order to stay with it. And then, second, I know there will need to be a point at which I go back and try to make all the elements support one another. Or, at minimum, ensure that none of the components (concepts, characters, style) are actively working against the others.

JM: It seems to me that each option of how to start would bring with it its own benefits and difficulties, and which method works best would be determined from the personal strengths and weaknesses of the writer—as well as what each story calls for. Have you found that one method works better for you than others?

CW: Strongly agree! A lot can influence what's going to actually "work" when it comes to creating a story. But, in general for me, starting with the character(s) seems to work best. Whose head am I going to try to be inside and how do they see the world? And, very often, where I decide to start comes from something that I've been thinking about relative to *myself*—even if I don't know it when I begin. I suppose I'm getting awfully close to the whole "writing is therapy" cliché, but I have to admit, even when I try to construct a character and/or scenario that is wildly outside my own lived experience, there's often a moment when I realize what I'm really doing is working over a bit of my own grief or insecurity or jealousy.

One other thing I've experienced over the years: my "mood" when I sit down to write does not need to influence the writing. My memory of what it was like to write stories in college, for example, is that I had to be in a very specific frame of mind and I needed a lot of specific supports (music, beverages, setting, time of day, type of paper, etc.). Thankfully, now, the experience is much more heavily influenced by staying closely connected to the words on the page. They create the mood. And I try to follow that. (I mean, as long as I also have a cup of coffee...)

JM: We spoke during revision, too, about how rhythm takes precedence over grammatical rules. As an example here, a comma typically comes before a conjunction when separating independent phrases, but a sharp author might eschew this rule if the comma negatively impacts the rhythm. Of course, obviously, commas carry a slight beat, a pause, in the rhythm, and that pause doesn't always make sense to the flow of the narrative and/or reading. For the keen-eyed, seasoned writer, selectively ignoring grammatical rules in favor of rhythm is best—provided that ignoring the grammatical rule doesn't create confusion. Of course, the primary purpose of grammar is to alleviate potential confusion, but do you ever run into situations where these two goals—rhythm and clarity—are at odds? What wins out, and why?

CW: I'm not proud to say that my relationship to the rules of grammar is at best second cousin. In seventh grade, while enduring instruction about how to diagram a sentence, we had to stand up in front of our classmates and draw all the appropriate lines and symbols to identify whatever grammar magic was being tested. I was miserable at this, so I think I've been allergic to really *learning* grammatical rules ever since. That said, I think my response to this question is that clarity needs to win out… and, importantly, if you work it long enough, there's no reason that you can't have both. Rhythm considerations certainly come more naturally to me. But thankfully, I have been able to work with other writers who see what I'm missing and help pull me back toward clarity!

JM: I love your note here about how both can win simultaneously, these goals aren't mutually exclusive. My question was phrased as a binary, but more writers need to understand that you can work hard enough for both ends to be attained. We don't need to sacrifice one in favor of the other. I think that's a frequent fear for writers—that editors will destroy the experimentation and pull them back to standardized convention. But of course, readers of *Driftwood* know that we succeed in both: experimental language, punctuation, grammar, narrative, etc., without confusing our readers too much in the process.

There's so much happening formally in this story! Please talk too, about the difficulties (or joys) in rooting each paragraph in a different collective POV, then shifting to individual POVs.

CW: As I mentioned earlier, this story required some elaborate support techniques and a large bulletin board to keep things straight. It also required—for me—some strict segmenting in the writing process. While my life is not such that I can typically write for the entire day, I can often dedicate at least the morning. For this story, however, my clock was more definitively the one page, one paragraph, one point-of-view structure. I only tackled one a day.

In addition—and this is something I tend to do with all my writing—I usually take the last 5-10 minutes of any writing session to quickly free-write (usually in block capitals) my thoughts about what I want to work on the next time I'm able to sit down with the piece. (I'm sure this technique comes from someone else; not claiming originality here!) This approach helps in two ways. First, it sets my brain to thinking about what's next even when I'm not writing and even when I'm not conscious of it. It's just helpful to have some sketch of ideas parked in my close consciousness for the balance of the day(s), and I find that new ideas or refinements often arise just by letting things sit. Kind of like a good stew or a loaf of bread. The second thing that happens is that when I do return to work on the story, I have something concrete to either execute or push back against from the minute I open the file. For me, that's extremely helpful. I don't find it hard to sit and write. I love that part. I just hate the first ten (or one hundred) minutes when you're sitting there and looking at the page and all the doubting voices show up to say all their negative things. This technique helps me leap-frog over that unpleasantness.

JM: Similarly, Hemingway advised that you stop writing for the day when you still know what's happening next. If you stop writing when you don't know what's next, beginning again the next day will be very tricky. I think most writers—particularly those with full-time jobs and/or family commitments—have a difficult time giving structure to their writing habits as you've outlined here, so hopefully your method inspires others.

Guest judge Daniel Wallace, who selected this story from our editors' finalists, noted in his acceptance blurb that these characters are ready for more action. Is "Of Course" an excerpt, or is it part of an upcoming collection?

CW: I was quite happy with that acceptance blurb… very generous. This story is *not* an excerpt—at least I wasn't thinking about it that way until I read Daniel Wallace's comment! Definitely open to revisiting some of these folks, especially LeeAnne and Clem. And perhaps the hapless Duane after he gets his band back together…

I am often surprised, when I look back at things I've written, to find commonalities across stories that were either very different in tone or subject or were written at very different times in my life. Some of these things are just quirks. For example, I've noticed that I often tend to put tattoos on my characters (and describe them) and my first & always hair color choice is red (despite knowing only one or two redheads). Other things—like the battle I was describing earlier between trying to get the world to bend to your wishes vs. accepting what's actually happening—are probably deeper themes that reflect my own real-world struggles and experiences. So the format of *linked* stories (within a collection or over the course of a writing career) makes a lot of sense to me.

At the same time, I will say that the more I approach the writing of a story with some very specific idea in mind—for example, what happens to LeeAnne after Jimmy dies—the more likely I am to write something very flat and unsuccessful. Even when it's a story that I really I want to tell! I guess what this says, for me, is that the sense of mystery and discovery—what is this story really about, where is it headed, who the heck are these people—has to be strongly felt in order for me to create something that has a chance of being compelling. I can imagine doing that with some of these characters as the basis, but I'd definitely have to go through some initial *forgetting* process before starting so that I could keep it fresh. Maybe that's helpful to do in all cases!

JM: I tend to think carry-through preoccupations are typical of all writers, and one's preferences in (assuming all things equal) writers you love or don't care for tend to reflect your own preoccupations. What other thematic considerations stick with you throughout your other works? What, if anything, is unique to "Of Course" when compared to your other writings?

CW: I think the most common preoccupation in my writing is self-sabotage, especially in male characters. Whether because of specific trauma or a generalized loss of faith, a lot of my characters do seem to have trouble getting out of their own way. They usually mean well, and sometimes they take significant steps toward the light, but insight comes slowly. Art imitating life, in my case! As for this story (and a few others I've been working on), the new & different element is probably the effort to portray the group as well as its members. I like the challenge of trying to work with a lot of characters in a relatively "short" space. It goes back to the idea of compression: in order not to confuse/lose the reader, you're required to make the images as sharp as you can. What's that one thing you can describe—the mannerism or the piece of clothing or the dialogue choice—that will truly stick in the mind of the reader?

JM: Who are some of your favorite writers? Which ones inspired "Of Course" most?

CW: As you mentioned above, I think certain of my favorite writers are dear to me because I experience them as wrestling with similar issues. So for "Of Course," with its domestic dissatisfactions, I think of stories by legends like Grace Paley, Lucia Berlin, Raymond Carver, Flannery O'Connor, and Richard Russo. But I'm also heavily enamored of authors that push toward the fabulist, including Robin McLean, George Saunders, Samantha Hunt, Ben Marcus (who I was lucky enough to go to grad school with!), and Italo Calvino. It's tough to make favorite author lists. I feel like I develop actual relationships with the books that I finish, so I want them all to be on the list—to acknowledge all the work that went into making the worlds they portray!

JM: Do other mediums influence you at all?

CW: Well, I've already confessed my admiration for poetry. I'm a deeply, painfully slow *reader*, mostly because I love to hear how the words sound. I can't do the glance & comprehend thing that speed reading requires. I wish I could... I'd love to read more! But I'm also heavily influenced by film. It makes me jealous: films get to use words, pictures, and music (and some theaters, I realize, also have smell, although I don't think that works too well). So, like Jimmy in this story... when I'm writing, I'm often imagining the scenes as if I was watching a movie.

JM: Which filmmakers inspire you most? Did any play a role in the creation of this story?

CW: Oh boy... that's an interesting one. I would start with Michael Cimino's *The Deer Hunter* and the wedding scene in the fabulously ornate and incongruous (for that neighborhood) Catholic Church. It's a scene that very much wrapped completely around me, especially because I grew up not too far from where that was set (Pennsylvania). Another hugely influential film for me is/was Francis Ford Coppola's *Apocalypse Now*. The plotline was compelling, but, additionally, the way in which the movie almost literally assaults you with colors (all the smoke and fog) and music has always stuck with me. And for pure world-creation and hero's journey stuff, I absolutely love Hayao Miyazaki, especially for *Spirited Away*, which we watch at least a few times a year! But your question also reminds me that for years, when our kids were young and before the Internet, we had the "lovely" task of going to the video rental shop every Friday evening to pick out the weekend's entertainment. I developed a reputation in the family for picking movies in which *almost nothing happens*. These were often French films, but also sometimes American "drifter" movies. I'm all for a filmmaker who has the courage to show you an empty street or a quiet hay field or a grumbling Camero on the interstate for an uncomfortable amount of time! To me, films that make these spaces end up feeling more intimate. I feel invited to be inside whatever world is being depicted. And, yes, sometimes that's boring! Probably a more successful, balanced example of this style would be many of the Coen brothers films. Plenty of "action" and plotline in a movie like *Fargo*, but also many scenes that allow the visuals (and soundtrack) to do the talking. And the viewer gets to decide what the message they want to hear.

JM: What are you working on now?

CW: In addition to a few short stories (including another "set" of characters that might come to life in multiple stories), I've just finished the fourth re-do of a novel that I started longer ago than I care to admit. It features a guy who can't get out of his own way (of course…) and who makes the unfortunate and illegal decision to drive the unprocessed body of his deceased grandmother from California to Rhode Island for a green burial. He's also trying to save his marriage and metabolize the fact that his wife is pregnant with what would be their first child. It's a mess. (Hopefully, the manuscript itself is becoming less of a mess and might find a publisher one of these years!)

JM: Any parting words to leave our readers with—either about "of Course" or writing in general?

CW: Just to thank you and *Driftwood*, again, for giving me this opportunity and facilitating the connection between readers and writers and writing. The writer I mentioned above, Robin McLean, has done a lot of her writing in deep isolation (including sitting inside an earthen root cellar), but at a reading she said she views writing as a *group sport.* I love that. Yes, there's plenty of isolation. And there's definite value, I think, for a writer simply to write (regardless of outcome). To try and see and understand experience. But when that process extends to editors and publishers and readers—the stone making the ripple in the pond—it's a new and different thing that goes way beyond whatever the author might have contributed. That's certainly a big reason why I write. That, and the fact that, for me, it's (usually) fun!

REDBIRD

Danielle Barr

The priest called up from Geezer Gaye's died as he was giving Mama her last rites, which seemed inauspicious to me. He was stood on a milk crate, looming over Mama's sickbed, where she hadn't moved from since the birth, coils of amber smoke snaking through the air like shooting stars, the stillness of all but Geezer Gaye's man's lips murmuring half-whispered invocations heavy velvet curtains that left me feeling smothered such that I gripped Figgy's hand all the tighter. His private sermon to Mama, her last directive to carry with her like a hall pass into the next, was gathering force, building up to the climax which, timed right by a seasoned fatherpriest, would coincide with the moment of her passing exactly. His volume growing still more, he suddenly snapped upright, uttered the feeblest gasp, and fell with a thud onto the shag carpet, a galaxy of lint and dust kicked up into the air by the particularly propulsive quality of his impact. In the fracas that followed—Figgy had been sure this was part of the last rites all along; after all, we'd never watched someone die before, so we'd stood stock still for fear of interrupting the handshake between the ordinary and the divine, even as the fatherpriest's attendants rushed to his aid, notably not to begin his own rites but rather to bludgeon his sternum with their open palms, like Mama used to do to Father's old duck hound that sought to bolt through the open door and into the wild of the swamp each time the opportunity presented itself—it went unnoticed when Mama took her last rattling breath, her rites unfinished.

The night before, once I'd pricked the soft fleshy soles of her feet to no response, just to be sure she was truly unconscious, I climbed into bed and molded my body around hers, just to see how it felt to be so close to her. I laid my head on her bony shoulder, cheekbones resting on the biting edge of her clavicle, and breathed her in. She smelled of iodine and castile soap and perhaps a dusting of baby powder to ward off the creeping, inexorable advance of the scent of blood and near-rot. I'd never met any real-life babies that smelled like baby powder. Babies whose sweat smelled inexplicably of school glue, or sickly mustard blowouts that bathed the air in the scent of buttered popcorn, or the occasional curdled, cheesy aroma of breast milk congealing in doughy neck rolls—but never baby powder. Somewhere in the bowels of the house, I knew, wrapped in a length of nubby calico, on a bed of ice there laid a silent swaddled baby that smelled neither like powder nor popcorn; I imagined the old double-walled Igloo, once opened, and after the initial gust of air perfumed by dried sprigs of lavender and thyme, smelled much the same.

Mama's skin—I'd imagined it warm and soft, a goose down-filled comforter—was instead waxy and cool and very slightly damp. Figgy had once caught a tree frog bedded down in the hollow of an old tree on the ridge where the hedge apples grew, which escaped his clutched fists just as it crossed the threshold of our home, to great fanfare and not a few curses from Mama, and its pale green skin, slippy and grabby both as it squirmed under the pads of my small victorious palms having caught it, had the same dimly alive feeling as Mama's did then, and I drew a sharp intake of breath in disappointment but didn't move. Instead I burrowed further into the bow of her neck and let the wild coils of matted white hair fall across my face until I could see nothing else but the wiry strands, a forest of birch trees in a winter thicket.

There was a guilty excitement buzzing in the house. Sad, yes, all very sad, but there was the undeniable crackle of electricity in the air, a collective breath-holding because something new was sure to happen next. After the granny ladies shooed away the gaggle of premature mourners, who seemed to have intuited at least half of the tragedy that had befallen our home that evening, Mama was whisked down to the basement and into the chest freezer. "Quick-like, now, before the rigor!" Muffett Gaye commanded as they fumbled down the narrow plank stairs and their petite leather boots with mother of pearl buttons padded across the dirt floor toward that most undignified of morgues. Then Muffett bundled the fatherpriest's rotund little body and someone rang Geezer round to tote it back to the parish. Figgy and I were tucked away to our room by the flitting hands of the aproned aged who now spun themselves into action, a well-honed engine what whirred to life on the heels of death.

Dovie Newbury and Sister Driscoll busied themselves darting room to room and throwing open the windows even in the chill of December twilight. "Make a way, make a way," Sister Driscoll called, and the faceless drones behind stacks of moth-eaten quilts retrieved from musky oak memory chests parted in sync to let her past and into the nursery, where the undulating leaded glass pane stuck fast in its casement, immovable despite the quick, studied upward jerks of her hamhock wrists. When at last Dovie bounded into the room in a flurry, the pair of them pried the thing open together, Dovie wedging herself, supine on the clapboard floor with the sole of her boot flat against the brass lift with her skirts spilling out around her, into the space beneath the sill. From the adjoining room, Figgy and I sniggered despite ourselves, which caused Sister Driscoll to admonish us smartly before she snapped the door shut.

The hum of the house lulled Figgy and I to sleep, gangly limbs like pick-up sticks strewn across the horsehair mattress, woven in and out of heavy patchwork coverlets. I dreamed of starless night skies stretched inky black over our cabin, of a sea of cardinals peppering the front lawn, of Mama's essence colliding with the window I'd inched silently closed at some midnight hour to ward off the fingers of cold that had filled the room in gusts like a chimney bellows, trapped on this plane, in this house, with us, forever, desperate for the release of death she'd been promised.

In the morning, blue and lazy as December sunrises are, the heater thrummed awake and the whole of the house roused themselves from bed to scuttle themselves over the floor vents, where the warmth radiated up through our toes like static, spreading slowly through our bodies until all at once it felt too much and we flitted away. Even Sister Driscoll perched above the metal teeth in the kitchen, and her dress sprang to life around her, billowing out such that I worried she may float away, a trapped hot air balloon bobbing around in the corners of the parlor, like the Mama of my dreams. "Hurry now, Bobbyette," she called out, batting me away when I blearily stumbled upon her would-be ascension, "close all the windows 'fore the hot gets out." I paused, chewing the inside of my cheek, and cast a doubtful glance toward the feedsack curtains fluttering in the breeze above the sink. "If she's goin', she's gone, Bobbyette. And I, for one, think one night in the cold's enough penance for us all."

Buckwood would've been sent for by now, I was sure, though I doubted he'd come. Mama'd once said, while she sat darning another of his thick wool socks that seemed to shrink two sizes something near monthly, if you took her word for it, that it was Buckwood who had sucked the color from her skin, first. Then, when Figgy was born, he siphoned the pigment straight from each hair follicle, leaving her with her wild, brittle mane of pure white. Finally, when I arrived not even a year after, the last of it had faded from her eyes. "God-colored," the fatherpriests of the greater Bowlick County called her, a preternatural silver-white being, but her blazing red irises looked more like licks of hellfire to me. Once, in the parlor of the father-priest from Heddy Garry, while we waited for Mama to finish her confession upstairs, Buckwood had whispered to us through gritted teeth that even when he was young, before Figgy or I'd been born, she'd been that same frosty white, head to toe, the pink networks of her insides peering through her skin like vellum. If it had been true, though, that each subsequent one of us had drained the color from her life in a manner both literal and psychic, it was no wonder to me, and perhaps something of a gross oversight on her part, that the arrival of still another Fulsom child found her wanting for anything else to be stripped of, and thus it seemed inevitable, right even, that there was simply not enough life left to go around between the two.

The next day, the womenfolk hauled Mama up from the chest freezer and painstakingly uncurled her icy limbs, which had been folded up like origami such that her compact frame could fit along-side the rack of venison that we'd only just processed and stored away in the very same repository not a week before. Sister Driscoll plaited Mama's hair and dressed her in a simple chambray housedress.

Muffett Gaye retrieved and tucked the neat bundle of my ill-fated sibling up under Mama's bent elbow, and I hazarded a peek, peeling back the scratchy calico to reveal its face: bruised, with purple lakes of congealed blood settled behind its closed eyes, but still indisputably the same shocking white of my mother.

The customary bloodroot and aster blooms lay dormant under the thin crust of ice in the thicket beyond the house, so instead Fig-gy and I were dispatched into the woods to collect a basketful of evergreen needles to adorn her hair. In a hushed voice, our boots crunching across the expanse between the cabin and the treeline, I asked Figgy if maybe it would make more sense to gather a bundle of switches from the hickory around back instead, since she'd seemed so fond of them in life. He smiled despite himself, but quickly pulled his face back into the pinched, severe expression he'd adopted since the birth. *Don't think ill of the dead, Bobbyette,* Mama used to warn, so I didn't, instead imagining myself pruning those indelicate thoughts like a bonsai, but my body remembered.

Deep in the trees, Figgy and I set to work, him at a hemlock and I at a fir. A cardinal, drab and brown, the unfortunate female, alit on a sprig of pine just beyond my reach, its black domed eye trained on me, unflinching. I retracted my mittened hand and watched as it considered me. "Mama?" I whispered, and my frozen breath was a mushroom cloud between us. I hesitated, heart thumping double-time, before I thrust my arm deep into the boughs regardless, past the startled bird to clip a final stem.

"It's no matter if it is you," I hissed, not wanting Figgy to hear the true ugliness of my craven heart ("the heart of a woman knows no other way than this," the fatherpriest from Yeadon Hall had once affirmed to me, real mournful-like), "on account of I'm alive, and you're not." I turned clean on my heel and tromped back to the cabin, willow-reed basket swinging from my arm.

I folded the sprays into Mama's braids, and then carefully wrapped the baby's fingers around another still. The deep green of the needles framing the pale milky white of Mama's ruined face reminded me of a stained-glass panel I'd seen once when Buckwood had toted us up to Richmond for his enlistment: Mary, the disgraced woman, clutching her baby, a golden disk encircling her head. Things had turned out only slightly better for her than for Mama, what with the public execution of her son and all.

On the third day, the granny ladies and Figgy and me lined up out front in our heavy wool coats, eight of us all told, Mama and her baby in a simple pine box and the fatherpriest in another, atop a bed of kindling on the frozen ground. The officiant fee, I heard Sister Driscoll say, was much more manageable split halfway with Father Burgis' estate: a two-for-one special.

Geezer Gaye's man's substitute, a lanky, humorless specimen, with a port wine stain splashed across the whole of his face struck a long-necked match against the roughhewn side of the pyre and intoned a final request for salvation for Mama, and for Father Burgis, before he dropped the flaming thing into the folds of Mama's skirts, where it caught and kindled and curled its fiery tongue around her, and the wasted baby in her arms, before spreading, crackling like a thousand shattering panes of glass, to the still-round but slightly sunken body of the fatherpriest who had been swept away into the ether right along with her. "Her ability to ruin a man," Muffett Gaye whispered hatefully, "was unmatched even in death."

We were supposed to be quiet for this part, but the blurry silhouette of a bird in flight against the twilight sky compelled me to poke Figgy in the ribcage.

"D'you think maybe Mama's a redbird, now?" I asked Figgy, thinking of the open windows that had unleashed Mama's wayward spirit onto the unsuspecting world at large.

"Well, she didn't get her rites finished, so she's bound to be out here somewheres, if you believe the parson." He jerked his chin in the direction of the fatherpriest with his purple-red face shiny from sweat.

I nodded solemnly, then folded my hands to hang down in front of me the way Mama'd said I should such that no one would think I was a ruffian.

Standing sentry there over the burn pile for hours, I watched the God-color of her char and bubble and then melt away, and the smoke from the flames that undulated like a mirage, greasy with perfumes and tinctures to hide the stench of the whole affair. When the flames died down at last, long after Figgy had gone in to the threadbare coverlets and the fitful sleep they afforded, and Muffett Gaye and Sister Driscoll and Dovie Newbury had assured us the lady from Children's Services would be along first thing in the morning and gone home to their respectable husbands and their neat, pink-cheeked children to wash away the grime of Happenstance Bog, I peered down at the sharp black nothingness of it all, breathless at what precious little she'd amounted to.

A MILLION THINGS AT ONCE

A Conversation with Danielle Barr

James McNulty: Welcome to the pages of *Driftwood*, Danielle! I'm so pleased this story won our In-House Short Story Contest with a unanimous vote total. I can't wait for readers to get their hands on this one.

Danielle Barr: Thank you so much for having me! I'm still pinching myself that this is real.

JM: From the start any reader will notice the innovative, sprawling sentence structures and inventive language on display, my personal favorite quality in this—or any—*Driftwood* story; the second half of that opening paragraph is a single sentence aided by commas, dashes, and even a semicolon. Talk to me about the process of drafting these sentences. Do you consider the content, then slowly sculpt the sentence's phrasing, or does it all rush out in a blur?

DB: I wish there was any conscious logic to it, but I just let everything come out as it comes to me. I rarely know where the sentence will go when I start it and move by feel, like I'm working my way through a dark room. The act of putting in tiny details and flashbacks sharpens the character from the start and mimics the way that I think inside my own head; it's never linear and polished, but rather a million things all at once. You add to that the fact that Bobbyette is eight years old (I'm a mom to four, the oldest being nine, so I've got some experience in this regard!), and to me, it's more realistic that you'll get an all-over-the-place POV, expanding, contracting, taking tangents. I just let Bobbyette, the narrator, and Bobbyette, the child, loose to pick up and show me bits and bobs of her existence. And then I wound up with a 154-word sentence.

JM: Do you worry about readability? Arguably the writing here is more rewarding *because* it's slightly more dense.

DB: Probably the most integral tenet of my personal writing style, for better or for worse, is "really long sentences." I think the form—packing as much as you can into any one sentence without bleeding into being purple—is really interesting. We have so many tools at our disposal—you mentioned all the punctuation that lends itself to this—to build and layer and make exciting choices with. And in this story in particular, there are things in that first paragraph's longest sentence—exposition and backstory and description and world-building—that I couldn't rank-order in terms of importance, stacking them in first, second, third sentences, and in fact, somewhat disparately, I think it would have been clunkier and too formulaic to have four separate sentences establishing all of those different things. But to exhale them all at once in the way Bobbyette does weights them all equally, and I think also, surprisingly, makes the act of reading and digesting all of that setup go faster, because it feels more stream of consciousness rather than info-dump-y (at least to me!).

JM: The stream of consciousness is using the character voice to camouflage the exposition. What other ways did you camouflage your exposition in "Redbird"?

DB: So much of it is implicit, where I'm hoping the reader draws the same conclusions I intend (or even invents something better!). There are a few details Bobbyette alights on that I think ground the piece but also provide some of that implicit exposition. I'm thinking, for example, of the leather boots with mother-of-pearl buttons that Muffett Gaye and her battalion of granny ladies wear. It's a really specific image that, for me, conjures a wardrobe comparable to early settlers, and I think that builds in some of the background information, helping the reader to make assumptions about this community based on how they dress.

JM: You note how seemingly improvisational your sentence-building is, and yet each paragraph feels very focused and structured as a separately functioning unit. Each paragraph here makes a statement, and each ends with a punch. Surely you're shorting yourself here a little bit: there's too much intention and focus in each of these paragraphs to be *entirely* improvised. Do you work with an outline, or are your revisions following a first draft heavy?

DB: I am 100% a pantser; I do not know where a sentence, or a paragraph, or even a story is going to end when I begin it. In the past, when I've attempted to make an outline, I've felt the writing has ended up very prescriptive, kind of soulless; I'm just trying to move the story from point A to point B.

"Redbird" specifically came about just because I thought of the first sentence and thought it was a hilarious way to begin a story, then I started padding everything else out to serve as scaffolding that would support that premise.

There was very little formal revision involved in the end. Because of how attached I get to the way words sound together, if a sentence doesn't feel exactly right when I write it, it will linger in my mind and I'll rework it once I think it's right; that definitely happened a few times, although aside from that, the first time it was actually committed to paper, I was pretty happy with it.

Originally, I had an ending that strongly implied Mama had in fact been transmuted into a cardinal, but it felt too neat and tidy, and it gnawed at me for a few days; I knew it wasn't quite right—it didn't fit with the overall tone of the story, and I wanted to leave things more open-ended. I deleted what I had and wrote the final paragraph in the space of about five minutes, and after I'd put the period on the end, I remember sitting there a bit shell-shocked, because I truly hadn't seen that ending coming, and it was only once I typed it out that I realized, "Oh! That was it! I guess I'm done, then." It felt kind of like magic.

JM: Sometimes, a writer will just be *tapped in*, so to speak, at the top of their game and able to juggle everything they've worked hard to learn both explicitly and implicitly over the years, producing a draft without a strong need for significant revision or outline. My worry with *Driftwood* readers and new-to-intermediate writers is that they'll take this as the norm. Do you have any processes or methods to get yourself into this writing headspace?

DB: Completely agreed here; definitely not the norm! I absolutely could not be the type of person to sit down every day at a prescribed time and write a set amount of words and have it be any good.

I only write when I am so completely overwhelmed by the ideas in my head that they're just beginning to seep out, essentially having worked myself into a frenzy mentally free-writing over a period of days or even weeks. So it's a long pre-heat, so to speak.

I also read, literary magazines in particular. Being swept up in other people's incredible work motivates me; I'll pick up on some small thing another writer does, some technique I've never tried that I admire, and before I'm done reading the story chances are I've written a few lines in my head that I've tried to apply the new approach to, and then we're off to the races.

JM: Keeping on this topic of language, I noticed at least one descriptive stunner per paragraph, from "a galaxy of lint and dust kicked up into the air" to "the wild coils of matted white hair fell across my face until I could see nothing else but the wiry stands, a forest of birch trees in a winter thicket." Please talk to me about the process of association here, and how you craft these associations.

DB: This is also very similar to how the thoughts arrange themselves in my head. I am constantly (the developmental editor currently slogging through my first novel may say too often) thinking and writing in similes. I think it's the most profound act, to liken something humdrum, like dust kicked up from the carpet, to something existential and momentous; everyday life read as if it's a classic. So small things are often comparing themselves to celestial bodies and immemorial fragments of the natural world in my thoughts and in my writing. It makes everything feel significant.

Moreso even than the narrative, my passion in writing is selecting the perfect words and stringing them together into something beautiful. So when I am writing those moments in each paragraph, I'm at my happiest. And if they make someone stop for a moment and go, "that was beautiful," but they're just talking about strands of hair, it feels a bit like I've done something impossible.

JM: Your love of language is made evident by the story, and this passion fits well at *Driftwood*. Ingenious description often takes extreme patience to craft. You have to look at the most normal things—dust, strands of hair—for a long time to see them differently, or to find an association to jump off of. How long did it take to craft the initial draft of this story, and what revisions did it go through?

DB: The beginning whispers of this story had been percolating around in my head for a few days before I finally decided to let them out, and because of that, it came out in a bit of a rush. I'd say cumulatively it came together in about three hours, snatched while waiting at school pickups, during children's sports lessons, and during the baby's naps. I expelled three stories, "Redbird" included, in a several-day span this past winter, and that tracks pretty well with how I operate: I have a flood of actionable ideas I churn out as quickly as possible, and then periods of drought where I have to let that well fill up again.

Similarly, and I know this is fully "bad writer" territory, I don't do much editing or revising of my work once it's written. That's not to say it's any good right off the bat, but because I spend most of my time tending to other things (a small herd of children has that effect, I've found), I have to let ideas bounce around my thoughts for a while before I'm able to do anything with them. While that's happening, I usually refine at least a paragraph at a time mentally. That process happens until I get so satisfied with it that I get scared of forgetting it (the worst game of chicken!), and at that point, I'll commit it to paper. Then the process repeats for the next paragraph. So, by time I type the words out for the first time, they've likely been edited in my head four, five times over. So there's quite a bit of revision, just not in the traditional sense, and it's much more real-time than after the fact.

JM: I would argue that the process you described in these paragraphs—"I have to let ideas bounce around my thoughts for a while"—is a form of outlining, just not manually written down. Gestating on ideas & internal "revision" pre-drafting are ways of building a story before pen hits the paper. Your reluctance to write down the idea despite being fearful of forgetting it is probably an effective tactic to get you writing, though. Of course, all writers figure out what works for them and their busy lives.

DB: Definitely. I think for a long time I felt like I was going about this writing business all wrong; I started stories aimlessly, without a clear direction, just putting pretty sentences together, and once they were written I sent them out into the world without much traditional editing. And that felt scary because I saw a lot of my peers agreeing that stories needed multiple drafts, or novels needed detailed outlines or what have you, so I had this sinking feeling that I couldn't possibly be successful because those things felt wrong to me. But learning my own individual process and learning to be okay with it and not compare it to anyone else's was a huge relief. And like you said, I think I do engage with my work in those ways, but it's much more internal as opposed to, say, a bulleted outline.

JM: Talk to me about using suggestion techniques in writing. Note this excerpt here, bolding mine:

> The customary bloodroot and aster blooms lay dormant under the thin crust of ice in the thicket beyond the house, so instead Figgy and I were dispatched into the woods to collect a basketful of evergreen needles to adorn her hair. In a hushed voice, our boots crunching across the expanse between the cabin and the treeline, **I asked Figgy if maybe it would make**

more sense to gather a bundle of switches from the hickory around back instead, since she'd seemed so fond of them in life. He smiled despite himself, but quickly pulled his face back into the pinched, severe expression he'd adopted since the birth. ***Don't think ill of the dead, Bobbyette,*** Mama used to warn, so I didn't, instead imagining myself pruning those indelicate thoughts like a bonsai, **but my body remembered.**

I'm interested by how you lay out the information with suggestion, with implication, and gradually. The first mention is that their mama liked hickory; of course, this could be a harmless preference for a type of tree. But the transition: from a revealed preference to the statement, "Don't think ill of the dead," implies there's something negative about their Mama liking hickory. The perceptive reader will likely stall on this for a moment. It might take a minute, but there's a suspicion there; we can maybe assume that the hickory was used for some illicit means. And then the finale of the paragraph confirms it: "my body remembered."

I've broken the paragraph down with a close reading to ask you this craft question: a large part of the struggles of young writers—or even veteran writers—is trying to figure out how to convey information naturally, or hiding exposition. Implication via transition is a very clever way of doing so, but of course, there are dozens of other techniques. Can you talk about your process here, and how you personally work to discover new ways of subtly conveying information?

DB: This story was a first for me. I challenged myself to not explain anything, whereas my instinct is to rush in and say, "this, of course, is because xyz," so I really had to fold in tiny clues here and there that point towards the conclusions I'm hoping for: Mama was not a nice woman or a loving mother; Mama was likely up to some illicit things with the fatherpriests of Bowlick County "upstairs," drawn to her on account of her looks kicking up some long-held rural beliefs about the likeness of god; the prevailing belief was that since she hadn't had her last rites completed that her soul would linger; and so on. Then in the section you mention, there are a few pieces to put together: one has to know that hickory switches, in rural communities, are often cut from the tree and used to spank children with, but even if they don't, maybe especially if they don't, they're still left with that feeling of unease over it.

And if you think about it, not much happens in the way of plot. Mama dies, preparations are made, she's cremated out on the lawn. But there's so much more going on beneath the surface, so many beliefs and traditions upheld and judgments made that the out-group never quite gets a handle on. That unease at the end, the feeling of *did I understand what was happening correctly?*—that's the payoff.

JM: I think your gut-call to not explain anything is what led to a contest-winning story. You mention there isn't much plot in the story (though the amount of plot feels right for a story of this length). How do you build plot? Say, pick one direction over another? What mental work goes into the generation of plotting out a story?

DB: In "Redbird", before I had any idea of where it would go, I knew Mama's body was stored in a chest freezer in the basement, because it was part of that initial burst of inspiration. I also knew I needed to bring the story back around to the fatherpriest who died while giving her her last rites, because it wasn't the type of thing you can bring up once and then never mention again. So the darkly comedic idea of a two-for-one special on funeral services occurred to me and gave me a landing place to shoot for.

That process is true of most of the writing I do. Those first "wouldn't that be a funny way to start a story?" lines hold details that I take note of so I can come back around to them. That generally leaves me with something like a jigsaw puzzle where I have a very basic premise and some details that need to be resolved. Finding ways to fit those pieces together reveals the plot to me, or at the very least gives me a direction to steer.

JM: Shifting finally here to the narrative itself: what was the impetus in your own life that inspired the premise?

DB: I live in rural Appalachia—southwest Virginia specifically—and I love the mystique of communities sequestered out in the backwoods, isolated enough that their belief systems and cultures have evolved in something of a silo, and the unspokenness of a lot of that. The self-sufficiency of handling and preparing your own dead butting up against "the lady from Children's Services"—the tension that exists between those two things. The inscrutable belief system that reads like Christianity tinged with something more vaguely sinister. The way thoughts and sentences dawdle and we linger in them for a while because no one's ever in a hurry. It was the language and the piecing together of the very clear in-group way of speaking about what was happening without thought for explaining to the readers—a de facto out-group—what was going on that excited me and propelled this piece forward.

JM: What did you learn while writing this?

DB: Truthfully, I had resigned myself to never being a writer anyone considered "economical," by virtue of that propensity of mine toward long, meandering sentences. I'd read reviews of other authors' work where the word economy was celebrated and feel a particular way about it. Writing "Redbird" was a eureka moment for me: it's possible for my natural style to also be economical; that's not only something reserved for terse, propulsive prose. The things left unsaid—that negative space—did as much work as the words on the page.
So it really felt this was a turning point in refining my writing. Discovering that key and explicitly naming it was transformative.

JM: It's an important lesson. Pacing and word count aren't synonymous. A Faulkner short story can often be just as tight as a Carver piece. Who are some of your favorite writers? Which ones inspired "Redbird" most?

DB: Part of the reason I'm so thrilled that *Driftwood Press* specifically will be publishing this story is because of how much I enjoyed Mason Boyles' *Bark On*, which was published by *Driftwood*! The repurposing of words and the surgical way Mason wielded them inspired me in so many ways to not only search for the perfect words, but to bend them to my purposes. Additionally, the narrative voice in *Bark On* was so strong, and that's something that is integral to all of my protagonists as well, so I took notes there! When I feel myself slipping out of the voice of my narrators now, I sometimes reference Mason's work to give myself permission to rough up some of my language and syntax to be more true to the character.

Also, since so much of my work references rural areas generally, if not Appalachia specifically, I'd be remiss not to mention Barbara Kingsolver. I admire the grittiness of her view of this region, and how she manages not to render judgment against it even in light of its faults.

JM: Whew. Quite the full circle moment. I'm thrilled to hear that Mason's work is inspiring other writers as it inspired me when I read it as a submission—and that those writers are submitting and winning contests here. *Bark On* is easily my favorite debut novel by *any* writer, and we were lucky enough to publish it. I like what you said about *roughing up* your language; I sometimes worry that contemporary agents & editors shy away from that, though it aids the voice and specificity. Do other mediums influence you at all?

DB: Life-as-performance, by which I mean social media, reality TV, and their ilk, have provided a not-insignificant amount of inspiration in my writing. I am naturally fairly adept at crafting characters and stringing words together, but when I'm trying to summon inspiration for conflict, my secret weapon is Reddit, believe it or not! The trick is to take a stroll through the "Am I the Asshole?" subreddit; only read the post titles, and then let your mind run wild to spin the story of the actual conflict. What's the context? Who are the characters? Often the titles are boiled down to the most basic, generic, click-bait-y components of the conflict, so you're free to fill in all the details, trying to make the disparate initial components make sense in the way brains are wont to do. It's a fun mental exercise no matter what. Sometimes when I'm done writing I'll go back and read the full post that provided the jumping-off point, and it's always something completely different from what I'd imagined.

JM: You mentioned a novel earlier. What are you working on now?

DB: I'm in the very early stages of querying my novel, so that is where most of my precious little time for creative pursuits is being channeled. It's a literary coming-of-age story that follows the widow and daughter of a famously lost-in-space astronaut ten years after his death, as the space program mounts a crewed mission to recover his remains. It touches on the disparity between what the media says and what is true, how our perception of our parents' faults and successes influences our sense of self, and wrestling with the duality of people we love being two very different things at once. And of course, for at least the first third of it, the setting is deep in the Appalachian mountains.

True to form though, the idea for my next novel has been taking shape as I go through the motions of other things, and so at some point soon I expect to give in and begin putting pen to paper!

JM: Any parting words to leave our readers with—either about "Redbird" or writing in general?

DB: Only thanks for reading what I've written, for being willing to chew on the images and sit in some of the distressing themes with me. I'm immensely grateful to *Driftwood* for giving "Redbird" a home.

STAGGERED BREATHING

Phoebe Phelps

Our musical director plays the starting note before counting us in. We stand in a circle around the piano with the lights off and our hands clasped together to run through the Final Madrigal before our concert. It is tradition and we are proud of it. We hum quietly, find our part's starting note from the chord we construct in the darkened air. One, two, three, and with one collective breath, four, we begin.

It's possible a few of us hold hands with someone we're not speaking to at the moment. Outside of the confines of this song, some of us hold grudges. We're not naming names, but someone here slept with one of our boyfriends, and we all know about it. The ramifications have rippled their way through our ranks. But right now there is no way to discern who is singing what or whose hand is holding whose.

Without sight, it is no longer a room with bodies. Even in the dark some of us close our eyes and we feel every bit of the four parts in our chests. The sopranos could just as easily be the source of the low, steady thump of the baseline. The tenors can take credit for the light melody that lifts above our heads. Two girls in the midst of a love triangle might be grasping each other's fingers. Our hands grow slack in each other's palms, or more tightly grasped. We have well-styled manicures or bitten fingernails but the veins in our intertwined fingers beat out the rhythm in synchronization. This is our last rehearsal before the end of year concert, where we will all wear black dresses and pin a red flower in our hair. We may grumble about the formality of it, that our outfits are dour and stuffy, but it is tradition and we are proud to be a part of it.

We have a visitor with us tonight. She holds our hands. Although she originally introduced herself as Mrs. Cooper, she was quick to correct herself with her first name, Jessica. She had been in our group thirty or so years ago; she mentioned the date, but we didn't listen. We tear her apart in our one mind's eye. Her hair is manicured and her makeup does not quite conceal her crow's feet or laugh lines. She wears jeans that look expensive but bunch on her waist and sag in the butt. That is just what happens with age, we tell ourselves. Still, we're on our best behavior because there's a rumor she's going to donate quite a bit of money to our album recording fund.

Of all the days to have a prospective patron drop by. We can't gossip or roll our eyes. It was a senior who'd gotten cheated on, a junior who'd done the cheating. Allegiances seem to have been drawn based on class, not voice part. Us Juniors think it's not on her, that it's always the guy's fault, because of feminism. We the Seniors think she's an absolute homewrecker and we're shocked at this bitch. How could we do that to someone in our own group? One of us? The Freshmen and Sophomores among us are more split, mostly we fall in line with the Seniors because they're more established.

Or we don't care at all. We hold all viewpoints in contradiction and they flow in and out of each other. But now we are arranged by voice part and in the folds of eight counts it falls out of our consciousness. We stagger our breathing to produce one constant sound. The first verse bleeds into the second.

This is our only song with no soloist. Each part takes a turn at the melody, snaking in and out of words and syllables. Many of our songs are pop covers and require one of us to step up and sing the words into a microphone by ourself. Different songs showcase individual voices, and on our own we each sound very distinct. Some of us get solos more often than others. Sometimes some of us get mad about that, but, in the end, we are not a democracy. We're a single entity and glory for one is glory for all.

Mrs. Cooper, excuse us, Jessica, had surprised us from somewhere in the darkened room and asked to join us for our last song, the madrigal. *We've been singing this song since I was a member*, she said with excitement slung through her voice. *I'm so glad to see we're still doing it.* So we broke our ranks to include her and she assumed her old position among the Soprano 1's, muttering jokes about how she hadn't warmed up. The Junior who slept with one of our boyfriends is also a Sop 1. *Excuse me if my voice cracks,* Jessica said.

It's been a while, we thought maliciously, as we let her in our circle. Held her speckled hand. We were half surprised when she fit right in. We'd almost expected cobwebs and dust to puff out of her when we started. Even as she holds her own, layers her voice into ours, we can not quite accept that she had once held hands that held hands that held the hands we are holding now. Or worn a red flower in her hair. Perhaps she'd even lived in the now mythic a cappella house.

There had been an upset with the passing down of the a cappella house to upcoming seniors the year before, the soccer girls signing the lease out from under us even though we've been in that house for almost a decade. Years of initiation parties and post-concert parties and regular parties. A lot of parties. But no more, thanks to the soccer girls. Fuck the soccer girls.

The chorus brings everyone's mouth to the same shape. We fall into the familiar grooves of the song we've sung year after year. Our bodies rock slightly back and forth. We are not flawless. Some of us have the song more memorized than others—the longer we've been in the group, the more confidently we sing. Each note is a matter of fact, tying us to our history with this collective, solidifying our belonging. But even the mistakes are easily absorbed into this thing that we are creating. Simple vibrations, such a common occurrence, arranged in such a way that it builds mazes in the airwaves. A few notes slip, a measure confused for one that comes later. It is to be expected; we learn five new songs every semester. We are not professionals. Among school and work and internships and keg stands, we rehearse twice a week and rarely practice on our own. Last semester we were in rough shape, our musical director lost it and yelled at us at the top of rehearsal when one of our new songs fell apart. Those of us who live with her didn't speak to her for the whole ride home. But this song we sing year after year, so mostly we know it all by now. The newer we are to the group, the more we struggle.

We know we should memorize our little string of notes on the treble clef, these puzzle pieces that fit into something bigger than the sum of its parts. It becomes worth it in moments like these, when the lights go off or the spotlight goes on and we fuse together sonically. Constantly chasing, reaching towards this feeling. From many lungs comes one chord.

Enjoy it, Jessica had sighed at the top of rehearsal before we'd turned out the lights, shaking her head with longing in her eyes. *After you graduate there are so few opportunities like this.*

We nodded solemnly; we know she's right. We've heard this sentiment before, from our older siblings, our parents. Take advantage of every opportunity in college. Afterwards everything changes. We accept this as truth, but the reality of it slips away before we can really ponder what it means.

As the chorus lulls into the second verse, we hear the boys out in the hallway. Traditionally we both rehearse at the same time, in rooms across the hall from each other. Us Seniors remember when there was bad blood between the two groups, but now we are buddy-buddy with those boys. We think some of them are cute, even if they are overly flirtatious with us. Some of us have crushes on some of them. We're pretty sure that some of them reciprocate. They jostle us after our shows and steal the red flowers from our hair, they clip them behind their own ears. Like children. They think they're all that because they can hit real base notes. But we have our traditions, and we have each other. After the song is over we will dissolve, regress to our petty problems with each other, but now we strengthen our circle and our voice and sing together over the boys.

Our bodies move on the same beat, and we rev ourselves up for the energetic crescendo of the bridge. Somehow we each sing just a little bit louder, but the whole vehicle swells around us without our even trying. Like blowing up a balloon. We wonder if Jessica will miss the key change, falter or fall when we take a breath and somehow sing the same song with different notes. Our musical director is the sole one among us who truly understands how key changes work, the science of it, the rest of us only feel it implicitly. We hate that music is math, that it can be boiled down into dots and symbols as a language on a piece of paper. Rather than what it is, running through our veins and coursing through our bodies, our one body. Making us immortal.

Jessica sings through the key change without faltering and we are a bit disappointed. *I still got it*, we can almost hear her thinking. She had truly been a part of us for a full four years, we realize. She had once owned these notes the same way the Seniors do. We think of the hands she's held in the other direction, not connecting her to us, but back in the past, holding a hand who held a hand who held a hand, once a we and now working in a corporate office in the sky somewhere. Old enough to be our mother, maybe our grandmother. Our palms are sweaty, slipping within each other's grasp. We stand up a little taller, craning our necks to reach the notes. New members will join the group and we will continue singing the Final Madrigal. The song continues, the same but different. One last chorus, in this new key.

Suddenly, the scandal, the divide between the Juniors and Seniors, seems a little less important. Jessica sings even louder, almost shouting the final measures. She illustrates the inevitable outcome that Seniors will leave us and die. They will never forget their part of the Final Madrigal, but neither will they be a part of us. We think of those hands she's held with horror. Once young flesh, ligaments pulsing in time with the beat of the song we are singing, counting us in with a snap of the fingers, now just bone against bone. We reject the thought. We will live forever. We squeeze each other's hands tighter within the rhythm of our darkened circle and let the last note hum against our skin.

HOW DOES THIS ONE START AGAIN?

A Conversation with Phoebe Phelps

Michael Stewart: Hey, Phoebe, and welcome to the pages of *Driftwood*! It is a pleasure to have an opportunity to talk to you about your story. It is such a beautifully crafted piece, and I'm curious about the work that went into making it. But first, the little details throughout the story are great, so I have to ask: were you in a Madrigal choir?

Phoebe Phelps: Hi, Michael! Thank you for having me. It's so cool to get to talk about my work with you. I'm very excited.

Yes, this piece is very much inspired by the a cappella group I was in during college. I'd been in chorus and singing lessons since elementary school, but there was something about the way that we made all of the music ourselves during a cappella. I had no problem waxing poetic about that. I had to cut down a lot more of the flowery stuff about it.

MS: One of the most striking things about your story is your use of a collective voice. The Madrigal choir, a kind of Greek chorus, addresses the reader directly as a single entity. Did you go into the story knowing that this was the perspective you wanted to take? Did you find it limiting, freeing, or a bit of both?

PP: That was the only thing I knew when I started working on this—a story about an a cappella group, written in the collective voice. The first time I encountered the first-person plural was during undergrad, when I was in an a cappella group myself, and I immediately thought that the two things were perfect for each other. I'd had that kernel of an idea kicking around in the back of my head since then and finally started writing it about seven or eight years later.

It was definitely both limiting and freeing, but much more freeing. There were a few technical constraints I came across when trying to describe the internal drama in the group—how do I do that when they are all talking and they are all "we"? Some things that I originally tried just didn't work. I had a few of the girls in the group named, like the president and beatboxer, but that made them stick out in a way I didn't want them to. In a way, the limitations led me right to what the story was about. That struggle between the collective and the individual and the power that the group has over each of them.

MS: Do you often hold stories in the back of your mind for years, or was this an exception?

PP: Yeah, I guess I do. I definitely always have more ideas than I can work on at a time, and it wasn't until a few years ago that I really started focusing on my writing consistently, so I have a lot of ideas that I'd been compiling before that. I also hold on to stories that I've already written but maybe aren't as good as they could be, and then they find their way into larger things I'm working on. Or I rewrite them completely into something new. I just revisited an old essay that I was writing three or four years ago. It was about fifteen pages because I was rambling on trying to find the meaning, and I cut it down to 750-words, and now I think it's exactly what I was trying to say since the beginning.

MS: Your story is told from inside a circle, and the central tension seems to be about being in and out of that circle. Individuality feels vulnerable, and the chorus, more than a group, is an identity. Could you talk about this circle and its importance to these women?

PP: The more I worked on this story, the more I thought of Vonnegut's concepts of Granfalloon and Karass from *Cat's Cradle*. A karass is a group of people who are linked cosmically, and a granfalloon is a "false karass," a group of people who think they are linked but it is only superficially—like being from the same state or a baseball team, etc. They are silly made-up words, but the ideas have always resonated with me, especially watching how people feel more protected when they're a part of something. You can see it very transparently on college campuses, with people joining clubs or Greek life, but it happens everywhere. There is strength in numbers, but it is a constructed and false kind of security. It comes out in politics, in war, in sports, or other kinds of fandoms, everywhere.

For this group specifically, that security is also about youth and being able to deny their future. While they are in this group, they are young and in a suspended moment. There's no need to think about graduating and leaving to become something else because they have already defined themselves with this group.

MS: I'm curious about your title. For someone like me with no background in music, could you explain "staggered breathing" as a technique and its relevance to the story?

PP: Yes! Stagger breathing is a term used in choir where each singer makes a point to breathe at different times during the phrase or measure, so that there is a consistent sound with no gaps for inhales. In my experience, it's mostly used in a cappella, when the singers are creating all of the sound of the song including the accompaniment. Whereas in a choir with a piano or orchestra, you might try to breathe all at the same time to create crisp words.

This story didn't have a title right up until the end. Or, it had many titles and I hated all of them. "Staggered Breathing" really came to me all at once, the idea that everyone is actually working asynchronously to create the illusion of synchronized sound. It's kind of a catch-22, and I felt like it really worked with this story, being told in one voice but all these different perspectives being contained within it. Working out of sync to create one consistent story.

MS: I love the evident care for language and sound you show in this piece. For example, the way you let the choir's voice build. Their opening statements are couched behind "might" and "possible," but as the story progresses, the voice becomes more sure, speaking in these wonderfully confident sentences. I am curious about your editing process and how you developed this story. What do you pay the most attention to when you are revising a piece?

PP: That's a great question. I wish I knew so my process could be a bit more methodical! My attention is usually all over the place in revision. I try to focus on big picture stuff before spending time on line edits, because I don't want to spend a lot of time on a sentence I wind up cutting. I move stuff around constantly and change up the order of paragraphs, my copy/paste buttons are well-used. My editing process can probably just be described as obsession and perfectionism. But I do find revision to be the most fun part of writing; it's where all of the experimentation and discovery happens. It feels like a puzzle to me, or a treasure hunt. The first draft is a slog; the second draft is a game.

Actually, now that I'm thinking about it, I think that my editing process is to let it sit for a little while and try to put it out of my mind. What I keep thinking about, what I keep coming back to while I'm doing other things—that's what I pay the most attention to when I return to edits. And that is different for every story or essay, but I guess I generally focus on the structure and ordering of a story.

For this piece specifically it was easy to follow the rhythm of it, and I mean that literally. It took me a while to realize that this story could be told within the time they sang one song, and then it became pretty easy to structure it. Verse, chorus, key change. I tried to lean into all of those concepts narratively. Starting off quietly and crescendoing, repeating and then changing.

MS: I am eager to read more of your writing. Would you say this story is representative of your work as a whole? Do you return to these themes of youth, identity, and acceptance?

PP: I'm not sure I'd say it's representative, but it definitely showcases my interest in point of view and craft. Mostly my ideas start on a technical level like this one, and then I have to work down to a story from there. So, a lot of things I'm preoccupied with come out almost unintentionally. When I finished writing the first draft of this I read it over and went, "Oh, I guess this is about fear of death? I guess I'm afraid of death?"

It's funny, you say it's about youth, but I'd say it's about aging or death or fear of dying. They're probably the same thing, just different ways of looking at it.

MS: Finding a story "unintentionally" fits well with your idea of second drafts as treasure hunts or games. I imagine this process leads to some surprising discoveries. Have there been situations where you think you are writing about one thing only to find out you're writing about another?

PP: Well, I think that stories definitely wind up being more complex than the initial idea or conception of them. I wouldn't say anything has ever done a 180 turn on me; it's moreso that they wind up being more interesting or complicated. This can be cool, like in this story, but I have also run into road blocks because a concept hasn't really turned out the way that I planned for it to. I've got this one story, for example, that started as a really simple scene with a couple in a bar and very quickly morphed into something layered with perspective about the bar as a whole and the life of the bartender and—long story short—I'm taking some time away from that one because it got too big for me for the moment.

MS: What are some of the inspirations and influences that shape your writing?

PP: Oh, this question is always so hard, because I'm not really sure what the answer is. I read a lot, and I am not really one to pick favorites—they seem so limiting and never exactly representative. I think that rather than just a short list of things I like being my influences, I am a collection of everything I've ever read whether I've liked it or not. The things I've disliked have led me to my style just as much as the things that have completely resonated with me because they have shown me what I definitely don't want to do. I'm sure I'm also influenced by many things I don't remember.

I mentioned Vonnegut earlier, and I can use him as an easy answer. He was someone I found in my late teens, and while I don't think my style is anything like his, I loved reading him, so I'd say he was an early influence on me.

Outside of reading I also watch a lot of stand-up; I think that influences me more than I know. Stand-up and music, because I think rhythm and timing (comedic or otherwise) in writing is very important and definitely underrated. I lived in Europe for about four years, and that had an immense influence on how I see the world, which of course is then translated to what I write.

For this story specifically, I tried to seek out other first-person plural narratives to read, and there were not as many out there as I'd expected. But then I was assigned "The History of Girls" by Ayse Papatya Bucak in a workshop, and it was just perfect. There is a slight shift in perspective at the end of my story that I'm very proud of, and looking back, I have no idea if I'd written that before or after reading *History of Girls*, which has a major and heartbreaking and completely effective perspective shift at the end. So whether it influenced me directly or not, it definitely feels worth mentioning.

MS: Sometimes, when working on a piece, I listen to the same song or a small set of songs when I write. I feel it helps ease me into the same headspace. Is there a particular song you associate with "Staggered Breathing," a specific Final Madrigal you hear them singing?

PP: Oh, this is a great question. No, there's no particular song at all! I listen to music constantly, although I'll often listen to instrumental or music in Spanish when I'm writing. In terms of what they're singing, that's so interesting; I'd never thought of it. I think it's because I never really experienced the songs we sang from outside of it. My own memories of a cappella are so fragmented that I can feel the rhythm of them all swaying their bodies together to keep to the beat, but all of the sounds I can think of are the assorted "ba dada do, ba dada do." I never remembered how a song started based on the title when I was in a cappella. We would be up on stage, about to start the next number, and the music director counts us in, and I would always have to turn to my friend next to me and say, "How does this one start again?" and she'd whisper the first few syllables, and then I'd be good for the whole song.

It's a funny thing actually, and I'm glad you brought it up, because I really had been thinking about it from my own experience, one voice contributing to many rather than the other way around. When you're in the heart of it like that, you can't even hear the full song that you're singing as it sounds to someone outside the group. You're just wrapped up in it, and you're singing your own little part, and you know it feels good to be a part of it.

MS: It's been wonderful having this back-and-forth with you. I truly enjoyed your story, and it has been fascinating to hear about how you work. As a final question, do you currently have any projects in the works?

PP: Always. I have a few stories that are at about the halfway stage that I return to every now and then, but I am in my final semester of grad school, so my focus right now is my thesis project. It's a novel, and I've never attempted anything so big. It is scary and daunting, but mostly I'm finding it to be a really interesting practice. Like, my brain doesn't feel big enough to think about the story as a whole, but somehow I'm making progress. It feels like I'm discovering things about myself and how I think even more so than the work.

Thank you so much for these thoughtful questions; it's been so nice talking with you.

QUIZ: HOW FORGIVING OF A PERSON ARE YOU?

Aziza Kasumov

1. Do you find that you tend to hold a lot of grudges?
   (a) When people step on my toes, I step back.
   (b) Fool me once, shame on you. Fool me twice, shame on me!
   (c) Generally speaking, I'm not really the type to hold grudges.
   (d) Holding grudges increases average wrinkle depth in women ages thirty-five and up by two nanometers per day.

3. Someone asks you whether you believe that people are good. You:
   (a)
   (b)
   (c) Don't answer that.
   (d)

4. The last time you were angry, how did it feel?
   (a) Storm clouds.
   (b) Hole-punch clouds.
   (c) Atmospheric-disturbance clouds.
   (d) Anger isn't actually anger at all, it's just sadness pretending to be anger. (Announcing-the-rain clouds.)

5. Consider the following scenario: In fifth grade, you become acquainted with a beverage priorly unbeknownst to you: Mountain Dew. You have one taste of this Mountain Dew and you are immediately infatuated. With every dollar you acquire, you purchase a bottle of Mountain Dew at the corner store across from your school. You drink the Mountain Dew during third-period history, otherwise known as third-person history, otherwise known as the opposite of first-person history/reality. A few weeks into your Mountain Dew infatuation, you leave the room in the middle of class to go to the bathroom. While you're gone, the kid sitting next to you—a popular boy you're a little in love with—shakes your bottle like someone working to mix you a drink. When you come back and open the bottle to take a sip, you splash Mountain Dew all over yourself and

over several children in close proximity. You know the prank was the doing of the popular boy sitting next to you because he ducked under the table as you reached for the bottle. The event teaches you the following: (1) never leave your personal belongings unattended, (2) people will, generally speaking, not have your best interest at heart, and (3) a person's capacity for goodness is inversely correlated with their capacity to act upon it—read: those with the greatest ability to do good will seldomly do so. Ten years later, you run into the boy on the street. He is still very good-looking, wearing a tailored suit and polished shoes. He looks like life, by all conventional measures, is working out just fine for him. No—better than just fine. Life is working out above-average for him. He doesn't see you, and even if he did, he may not have recognized you. Nearby, two kids on the sidewalk are tossing a bottle of Mountain Dew back and forth between them. Shouldn't you forgive him, for making you the person that you are?

(a) Yes.

(b) Assuming that the popular boy's life working out above average for him approximately equals a 81.5 (out of 105) on the quality-of-life scale, therefore suggesting a capacity of goodness of >73.5, the boy's capacity to act upon his capacity for goodness would, given the inverse correlation of the two variables, come out at approximately <3.1, altogether suggesting a forgiveness delta of 0.22.

(c) No.

6. Have you ever left your personal belongings unattended?

(a) Yes.

(b) No.

(c) Leaving your personal belongings unattended significantly increases your chance of serendipitously finding them again over time.

(d) Serendipitously recouping lost unattended personal belongings significantly increases your outlook on humanity over time.

7. If you responded (b) to Question #6, move on to Question #8. Otherwise, answer the following: Do you believe that people are good?

(a) No.

(b) Yes.

8. Consider the following scenario: Two girls grow up in a land far, far away. They grow up close—each other's closest confidantes. Once they are of marrying age, they both marry—the older one first, then the younger one. The older one marries a nice man, though soon after she becomes pregnant with their first child, the husband gets in trouble with the law. He has to leave the land far, far away, for a land even farther away. He asks his wife to come with him, even though this means leaving her closest confidante behind. Still, she decides to go with her husband. The other girl, upon realizing that her closest confidante has gone away with her husband, is shattered. Meanwhile, her own husband gets in trouble with the law, too, though for different reasons: he is not a nice man, not to her at least, and not to their child when it is born, either. The girl feels trapped and alone. Often, she thinks about her closest confidante and wonders how she's doing in the land even farther away. Finally, the girl manages to escape the far, far away land with her child and runs away to the land even farther away. She arrives there one day, years after the two girls have last seen each other. She knocks on the door. Her closest confidante opens. What do they owe each other, if anything?

9. Consider again the scenario from Question #8. Does it change anything that the two girls are sisters?

(a) As they say: Blood is thicker than water.
(b) Which is to say it matters more than it does not matter.
(c) Because blood is thicker than water, it is also heavier.
(d) Which is to say it does not matter more than it does matter.

10. Do you believe that people can change?

(a) Yes.
(b) No.
(c) Answering this question in the affirmative presumes that a person may, as part of her general ability to undergo change, also change her answer to this question at a later point, thereby acknowledging that the question may also be answered in the negative.
(d) Because of the paradox presented in (c), (b) is the only appropriate answer.

11. If you responded (b), (c), or (d) for Question #10, move on to Question #13. If you responded (a) for Question #10, answer the

following: Do you believe part of a person's ability to change is her ability to learn how to forgive?

(a) Yes.
(b) No.

12. If you responded (b) for Question #11, move on to Question #13. If you responded (a) for Question #11, don't you believe that answering Question #10 in the affirmative (=people can change) presumes that people can both learn and unlearn how to forgive, thereby acknowledging that there is no one-way correlation between a person's ability to change and her ability to learn how to forgive (=learning how to forgive is not a necessary condition for change), thereby acknowledging the only correct answer to Question #11 is (b)? Also, don't you believe answering either or both Question #10 and #11 in the affirmative, thereby acknowledging a person's characteristics and abilities (=ability to forgive) are subject to change over time, renders this quiz—which, given the nature of personality quizzes at large, assumes characteristics and abilities to be fixed rather than mutable—inherently paradoxical? What is, in your opinion, the necessary condition—if any—for people to change?

13. Imagine a country in which citizens are financially rewarded for performing good deeds. Forgiveness, in this system, qualifies as a good deed. Is this what true forgiveness looks like?

(a) True forgiveness looks like announcing-the-rain-is-over clouds.

14. Consider the following scenario: Once upon a time, in a land far, far away, there lived a grasshopper in a field of corn surrounding an old country house. One day, the grasshopper went into the old country house and came across, in its kitchen, a pot of fat. Excitedly, the grasshopper jumped into the pot and began eating. The grasshopper became so enamored with the fat that he didn't notice the bed of fat below him lowering, while the rim of the pot rose higher and higher. Finally, once the pot was empty and the grasshopper full and heavy, he looked up to notice that the rim of the pot was too high up for him to jump out. The grasshopper tried to climb up the sides of the pot instead, but his hands and feet were sticky from the fat, and he kept sliding down. Suddenly, a cat appeared and looked into the pot,

seeing the grasshopper. "You ate all my fat!" the cat howled. "Don't you have enough corn to eat out in the fields?" The grasshopper shrugged his shoulders. "I became enamored," he said. "I apologize. But now I am stuck, can you please help me out of the pot?"

14 A. Assume the position of cat. What would you do?

(a) Leave the grasshopper in the pot.
(b) Teach the grasshopper a lesson, though ultimately save the grasshopper.
(c) Eat the grasshopper. (One grasshopper fulfills twenty-three percent of your daily nutritional demand for protein.)
(d) Save the grasshopper.

14 B. Assume now the position of the grasshopper. Shouldn't you thank the cat, for making you the person that you are?

15. Consider the following scenario: You're twenty-three years old and your mother has recently passed away. At a bar, you meet someone you could see yourself falling in love with. However, this love union is conditional: for it to work, you must stop consuming substances and stop affiliating with people consuming substances, a group of people that includes your closest (and only) confidante. Upon careful deliberations, you choose to fulfill the conditions of this love union. You are happy. (Or believe that you are, which is essentially the same, given the difference between being happy and believing yourself to be happy is indetectable to the human mind.) A few months go by, during which you ignore your former closest (and only) confidante's attempts at contacting you. One evening, your former closest confidante consumes a large amount of substances and burns down your house. Subsequently, the confidante flees the city and narrowly avoids criminal prosecution. Meanwhile, your love union falls apart. Was it all for nothing, then? What do you owe your confidante, if anything? Does it change anything that you and your confidante are related by blood? Does it matter more than it does not matter? Do people owe each other anything, anything at all?

14 C. Assume now the position of the grasshopper. What does it feel like, to seek forgiveness?

BREAKING THE QUIZ

A Conversation with Aziza Kasumov

Stephen Hundley: Hi, Aziza, and welcome to *Driftwood*. Your ability to infuse a multiple-choice test with narrative, memory, and tension made this piece stand out to our editors. "QUIZ..." carries the humor that we expect from a story that subverts form norms—I'm thinking of the "List" pieces published at *McSweeney's Internet Tendency*—but beyond that, we found that framing this narrative within a series of questions defused character throughout the piece and complicated our approach to the story within the questions. How did you arrive at this form, and is it one you've encountered or worked with before?

Aziza Kasumov: Thanks so much for these kind words, Stephen, and I'm glad the story has found a home at *Driftwood*. I didn't think of *McSweeney*'s "List" pieces per se when I started drafting the form, though I do read and love many of them. More so, I've always had a weak spot for personality quizzes and still sometimes find myself indulging in them. They are admittedly quite silly, though over time I've come to recognize them not as a tool for self-discovery but more so for self-reflection. A personality quiz is not going to tell you that you are most likely to develop a lipstick addiction or will become an overbearing mom, but taking a personality quiz means taking time out of your day to think about who you are. At first I wanted this story to work more purely in that sense, as a tool for the reader's self-reflection, an actual personality quiz with an answer key and so on, that truly lets readers determine how forgiving of a person they are. Then I saw David Foster Wallace break the psychological quiz format in "Octet," a short story in *Brief Interviews with Hideous Men*. While he ultimately takes the format into more of a metafictional and different direction, I liked his use of narrative in the questions, or prompts, and how the answer options he presented felt kind of like non-sequiturs at first. It made me, as a reader, engage more thoroughly with the story, and it was also just such a fun, unexpected read. As a writer, it made me want to play around with the personality quiz form myself.

SH: That's fascinating. When breaking a quiz or other form, how does one break generatively?

AK: I think breaking is most generative when it is done for a purpose that clearly serves the story, that isn't just gimmick. In my quiz, I wanted to draw awareness to the quiz author's own struggle with the themes of the quiz. This is a layer I don't think I could've achieved without leaving certain answer options blank, repeating questions, and so on. In an earlier version of the story, when I was thinking through different ways I could break the quiz form, I briefly embedded the quiz—still in its flawed, broken version—as an annotated "teaching quiz" into a fictional guide on professional quiz-making that I wrote for that purpose. Ultimately, I found that this "teaching quiz" frame didn't serve the story, though. On the contrary, the effect of presenting the broken quiz as a "teaching quiz" served to sanitize and deaden the emotional impact—it was now a quiz that was purposefully written incorrectly for educational purposes, rather than for the purpose of reflecting the author's emotionally volatile state. I think there's something to be said, in general, about emotionality and breaking narrative frames. Breaking, to me, suggests a loss of control. We lose control when we are overwhelmed with emotion. We write novel-length text messages when we've got things to get off our chest emotionally—I'd argue this is one way we, in real life, break the standard "text message" form.

SH: How was the process of drafting this story different from a more traditionally formatted short story, and what did this form allow that was unique or important to your vision?

AK: I think one big joy I got out of writing this story was that I got to work on a scenario or question I liked and then, rather than moving chronologically to build meaning and/or advance plot, could jump to a totally different section and work on that, whatever section called to me. To me, it made moving through the drafts more pleasurable than usual. As for my vision as a writer, something I keep returning to in my work is trying to use forms that mimic how people most commonly engage with the written word in their day-to-day lives. Other pieces I've written use the format of a Reddit thread, a Wikipedia article, a customer service chat and so on. As a reader, I myself love spending time reading in these formats online, and I find a lot of what I come across there actually strangely artistic and literary, without there often being any intention by the author to present their writing as such. It's something that's always fascinated me and that I try to capture in my own work. Also—I'm bothered by this notion that people aren't reading anymore. People read all the time! People literally spend hours on Reddit everyday, reading about gastrointestinal diseases or whether M37 should break up with F29 because she slept with his cousin or whatever. I'm interested in what happens when literary writing attempts to operate in these forms.

SH: I'm very interested in what you've said about finding the places where everyday discourse and literature meet, and I would love to see more of these kinds of pieces. How would you characterize the form of a post? What opportunities does it provide?

AK: I should say I'm obviously not the first one to play around with form in that way. Jennifer Egan does it famously in her PowerPoint chapter in *A Visit from a Goon Squad*, Tess Gunty's *The Rabbit Hutch*, which won the National Book Award in 2022, has several online-format chapters, and then I just read a great new story collection called *A Couple of Things Before the End*, by Australian writer Sean O'Beirne, which includes a whole stack of stories mimicking everyday discourse online, be it emails, online newsletters, comments below YouTube videos, etc. And it makes sense that the means by which we communicate with one another are making their way into our literature—they always have. Think about the epistolary novel, the novel in letters, which has probably been around for as long as people wrote letters. Today, so much of our discourse, our communication and our reading, takes place online, and literature should and does reflect that. But I believe we have room to push further. Right now, I think a lot of writers are experimenting in this direction, but ultimately find they need to supplement their narratives with more traditional first- or third-person design. I disagree. Senthuran Varatharajah wrote an entire novel, published in German and unfortunately not (yet) available in English, in the format of a Facebook Messenger conversation between two people. Other recent German literature has been written entirely in WhatsApp chat or email format. I'm not saying every single time this is done, it's done successfully—but it's possible.

As for the opportunities it provides, I think the advantages are obvious: meet readers where they are. Fiction imitates life, right. Well, then it should imitate all parts of it, including the four-hour-daily-screen-time part, though I'm certainly not advocating for that. Even from a craft perspective, I think there are clear opportunities for writers. Personally, I find it easier to write within the set constraints of a container, because the limitations are clear from the start, even if I find myself re-drafting the same story five or six times from scratch, each time in a different container. To me, that's still less intimidating than the blank white space of an empty page.

SH: Working out of the quiz form, what were your expectations for facilitating collaborative meaning-making with your readers? What is the role of choice (or its illusion) in this piece?

AK: Once I decided to move away from the traditional quiz format, that this would not be an actual quote-unquote functioning quiz, I began thinking about the piece more as a traditional short story that's perhaps more one-directional in meaning-making. What I mean by that is, I finish writing something, and then you as the reader take from it what you want, meaning-wise. Only later, when I shared a draft with friends and they told me they began their reading experience of this story by getting a pencil and marking their answers to the first few questions did I realize something else was going on here. It wasn't intentional, but I liked that. Of course, eventually they realized the story didn't actually require them to mark their answers, but I liked that they were prepared to engage with this piece in a different way—that they slowed down to think about their responses. My hypothesis would be that a quiz-taking mindset makes you more self-aware as you're reading the prompts, makes you think about your own behavior or preferences as well as the actual story on the page, rather than disappearing into the story entirely. Again, I'm not sure if that's what's actually happening, but the idea excites me. Especially when it comes to stories that deal with ethics, a subject matter that interests me very much, I'm curious about the potential of the quiz format to engage readers on more than a storytelling level. It's something I've started exploring more in other pieces I've begun working on.

As for the role of choice in the piece, I think it goes back to what I said earlier about personality quizzes being tools for self-reflection and not self-discovery. If a quiz asks you whether you would be angry or not in response to your roommate eating your last can of soup, you're not going to "discover" the answer while taking the quiz—you already know you'd probably be pissed. Taking the quiz, you solely reflect on it. The quiz story is actually a chapter in my novel, written from the perspective of a character who's supposedly trying to figure out whether or not to forgive a family member for a terrible thing that person has done. I liked the idea of using the quiz format for this chapter, because even though there may be the illusion of choice, in truth the character already knows what she's going to do—she will forgive, and the quiz is only a tool to reflect on that choice. For readers who come across this chapter as a standalone story, without the context of knowing that character, I'm hoping the illusion of choice is still reflected in their own reaction to the prompts. Even if they're not actively marking their responses with a pencil, I am, like I said earlier, hypothesizing people would still think about how they react. But in doing so, they're not "choosing" a reaction—they're only articulating what they actually already know to be true about them. For the record, I'm not making the argument people don't make active choices or can't change. I do believe they can. I just think that when you're sitting down to take a personality quiz on how great or shitty of a roommate you are in your shrink's waiting room, that's not the moment when you make those changes or choices.

SH: I see what you mean about the quiz form providing a break or change for the reader. Does the character behind this quiz break from normative prose in other ways? To diffuse a character over multiple modes in one book is exciting.

AK: Yes, throughout the novel, readers mostly encounter this character in modes that are removed from normative prose—we see her engaged in a lengthy conversation with a chatbot, for instance, and as the subject of a r/relationship_advice post. The same is the case, by the way, for my other main characters. The project at large, for me, is very much about building—and diffusing—character across different narrative containers. Not to mention *Goon Squad* again, but I think what makes this work so incredible—at least to me—is that we get to see several characters in different narrative containers. Rather than confusing or flattening our understanding of who they are, it deepens it. Obviously, the book is primarily interested in doing so by rendering characters at vastly different points in their lives, so that we may see the effects of time—the "goon squad"—on them. But I would argue the fact that we see Jules Jones narrated in third person after his release from prison, and then again in first-person when we are presented with the footnoted magazine article he wrote about the very incident that got him arrested, has a similar effect. People contain multitudes. Who you are when you're anonymously commenting on influencer snark pages on Reddit is not the same person you are when you're talking to a customer service representative on the phone, or writing a job application, or sitting at a bar with a friend—something you may not even be actively clocking.

The idea that a first-person narration can present us with some ultimate level of access to a character's interiority, and thereby most effectively show us who they are, is, in my view, flawed. I would argue presenting characters across various narrative modes holds the potential to get closer to the truths—plural intended—about them. Online containers are especially suitable for that purpose, because the internet gives so many people the illusion of privacy and anonymity, and thereby invites them to reveal hidden parts about themselves. What could be more enticing when writing a character? At any rate, I think it's a helpful exercise, even when you're not writing in "found text" form, to ask yourself which Reddit board your character would be most active on, and what they'd be posting.

SH: I was interested in the asides and back-channel voices you built into the vignettes, particularly in questions 12 and 15. Can you speak to the voice or voices you deployed in this story to produce such an energetic, urgent effect?

AK: Both in question 12 and 15, I wanted to play around and see how far I can steer away from the traditional quiz format and still make it work for the story. At the end of question 12, with the imperative for the reader/quiz-taker to "discuss" the necessary condition for people to change, the question reads more like an essay prompt than a question in a personality quiz. I think what I tried to capture with those back-channel voices, with the back-and-forths and rephrasing and reiterating of the same questions, are the mental gymnastics we engage in when we try to figure out a personal problem. Yes, mostly we know, deep down, what we'll do. (See response to prior question.) But still, we must often go through this process of looking at things from every angle, drawing logical conclusions and coming up with logical consequences and arguments to make us make sense of the thing we've long decided to do anyway. For question 15, I also wanted things to feel like there is some sort of narrative climax being reached, despite the fact that there's no traditional narrative plot to follow throughout this story per se. I hope the repetition of some of the earlier questions, rephrased in a more urgent voice, worked in building that effect.

SH: How would you describe the role of forgiveness, memory, and debt in this story? How are they distinguished?

AK: In recent years—and this sweeping generalization may simply be a byproduct of getting older—I've increasingly felt that, for some people, it's become an acceptable mindset to believe that you don't owe anyone anything. Cut what doesn't serve you, set your boundaries, etc. The Kim Cattrall take of "I don't want to be in a situation for even an hour where I'm not enjoying myself." No actual dig at Kim Cattrall—I love her acting. And yes, boundaries are important. People who treat you poorly don't deserve your time and affection. But we've seen this language at times be pushed to a point where it's promoting a certain type of individualism that I find sad: egotism masquerading as self-care.

Maybe I'm old-fashioned, but I believe that we *do* owe things to others. The more difficult question, to me, is determining just how much we owe. One area in which I find this conundrum particularly hard to puzzle through is forgiveness. People, of course, do bad things all the time. But just how much forgiveness do we owe each other—and should this forgiveness be conditional or not? I wanted to explore this sentiment in a setting where people often still feel that they are indebted to one another to a large degree—the family unit—and juxtapose that with scenarios in which the familial relationship of the characters is not established yet. That's what I'm trying to do in question 8 and 9, and again in question 15. I think memory comes into play here, too, because forgiveness presumes a certain willingness on the part of the forgiver to live with the facts of what happened without letting them determine the present relationship—at times a very difficult feat.

Of course, there's also the argument that forgiving someone may betray one's own memory of the harm one has experienced at the hands of that person. I can think of situations where this might feel true, too. Well, perhaps the compounding of open-ended questions toward the end of the story hint at the fact that I haven't found a definitive solution to answering many of these questions either. I think the only thing that I ultimately landed on in trying to figure out what we owe others is that it's important to keep in mind the perspective of the person on the receiving end—the grasshopper asking to be forgiven, in this case. I tried to emphasize that in question 14. C.

SH: Thanks for sharing that. I admire your focus on the questions under the surface of this piece. Is it cathartic to see a study like this go from meditation to fiction piece?

AK: Yes, of course! To some degree, even though I may have not answered the questions at the center of this inquiry definitively and am, in fact, continuing to ponder them as I revise other parts of my novel, there's something about having at least revised this story or chapter to the degree where it is now "finished" that makes me feel like there's an element of conclusion, of having reached some sort of "truth," even if it's a messy one.

SH: How has your relationship changed with the piece since writing it?

AK: I feel like since finishing it, my relationship to the piece has not changed very much, but I do think there's something that always happens with drafts of chapters as they mature, which is that they feel less personal—in the raw, emotional sense—as they mature. This is the case here, too.

SH: Have other portions of this novel been reimagined or published as stand-alone pieces? Is the transition from chapter to story or poem a difficult process?

AK: My novel is highly fractured, and I wanted all of the chapters—while they serve the greater narrative—to also work as standalone pieces. My process on working on the novel has probably been closer to that of someone working on a short story collection; I've written all of the chapters completely out of order, with only some general idea of the larger narrative in mind. In that sense, all of them are technically publishable as standalone pieces, though none of them, aside from the quiz, have been published individually so far. I don't find the transition from chapter to standalone story difficult in that sense; actually, what's been more complicated is trying to turn all the standalone stories into chapters that actively serve the greater narrative, to deepen the links between the individual chapters. Sort of like weaving a loose net tighter together, which involves a lot of disentangling and re-weaving, unfortunately.

SH: What does this piece borrow or develop from fables?

AK: I've said earlier that I'm very interested in morals and ethics as a writer, in exploring the tension and complicated space between what's right and what's wrong. Well, there's one literary genre in which these sorts of questions tend to be not so complicated at all: Fables, generally speaking, follow a set of very simple but strict moral rules, and the scenarios they present are uncomplicated enough so that they don't brush up against the boundaries of the moral framework we are being presented with. I wanted to have one question in the quiz that uses the fable form but pushes it past the point at which a reader can walk away with a clean "moral of the story." I don't remember the title or author, but I believe there was a fable I heard as a child about a bug of some sort stuck in a pot of fat or butter because the bug had eaten up all the contents and then couldn't get out because the sides were too slippery, and the bug itself too heavy. I wanted to start there—of course, the moral here being that one shouldn't be gluttonous, that greed is bad, etcetera. Then I'm asking the reader to assume the position of cat—a position of power in the fable—and make a decision on how to proceed. To punish or to forgive? In the traditional fable world, the obvious resolution would be to punish the grasshopper. But I think inviting the reader into the fable as a decision-maker also invites our whole world of complex ethics into the fable, a world in which we typically consider things like power dynamics and forgiveness when making moral decisions. I'm hoping that what's right and wrong at this point isn't so clear-cut anymore, despite the fablesque presentation of the story.

SH: Does this story have a sense of place? What was the role of scene and physicality in this piece?

AK: Because I've written this story with the rest of my novel in mind, I'm hoping that readers of the full book will eventually recognize some of the scenarios as scenes from other parts of the narrative. Of course, as a standalone story, this effect is lost. But to some degree, I believe this can also be an advantage, because the scenarios presented remain much more anonymous and in doing so adhere more closely to the form I'm trying to imitate. The reader is invited to think through the questions and scenarios presented with only the information given on the page in mind. Also, if I'm successful in my casting of the reader as quiz-taker, inviting the reader's presence, self-perception and self-reflection into the story, then the sense of place becomes something else altogether—a collaborative space in which the reader is taking the quiz.

I do, however, believe that there is scene and physicality in this story in the more traditional narrative understanding of these words, and creating that was important to me in writing this piece. Yes, not all of the questions live up to this, but questions 5, 8, 14, and 15 ultimately were attempts of mine at getting there. I love flash fiction, and, while writing, I was thinking about the scenarios in these questions as stand-alone flash pieces. For me that meant that, even within the constraint of none of them being longer than a paragraph, I attempted to build in mini-scenes, a mini-sense of place, characters, and physicality. I think in order for the story to express the kind of emotional urgency I hoped to convey, I couldn't have done without those moments.

SH: Where can our readers find more of your work, and what are you working on now?

AK: Nowhere, as of now—though I'm in the final stages of revising my novel and hoping to start the process of eventually getting it published. I might try to place a few chapters in magazines as individual stories before then—to be determined. The quiz felt like the most natural piece to try to get published individually, and it was also the first chapter I felt was truly "finished." I'm also working on a few literary translation projects—I'm translating from German, my mother tongue—on the side, and am hoping to get those out soon.

SH: What are you reading?

AK: A friend of mine recently got me onto Salinger's work—his novellas and stories beyond *Catcher in the Rye*—and I find his writing narratively incredibly inventive and exciting. In *Seymour, an Introduction,* he offers the reader an "unpretentious bouquet of early-blooming parentheses: (((()))).” I nearly fell off my chair when I read that! Also, because he keeps returning to members of the same family in so many of his stories, it feels like with every new text of his you read, you get another piece of some greater canvas, which feels very rewarding. Other than that, I try to read a lot of contemporary fiction to see what new forms other writers are coming up with. And I re-read Siri Hustvedt's *The Blazing World* probably once a year. It's my "found text" bible.

SH: Do you have any advice for writers looking to expand their relationship with form?

AK: I think, similarly to what I said earlier about "breaking generatively," the biggest thing that can go wrong with form experimentation is when it's done as a gimmick, with no meaning behind. Someone picked a random form that they were interested in and then shoved a story into it. The work that results is, in my view, often without much meaning. That being said, figuring out what the "right" form is for a story is often not obvious, rather, there are many possibilities. At this stage, I find myself often re-drafting a story several times completely from scratch, in a different container each time.

I think, despite the amount of work this takes, it's important to recognize when a container isn't working, and to not be afraid of scrapping it and starting anew, even though that, of course, is incredibly frustrating. But you'll also get a little euphoria-high when things are finally clicking and you realize you've got it right this time, that form and content aid each other in creating and amplifying meaning. Other than that, the only advice I can give is to pay attention to the world around you. You'll find "found text" in the randomest of places, and whenever you do, you have a new potential form to play with. Take this line, from New York City's Smoke-Free Air Act, which I was browsing for some random reason recently: "Smoking is prohibited in [...] 17. Zoos. 18. Elevators. 19. Public areas where bingo is played." Assignment: Write a story in the form of an anti-smoking regulation. It's possible.

MICHAEL FURY VS THE DEAD

R. Hunter Whitworth

I wake up early and dollop wet food out onto baking trays, and the cats emerge—dozens of them—from the corners of the house. I have to do it all myself now: see to their breeding and feeding, shear their fur in the summer, moisten their assholes with warm wet cloth to teach them how to shit when newly born. And yet Trisha would always ask me what was so horrible about my own life that I wanted to escape it by trying to be a professional wrestler.

The Persians look foolish in their summer cuts. They're almost bald everywhere except for shocks of white hair at the head and tail, but still they walk proudly. Their heads jerk up and down when they eat and they can be angry and unkind, as much as any human can. They had yowled during the haircuts, knowing that they were being made to look undignified, but let the offense go at the first meal afterwards. I ponder the volume of shit they are responsible for and think, as I often do, that if they can find a way to forgive, a person ought to be able to.

I walk up the stairs to Travis' room, clean, off-limits to the cats, and open the door. It looks the same as when he lived in it, frozen in a moment full of old wrestlers and bands that he doesn't talk about anymore. The bed is made from last Sunday and untouched since.

And I wonder, as I often do, what his room looks like in Ray the optometrist's house across town. A man, says Trisha, more content to live in the real world. I try not to think about Ray, but he has these billboards I have to drive past sometimes and Trisha keeps making a point of saying how good he is with Travis.

I leave the room, shut the door, take coffee to the van, and note the start-of-day mileage. The van has no seats behind the driver's or passenger's. It has a kind of slat in the middle of where those seats would be, for a body gurney, the legs of which fold in a neat way for being pushed into and pulled out of the van.

The gurney slides in better if I'm not pushing too hard, actually, and in the summer heat the van doesn't start as well. I learned on the job like that, like how becoming a better wrestler is about being on the job wrestling a lot and hearing what live crowds like and don't like. This is why a wrestler might not peak until his 40s, like I tried to tell Trisha. Like I tried to tell her that it might make long-term sense for our family sometimes if I drove four hours for a match on a Friday night to wrestle and be paid with a hotdog and a handshake.

Another thing I have learned is not to pull the van right into the front entrances of the nursing homes where everyone can see, so I park the van outside of the back gate of the Maple Grotto and buzz in.

"Here for," a sticky voice asks.

"Giving Mr. Bumgartner a ride," I say, checking my list.

The gate rolls open, the sun creeps a little higher on the horizon, and in I roll.

This part of the job is straightforward. Bumgartner is bagged already, so all I have to do is make some small talk, respectfully load his old bones up, and point the van back at the funeral home. It's good money if you can get it, though not enough to drop the cats. More importantly, I can think about wrestling matches during the driving time.

The funeral home is run by a pleasant man and that man's pleasant son, but the only person I ever get to interact with is Dale. The son and the father are shaped like a butternut squash and a larger butternut squash. Dale is shaped like the kind of insect that would have to disguise itself as a stick to avoid confrontation.

One thing I have noticed in years of hoisting up for body slams (even if the guy is jumping a little to help you) is how much heavier a living body is than a dead one. Bumgartner, for instance, practically requires no effort for me to push down the hallway to Dale's lab. It's like they lose some burden at the moment of departure.

Dale is in there, holding the corners of a corpse's mouth open in something like a smile and mirroring it as best he can on his own face. He's got a flashlight between his teeth, pointed down, and the right sleeve of his lab coat hangs deflated at the shoulder, tied into a knot at about where an elbow would be.

He sees me, lets the flashlight fall, and catches it. The fingers do a little spin with it and he sets it down on a counter by where some other instruments are sitting on a tray. He yawns theatrically. "Caught a live one last night," he says. He works the eyebrows, expecting follow-up questions.

"Bumgartner," I say. Somewhere in here, I know, he keeps a drawer full of breast implants removed prior to their hosts' cremation.

"These girls," he says. "Once they find out what I do..." and he looks at me like the sentence finishes itself. He'll go on, if I let him, about the women he finds online and what he can accomplish with only one hand.

"So nothing else?" I ask.

"I suppose not."

My thing is that if Dale can call it art to shoot a corpse full of goo to paralyze a smile onto its face, I can damn well call it art to be a wrestler. I can hear the rejoinder from Trisha though, as fresh as it had always been, that at least the man has made a career from his art.

Dale bites the glove off of his hand and spits it into a trashcan, then fingers his way into a new one for Bumgartner. The hand is spindly and delicate.

I pick up two more bodies (another old age, then an electrocution), and after that I load up the duffel bag with my wrestling gear, take note of the end of day mileage on the van, and drive up to Boone.

Whenever the boys see me arrive in the van, someone says something about how I should build my gimmick around the job, change my name to something like the Mortician or the Body Hauler. I try to be polite in those situations, but I am happy with Michael Fury, and I'm not looking to tweak the character.

Tonight, I'm the first one to park in the lot behind the warehouse. It's unassuming, off a mountain backroad, but the promoter owns the warehouse itself so we can advertise the wrestling with a banner on the building, and the shows draw pretty well.

I go inside, smell the stale beer and cigarettes and the faint stink of the canvas. It's a living place, unlike Dale's lab. Faintly the place buzzes with last week's cheers and boos.

The Boone shows are full of wrestlers on their way up and wrestlers on their way down. Teenagers just breaking in and 50-year-olds with knees that click who did a job once in the 90s on WWF television.

This summer, I've been working a little program with a kid on his way up named Gabriel. I like him: he's respectful, he shakes everyone's hand, he can do a backflip. I don't know his real name, but a few weeks ago I put a thumb in his eye while the referee wasn't looking and the people of Boone were ready to riot. Our story is a classic, and it's good: Gabriel is better at wrestling than me, but he can't win because I'm always cheating.

Last week, Gabriel was beating me in a match and so I got myself disqualified rather than face a real loss. A week before that he had pinned me, but in a tag team match, so I make much of the fact that he has never beaten me one-on-one. The people of Boone keep coming back for wrestling for the same reason they keep living: they have been made to see that good things are possible even as they fail, again and again, to actually happen.

This is the art to it: when I put a thumb in Gabriel's eye, I'm only trying to make it look like I'm hurting him. Ditto for when I punch him in the face or the groin. It's art because I can make the people of Boone believe that I hate this Gabriel—a friend with whom I have shared more than one beer—and am trying to cause him harm at the same time that I am protecting him from harm.

Whereas what Dale does, to make a dead body look nice, is a lie no one could believe.

Jonathan shows up, whose gimmick is that of an escaped mental patient who wrestles in medical scrubs. He is older than me so I go shake his hand. He's starting into the story about how one time Terry Funk paid him a compliment when Gabriel shows up. He is younger than both of us and makes sure to come to us for handshakes.

There are plenty of bad characters who work here (stuttering clown, football star, colonial bodybuilder), but Gabriel isn't one of them, and neither am I. We wrestle as normal people. Jonathan, in fact, tells us both from time to time (and now) that our lack of gimmicks will hurt our connection to fans. He suggests that I lean into the body van, and that Gabriel wear wings to the ring for his matches. Jonathan has been around for a while, and that gives him the right to talk.

The other wrestlers trickle in, shaking hands and allowing their hands to be shaken as etiquette dictates. Men put on their tights, their medical scrubs, their graduation regalia, become the people they want to be seen as.

Gabriel and I will not wrestle each other tonight. I will wrestle a college kid, a good hand working a misguided but locally popular zombie gimmick. Gabriel will wrestle Jonathan. We are both set to win our matches, so we both look good going into next week, when we'll face off in the first steel cage match in the history of this warehouse in Boone.

What troubles us is that this week's crowd is smaller than last week's, which had been smaller than the crowd of the week before.

"Heat wave," says Jonathan. "We can expect the same thing in winter cold." Which—it's fine that he knows that, but it doesn't help Howard, halfway changed into his karate gi and the primary leaseholder on the warehouse.

We sit in the locker room, and the first couple of matches fill the small place with noise. We hear the crash of bodies hitting the wrestling mat and the cheers or boos that the crashes elicit.

I emerge for my match through a curtain, a known and disliked entity by the regular crowd, to what I would call a respectable amount of heat. The kid comes after me, announced simply as 'The Dead.'

The match itself is straightforward. Shoulderblock, drop down, duck a clothesline. I win, and The Dead slinks back to wherever he came from. I take a microphone, to incite the crowd until Gabriel comes out to beat me up.

I tell the assembly that they are all fat, worthless, souls devoid of enlightenment. I call them hypocrites for booing me, add that if they told the truth to themselves they would have to admit to paying money to see me perform. I tell them that they will leave this building, the only place in the world where their lives have meaning, and go back to being toothless cogs in society's machinery. The anger of the group swells at this, and the warehouse is filled with noise.

And when Gabriel rushes out and kicks me, the joyous pop out of the crowd is magnificent.

He takes the microphone and tells me that next week, we will do battle in a cage from which neither one of us can escape, in a match in which no one can be disqualified. He calls it coward-proof and says the results will be final.

I make a show of rage at the injustice, storm into the back, collect my fifty dollars and a hot dog and make my way back towards my house of cats, but not before shaking hands with The Dead and thanking him for the match.

I endure most of a week. I move bodies, refuse Dale's offer of his fingers to smell, and throw away who knows how much shit. I put miles on the van, I sell one of the cats. Whenever I sell one, the other cats all look at me smugly, like they know they're the ones keeping my lights on.

All that until Thursday, when Travis knocks at the door. He comes in with a backpack and some justified irritation about the number of cats he is now encountering.

By the time I hug him and make it outside, Trisha is halfway back to her car. "I'll be early on Sunday," she yells without turning.

She had known about the wrestling when we married. I pointed this out to her once, and she conceded but told me she had assumed that I would give it up once I realized I was a failure. Did that hurt to hear, in the presence of our impressionable son and a marriage counselor from the church? It did, but not as badly as the concussion I was then suffering from being hit with a chair in a match with Simon Fua (a seminarian and former linebacker).

Maybe we were never rock solid, but things were good until she got me a job interview and I turned it down to preserve wrestling time. ("Some women have husbands who carve wood," Trisha had said. "Some women have husbands who smoke barbeque.")

I go inside and brush a cat away from the Tupperware of lasagna. A toilet flushes and Travis walks back in the kitchen, sits down, eyes his phone.

"How much are you weighing now, Trav," I ask, which feels like an appropriate question for a proud father to ask his growing boy, but it seems to make something well up inside him and he shrugs without saying a word.

I slide him a plate. "You were going to try out for something this year?"

"Dr. Ray says it's an important year for grades," says Travis.

"He makes you call him doctor?"

"That's what he is."

"Well," I say. "Optometrist."

"Mom thinks so too," he says. "About grades."

"Does she call him doctor?"

"That's *what* he *is*."

We eat for a while without saying anything. I am aware of a clicking in my jaw when I chew, and do my best to maneuver my food away from it. If Travis notices, he isn't saying anything. He takes small bites like he's testing it at first, and then finishes it way too quickly.

He agrees to help me feed the cats. When we open the door to the room where they spend most of their time I can see the smell hit him in the way it hits people who have been away from the cats for a while. "Shit," he says. The room itself is mostly baking pans for dollops of food and a network of things a cat can climb on.

"Actually, they smell like money," I say. The cats purr and churn around the food once it's on the tray.

I go to bed in the room underneath Travis', and as usual a cat or two intrudes in my dreams about wrestling and dead bodies.

I wake early next morning, eat an egg, make coffee, wait for my son to stir, think. Don't middle school grades go away when a kid makes it to high school? I believe they do. Who is Ray to pressure the boy? I chew the egg and begin steeling myself for the conversation I will initiate with Trisha on Sunday, about athletics and possibly also portion control.

Up in his room, I find that Travis isn't awake and hasn't opened his backpack either. I approach the bed and put a hand on my son's foot, like I used to do.

"It's time," I say. "Hardee's on the way, if you want."

Nothing out of Travis.

I joggle the foot again and say Travis' name. He makes an aggressive tired noise at me and yanks the foot away. I move the backpack so I can lean against the bed for a better angle on the toe.

"Travis," I say. He curls into a ball.

Then I feel a sharp nip at my heel. The cat looks up at me with its small motor purr and licks the corners of its mouth. I say Travis' name again while I bend over for the cat. I wait for what feels like a reasonable amount of time before I throw it. It spins in the air, with a degree of bodily control that if a wrestler had it, he could make a million dollars spinning in the air for crowds, before landing on the portion of Travis' face that isn't hidden in covers. The cat yowls and Travis rises in a burst of language and a few minutes later we are in the van, steam fluffing off some coffee in the silent air between us.

Travis sleeps the whole drive out to the Maple Grotto and wakes up on the drive to the funeral home. He's lit sickly by this green glow off of a game on his phone. Intermittently what sounds like exploding coins signify some kind of achievement.

"I'll let you push it when we get there," I say. "The body is big, but you won't believe how light it is."

Nothing out of Travis. The road stretches on.

"I forgot to tell you, I'm in a cage match tonight."

"I have to go to Boone?"

"I'm fighting Gabriel. You'll love it."

Last year, Gabriel had been his favorite. He loved the spins and flips, and when he entered the space for his match the screams in the crowd were high-pitched, from the girls and the children, Travis among them. A year ago, the prospect of seeing Gabriel would have lit him up, but today he stays quiet. The only sound is the phone game.

Travis barely touches the gurney once we make it to the funeral home. He just puts both hands on it and gives it a weak shove, and I take it the rest of the way. Dale's room smells as bad as it ever does. Worse, Dale is in it.

His table is empty, so I hoist the body up myself (a Mr. Borogrove—aneurism, a surprise) and Dale watches. It seems even lighter lifting it here than it did on the gurney. I set him to rest and notice Travis moving a couple of the instruments around.

"Don't mess with those," I say.

"He's fine," says Dale.

Dale picks up a set of large calipers and holds them out to Travis. He turns them in the air, snaps them open, and shuts in the light. Next to where they had rested are the reference photographs provided by the bereaved, which Dale ignores as infringements on his creativity.

"What does that one do?" Travis asks.

Dale clears his throat and raises one eyebrow at me. "Holds the mouth open," he says. "To keep a smile."

"You can make them smile?" Travis asks.

"Let's go," I say. "We have four more today."

"Let him stay," Dale says. "He wants to stay."

"You don't have to," I say.

"It's no problem," says Dale.

It's dangerous for me to try to pull Travis away from something he's expressing an interest in. If he doesn't enjoy these visits it won't be hard for him to make them stop, and I'm already pushing it with the wrestling. Dale can see my weakness even if he doesn't have the whole story. He pushes his advantage and leans his head close to Travis with the one hand theatrically failing to hide a loud whisper: "I can show you the tit-drawer."

Later, on the drive up to Boone, I find myself going on about Dale's arm.

"He didn't even lose it in a cool way," I say. "He was just born without it. He was just born with not enough arms." I can tell from Travis' eyes that he doesn't care. He has eyes in this moment like some crowds I've seen, where nothing the wrestlers can do will wring any kind of emotional investment out of them. For the rest of the drive his eyes are on the phone, but I can tell that his mind is back in Dale's lab.

We arrive, and I take my place by the ring, and Travis finds a seat. "Are you the main event?" he asks.

"We are," I say, "it's a big match," and Travis with a sigh makes himself comfortable.

I am not someone who prays, but it is my habit to take time at the beginning of these nights to think about my own safety and the safety of the wrestlers. If some higher power wants to do something with those thoughts, that is its business. As I think, I behold a ladybug on the canvas, and offer my fingertip to it. I walk over with it to show to Travis.

"Okay," he says.

The wrestlers arrive, from wherever their jobs are. In comes the grocery store manager, the carnival worker, the professor of Communications. In comes the radio DJ and the PhD candidate in British Literature. When the lights go down, they will all be someone else.

In comes Gabriel, full of respect, immediately shaking hands. We all agree that whoever broke him in broke him in the right way. Some boys start bumping around in the ring, and the warehouse echoes with the sound of their falls.

I don't take extra bumps anymore, but I do stretch. I'm watching Travis, whose hand keeps going to his pocket, when Gabriel walks up to me. He shakes my hand and lingers.

"Appreciate you working with me tonight," he says.

"Don't thank me yet, it could still be the shits." I have a foot in my hand, stretching out a quad.

The materials for the cage are against one wall of the warehouse. Four graded metal sides, a not insignificant investment on Howard's part.

"I want to take a big bump tonight," I say. I am looking at Travis. "Top of the cage to the mat."

"What's the finish?" asks Gabriel.

"The bad guy loses," I say, and clap him on the back.

I walk back over to Travis, still in the same spot, still on the phone.

"Travis," I say. "You know that Gabriel and Dad are friends, and even if it gets violent tonight it's all a part of the show."

"I'm not five anymore," Travis says.

What is there to say? "Okay. And all the things I say to the crowd tonight, I don't mean them. I just need them to want me to lose."

"I know," says Travis.

"Okay." I put a hand on the boy's shoulder and walk back into the dressing room.

Jonathan is holding court, giving the same advice to young wrestlers that he has been giving us all for years. "Sincerity is the key," he says. "So if you can fake that, you've got it made." In dark moments, I can't help but think about how much of my time here has overlapped with his.

He has put on the medical scrubs of his character's gimmick and taken out his earring. The dressing room is full of folding chairs on which the wrestlers sit, towels draped across their laps, so they can change pants without exposing themselves.

I am the first wrestler to emerge from behind the curtain, with the job of creating hate. I stand in the ring and thank the assembled crowd for putting the money from their low-pay, low-skill jobs directly into my pocket. The anger swells, and a man—full beard, strange eyebrows—in the front row of the crowd tells me that I suck. My rejoinder is that, hey, guy, I don't go down to the toilet-unclogging station and question your acumen. I ask him if he needs me to define the word "acumen." The anger grows again, and I inform the crowd that I don't go down to the dick-sucking factory and tell this man's wife how to ply her trade either, so why doesn't he just let me do the job I'm so good at.

The anger of the crowd roars, and my concern for exposing Travis to some perhaps less-than-appropriate language is lost in that noise.

"As far as Gabriel goes," I say, and wait long enough for the crowd to cheer a name they love. "When this match starts, inside a steel cage, I will kick him. When he's down, I will kick him. When he begs for mercy on his hands and knees, I will kick him where he kneels. When he bleeds, I will bite him where he bleeds."

I slide out of the ring and make my way back to the locker room, the sound of the crowd filling me with something that I could never make Trisha understand that I needed.

The Dead shuffles to the ring for the first match of the night, against Jonathan, and the two of them are bad dance partners. I have seen it go badly for them before, and it goes badly for them tonight. They return to the locker room with the crowd less alive than it had been, blaming each other for it. Jonathan is holding his eye.

"Stiffness I can understand," he says. "I can work stiff if you want. What I don't understand is you hauling off and goddamn punching me."

The Dead says nothing.

"It would be one thing if you hadn't been doing it for years," says Jonathan.

The Dead looks down, picks something off of his ripped jeans, knows that he is wrong and refuses to admit it.

***

The cage is assembled and Gabriel and I enter it, and here is the final chapter of our story: even though I am bigger and more devious and lack morality, I cannot overcome the heart of Gabriel. We tell it with Gabriel rising after every clubbing blow I lay into his back. We tell it with Gabriel leaping onto me from height. We tell it with Gabriel stealing the chain I had snuck into the cage to use as a weapon and hitting me with it himself. And at the end of the story, I am lying on the mat, motionless and vanquished, and Gabriel stands outside of the cage, bloody but having his hand raised in victory.

The people of Boone are vindicated. Even if it never happens in the outside world, sometimes in wrestling you can have what you hope for.

I have taken the big bump that I wanted to. The fall from the top of the cage was excellent and full of noise, but the landing was different than I envisioned and I am hearing the ringing in my head that I have only heard when concussed.

Back in the locker room, Gabriel tells me that he doesn't think our match was the shits.

"Where is everyone?" I ask.

But then I hear it, the fleshy contact and violent cheer from the door that leads out of the locker room to the gravel lot behind the warehouse. I walk through it and see Jonathan on the ground, bleeding out of his nose. The Dead is up, with a badly swollen hand and most of his zombie makeup rubbed off. The whole congregation of wrestlers is out here, plus some fans. With Jonathan down, the crowd disperses.

This is the reason for not letting the job hauling dead bodies become my character, like it has with our truck driver and our garbage man: even if the anger is real, a fight between a zombie and an escaped mental patient looks foolish.

Simon Fua sees me on his way back inside and asks how the match was.

"You didn't see?" I ask.

"These brothers were scuffling," he says. "I was out here."

I am feeling my pulse now in the throb of my head. Headlights burst on and sweep across the trees as cars parked on the other side of the warehouse depart. Each light strikes me as beautiful, though they all hurt to look at.

I change clothes among the wrestlers who are left and find Travis milling around, kicking gravel.

"What did you think of the match?" I ask.

"Yeah, good," says Travis. "Fine."

I feel a new rising of nausea.

"What about my big fall?"

"I think maybe I missed that part," he says.

"That was the finish."

Travis looks down.

"There was a real fight outside," he says. "I've never seen a real fight."

I walk faster than Travis to the car and sit in the passenger's seat. I think about the conversation that I'll have to have with Trisha about his nutrition and his screen time and his shit attitude. Even in my own head Trisha gets the upper hand. Travis clonks on the window.

"You gotta drive," he says.

"You drive," I say, and shut my eyes.

"I don't know how," he says. "I can't drive."

"I guess it's time to practice," I say. "Keys are on the dash."

I keep my eyes closed and try to guess where we are based on the turns Travis is taking. To the boy's credit, he quits bitching once he realizes I'm not going to dignify it. We make it home without incident, as far as I can tell.

Travis, shaking slightly, goes straight to bed without saying anything. I am able to make it to the shower before I throw up. After I have washed the stink of mat and blood off of me, I notice a bruise, from another part of the match, covering my left side from hip to armpit.

I fall asleep on the sofa to Western movies. But I do not realize that I have fallen asleep until I wake up there. There's some creaky movement on the second floor, and the sun is throwing pillars of dust in through the blinds.

I stand slowly and almost fall over. I try Travis' name but manage more of a croak. The cats, unfed, sense my movement and swarm. I pull two containers of the food out of the fridge, but the smell sets me off as soon as I pull their tabs, and I vomit again into the kitchen trash.

I can hear a car park outside and I hear the stairs bearing Travis' weight. He's startled by me in the hall, like I'm not supposed to be there, and tries to put something quickly back in his pocket before I can see. Only I do see it, before it slips back down Travis' gym shorts. It's the clear glob of a tit from Dale's drawer.

"You know," I say, "I would have killed to drive on the highway at your age."

I follow Travis out, but the sunlight stops me in my tracks on the porch and by the time I can open my eyes again Trisha is rolling away. I can't gather the thoughts about our son's health or activity into anything coherent anyway, but she still could have waited.

Before she goes too far, I notice, on the car that I helped pay for, a new bumper sticker advertising Ray's office.

Back inside, some cat finds it in its heart to rub against my shin. My phone rings: it's overtime if I can come pick up a body from the pool and take it to the county coroner. I know I shouldn't drive, but I go.

The girl is dry by the time I get to her, and the concrete underneath her is dry. Only her hair is still damp, dark and splayed around her head. The sheriff and a fireman seem embarrassed. They stand near the girl, hands on their hips. The lights of their vehicles still flash, even in the sun. Further away, a smaller girl with the same color hair as the girl on the ground is being held by a woman crying angry tears. A deputy is with them, doing his best. It is always harder to talk to one person than to a crowd.

I can't stand looking at the flashing lights, but even the sun reflecting off all the wet pavement is killing my head.

I expect to encounter some strain with moving the girl, but she is light and for a moment my head is clear. While I am loading her into the van, I try not to look in the direction of the mother, but I can't help it once I turn the key and start to drive. She glares at the van, and at me, while I take her daughter away.

When I have a body in the van, I do not listen to music, out of respect. I drive in silence, change lanes slowly, try not to stop at lights where someone might be able to peek in the back. I try to ignore the glare of the sun for a while before I realize that I have been driving without thinking, or that I have been driving and thinking about the wrong things. I have brought the drowned girl nearly to the funeral home and to Dale rather than the county coroner's office.

This is a narrow road, and it will be difficult to turn around here. Still, I would rather try to U-turn in the van than turn around in the funeral home lot and risk seeing Dale. I pull off to the shoulder, and I have to take a moment. I rest my pounding head against the steering wheel and let it pound.

In retrospect, maybe we weren't believable opponents, my van and house of cat shit up against a doctor and a guy with access to a drawer full of tits. Maybe there was no cage tall enough for me to reclaim my boy's affection. I think about the fight outside the warehouse, picture myself on the ground like Jonathan. Dale stands tall, outpunching me even with half as many fists.

The only sound now is the metronome click of the turn signal, but I find even that deafening. I note the mileage and try to figure how far I have driven in the wrong direction. With effort, I turn the van back onto the road and start driving the girl back to where she's supposed to go.

BEAUTIFUL THINGS ABOUT WRESTLING & STORIES

A Conversation with R. Hunter Whitworth

Rachel Phillippo: Hello, Hunter! I am so pleased to see your engaging story, "Michael Fury vs. the Dead," join the pages of *Driftwood*! Welcome!

Hunter Whitworth: Thrilled that you liked the story! *Driftwood* is beautiful, and I'm so grateful for your role in helping the story. Stoked to be here.

RP: This is such an enjoyable read. The voice of the narrator, Michael, is at once introspective, relatable, and oftentimes funny. Can you speak a little on your use of humor in this story? And how you're able to make humor work, even alongside such themes as death and estrangement?

HW: The stories that I'm drawn to as a reader are able to blend seriousness and humor in a way that I think is true to life. I'm also as guilty as anyone of using humor as a defense mechanism in serious situations, so I imagine that's part of it as well.

RP: I'm sure many readers will relate! Another great strength of "Michael Fury vs. the Dead" is your vivid development of character, particularly those of Michael and Dale. Do you find in your writing that character enrichment happens as you write the story? Or do you have a well-defined idea of your characters first, the story unfolding to suit?

HW: It's different for every story, but for this one the characters came first. They changed in some ways over the course of the writing, of course, but the starting point was Michael. Dale emerged as the kind of person that Michael would hate working with, and therefore became a sort of weird rival for his son's affections.

RP: This rivalry is very believably rendered. One thing that makes

Michael so appealing as a narrator is the authority with which he speaks on the many strange details of his life. Was there much research involved in writing about the Persian cats, the semi-pro wrestling scene, or mortuary transport driving? Did you draw on your own experiences?

HW: First, I'm a huge fan of pro-wrestling. I trained in college to be a pro wrestler, and so I spent a fair amount of time around some interesting characters. My trainer was current WWE Superstar Xavier Woods, and when he graduated I was left in the capable hands of the Greenville S.C. independent wrestling scene. I stopped after a little less than a year, but I'm drawing a lot on the experiences of the people I came to know in that world. I never personally knew a cat-breeder or a mortuary transport driver, but those guys are out there. I did know a wrestler who was a welder, one who managed a GameStop, and one who did very important work with special needs adolescents. They did the work they had to do to keep the dream of wrestling alive, some well into their 50s and 60s. Like writers, very few wrestlers are able to pursue their art full-time. Wrestlers are artists, and have intense respect for what they do and for each other, and I hoped to capture and to respect the reality of that.

RP: Wow! Your background in wrestling surely provides a lot of creative fodder. The culmination of all of these specific and odd details in "Michael Fury vs. The Dead" lends a sort of surreal feel. Heightened, I believe, by Michael experiencing a concussion. Do you feel that there is a surreal element at work? And if so, how does this serve the story?

HW: One of the ways I think pro wrestling is underrated as a storytelling medium is the way it asks its audience to hold reality and un-reality in tension with one another. A character like The Undertaker (my favorite), for example, exists simultaneously as this undead heroic archetype as well as the man Mark Calaway portraying the character, and his success hinges on both of those elements being engaging, as well as the fact that the story has to play out in real time. It's like if Michael Jordan was also Darth Vader. We impose narrative onto sports all the time, but in pro wrestling the sporting element exists to create justification for narrative, and those two aspects of each story feed each other. I don't know if that's surreal exactly, but there is a specific feel to wrestling I was trying to capture, where it has to operate on multiple planes of entertainment at once. The oddness is part of that, and I tried to give the story a sort of incongruous second layer of references to James Joyce's "The Dead" to achieve that feel as well.

RP: This also touches on the theme of authenticity. Michael's fellow wrestlers urge him to take on a persona, but Michael resists, content to play the character of himself. Is this theme of perceived and true identities something you were intentional about building?

HW: I wanted it to be that Michael took himself seriously and had serious ambitions as a wrestler. This would set him and Gabriel apart from those guys willing to be caricatures. You could also read it as him being less willing to separate the wrestling from his everyday life. The most successful wrestlers tend to talk about their personas as their authentic selves with the volume turned up all the way.

RP: On the topic of referencing Joyce; which other authors inspire or influence your work? Do you find that you are informed by other art forms, aside from the aforementioned wrestling?

HW: My favorite book ever is *East of Eden*. For short stories, though, George Saunders, Haruki Murakami, and Flannery O'Connor are my big three. I think they all in different ways can't be beat for style, but at the same time they always remind us that the characters in the story matter most. Also, I was in high school band and trying to draw comic books before I was ever trying to write, so I think I internalized the importance of practice and repetition as far as process goes. I get lots of practice by doing lots of drafts.

RP: Much like the Murakami works with which I'm familiar, your very character-driven story emphasizes the human body and its connection—or disconnection—to our being. Can you speak a little on your attention to this motif of the body, particularly in regards to the concussion? Do you find that repetition of an idea such as this occurs early on in the formation of a story, or does it emerge in the later stages of revision?

HW: A lot of what let the concussion really breathe was the good work of *Driftwood* editorial staff! The health of the body is so important (and so constantly at risk) in the world of wrestling, so attention to it would be a part of Michael's focus, if the narrative voice was going to be authentic. He would worry about his son getting out of shape, and he would have contempt for Dale's lack of physical strength. Originally, the story ended much earlier and more abruptly. The concussion just happened to him in his fall from the cage, robbing him and reminding him of reality in a moment of artistic triumph. That it could be more thematically resonant emerged later.

RP: It is always interesting to watch a story evolve during revision. I know "Michael Fury vs. The Dead" underwent its fair share of alterations before ultimately landing on this complex and lively version. What does your revision process look like, and for how long was this story in the works for you?

HW: My process is long. I alternate between longhand and typed drafts of everything, which makes everything take a bit longer, but I find it very helpful. I'm superstitious, so I never deviate from this method and I only write longhand with Blackwing pencils. The first draft of this story is from a notebook I started in April of 2019, and it's changed a lot since then. My little sister reads everything I write, so after I've let a story sit for a while she's my first editor. (I say "little," but she is more intelligent and mature than I am and loves me but doesn't take me too seriously, so she's the perfect reader). Her feedback is always good, sometimes drastic. She's never afraid to give a story the surgery it needs.

RP: Your sister sounds like a perfect first reader! It's possibly no surprise, then, that relationships are at the heart of your story, particularly that between Michael and his son, Travis. Yet, there is not a whole lot of dialogue on the page. Much of what drives their interaction is what is actually left unsaid. This is perhaps even truer for the tense relationship between Michael and his ex-wife. Can you tell us about your use of white space here, of dialogue and action left off the page? Is this balance between spoken and unspoken and seen and unseen something that happens intuitively, or is it cultivated during revisions?

HW: Trisha was a much bigger part of the story in earlier drafts. I realized that I was having trouble getting her voice exactly right around the same time that I realized that her impact on Michael could be heightened by her refusal to be around him more. It was also helpful for having Michael live in the past in some ways. The intent was that she loom in the background. Travis was easier, because I teach ninth graders and have a sense of what it's like when adults try to relate to them. The best advice I ever got for writing dialogue was that people almost never say exactly what they mean. Honestly, a fair amount of the time kids Travis' age also don't even say what they don't mean.

RP: This is excellent advice and observations regarding dialogue. With a busy teaching schedule and a lengthy writing process, how do you go about making time for writing and revising in your daily life? You mention having some craft superstitions; do you have a specific writing routine?

HW: I find I work best in the morning, usually, with some strong coffee and my phone not at hand. I am very superstitious, so much so that there are superstitions that I'm afraid to talk about in case exposing them diminishes their effectiveness. But sometimes, I have to let go of superstition and grab an hour when I can.

RP: The story ends somewhat quietly, with Michael making a wrong turn and planning how he will rectify his mistake and change course. Can we read this ending with a certain measure of hope for Michael? Is there still time for him to turn around and "win" back his relationship with Travis? And will this require Michael to sacrifice wrestling altogether? You've created him as such a relatable and deeply human character that I can't help but root for his success!

HW: I like to think there's time for us all, but I think you might be more optimistic than I am. But I do think that one of the beautiful things about both wrestling and stories is that we can't help but be in the corner of these flawed individuals, and that even the most villainous character can be one good deed away from a crowd roaring its approval.

RP: I love that concept. I would never have thought of redemption as a link between stories and wrestling. Do you have any other projects in the works?

HW: I sure hope so. My wife and I have a daughter who, when this comes out, will have just turned two. So all projects are undergoing some wonderful disruption. I have several stories that I'm in the process of revising, and I'm chipping away at what I hope eventually will be a novel.

RP: Congratulations on the most wonderful kind of disruption! As for the novel and other stories, can we expect to see wrestling as a recurring motif?

HW: I hope so. Wrestling is getting its due lately, with *Iron Claw* and *Glow* and *The Wrestler* a little longer ago, but I still think it's pretty rich and under-explored. I have a few more stories to tell, I hope.

RP: Lastly, Hunter, do you have any advice to impart to the artists reading, writers and wrestlers alike?

HW: Always be reading. The best reading advice I ever got was to read my favorite writers' favorite writers, as far back as I could go. I also like what Haruki Murakami has to say about reading, that if you only read the books that everyone else is reading, you can only think what everyone else is thinking. When I was training to wrestle, the equivalent to reading the classics were watching old Ricky Steamboat matches, and Ric Flair vs Kerry Von Erich. Those are great, and anyone who is skeptical about wrestling should watch the Shawn Michaels vs Undertaker matches from WrestleMania 25 and 26. Michaels vs Ric Flair from WrestleMania 24 is also a wrestling match that is a perfect story. Flair is fighting to keep his career alive; Michaels is fighting to be the best. Both men are desperate, and they love each other. It's also a generational showdown between wrestlers who could both reasonably claim to be the best of all time.

RP: Thank you, Hunter! This is great advice to writers, and you may just have won over a few new fans to the world of wrestling. "Michael Fury vs the Dead" is a memorable story, and I'm looking forward to reading your future works!

HW: Thank you so much! It's an honor.

SHRAPNEL

John Kaufmann

Everyone Ike knows is talking about space debris. *Time Magazine* says that a man-made satellite, nine stories tall and weighing 77.5 tons, is expected to slip into the earth's upper atmosphere, then disintegrate into a celestial shower of flaming metal as spectacular as a Fourth of July firework. Fragments, each weighing 1,000 pounds or more, will crash to earth at speeds of up to 270 mph. When the prior crew left the satellite, they stowed care packages of food, water, powdered lemonade, and magazines for the next crew, but Congressional dysfunction and budget cuts forced NASA to scrub the mission. With no one to right its course, the satellite will become shrapnel. The government suggests that people stay inside until danger passes, but issues no further guidance. If you want a nanny, move to Canada.

Across the country, people are organizing crash parties, wild bacchanalia with music, drugs, and orgiastic sex. A few entrepreneurs have bought up hard hats with SPACE JUNK stenciled in NASA font across the crown. Tin Hat Guy, in Lot 4A, tried to reinforce the roof of his trailer with metal and pressure-treated wood, but Lowes ran out of two-by-fours before he finished. He says that the bulk of the debris will fall on a hillside near Palmyra, a hundred eighty-four miles to the south and west of Ogdensburg. His brother-in-law—he says—works at NASA. When Ike and his father dun him for lot rent at the end of the month, he says he will pay on Tuesday and assures them that NASA has calculated the crash site to nine decimal places.

This time of day, the Saint Lawrence is the color of pot roast. The bridge is empty, the sky the color of the water. I'm a wetback, Ike's father likes to say. When I crossed the river, I didn't have a pot to piss in or a window to throw it out of.

Don't use that word, Dad, Ike says.

What word?

Wetback. It is nasty.

Well, I *am* a wetback. I can use it.

When he looks at the river, Ike thinks, *you could swim across—but*

God knows what shape your nuts would be in when you reached the other side. The snot green, scrotum-tightening, yak, yak, yak, they read in AP English. He adjusts his clipboard and shuffles the papers his father has given him. *We hereby require from you the payment of said rent (which would cure this default) or complete possession of said premises on or before the expiration of thirty (30) days from the service of this Notice.* Lots 9A, 5C, 13C, and 7B.

Hand these out, his father told him when he gave him the papers this afternoon. When I was your age, I worked.

What if they yell at me when I give it to them?, Ike asked.

Tell them to talk to me, his father said.

What if they chase me like Mr. Gagnon?

Tell them to talk to me.

Fuck, Ike thinks. *Fuck, fuck, fuck.*

The first time Ike saw Des was when he was five and she was six. Ike was at the bottom of a septic line ditch, watching his father square it up. Three faces appeared over the rim of the ditch. Desiree, Brayden, and Kayla McCarthy.

You want to go play?, his father asked.

I want to stay with you, Ike said.

Hold this then.

Ike heard, Hee, hee, hee, and when he looked up, the McCarthy kids were gone.

When Ike comes by, Des is on her porch alone. Ike says, Is your father here? He has folded the notice in three, like a letter, with the printing on the inside. The sweat from his hand has softened the outer fold and left a moist, thumb-sized lump over the notary stamp.

You're cute, she says. She is wearing army boots, jean shorts, and a white tee shirt. Her nails are black and her hair is—this week—pink.

You have Hamlin for math?, she asks.

No, Demaray.

Brainiac.

Is your father here? I need to give this to him.

Give it to *me.*

She is sitting with her knees together, pulled up to her chin. He sees that the skin above her knees is covered with fuzz, but her shins are smooth as a bowling ball. She lowers her knees when he hands her the notice, and he sees, printed on the front of her shirt, a series of dots and the text, 'Only losers read Braille.' She straightens her legs, crosses them at the ankle, looks up at him.

Kayla's a slob, she says. You should see our room.

There is plenty Ike would like to say, but all that comes out is, Uh-huh. He feels sweat in his armpits.

Brainiac, she says. Moron. Hee, hee, hee.

When Ike was six, he came out of his house on a Saturday and found Des sitting on the tire swing in front of their door. She had freckles, braids and—I swear to God—red ribbons on the end of her braids. She said, Push me, and he pushed. His father had hung the swing from a chain he attached to a hook he drilled into the branch of the willow tree in front of the park office. He had done that right after he tamped the soil around the sign for the park. His father told Ike that the sign read 'Leisure Living Estates Trailer Park – Lots For Rent', that the lei was pronounced 'lee', and that *estates* is 'estates', not 'states.' Ike asked his father, Why are you putting that tire there?, and his father put him on the swing, held on to his arm, and swung gently. It seemed to Ike as if the bottom had come out of the world and a rough hand was rocking the cradle.

After Ike pushed Des once, she said, Higher. Ike locked his arms overhead, put his hands on the treads, and ran underneath the swing. Her sneaker grazed the back of his head as she swung back. *Tap*. He pushed her again. *Taptap*. She said, Wheee!

As Ike watched Des swing toward him, Brayden walked up, put his arm across Ike's shoulders and his foot in front of his shins and shoved. The earth was wet, hard, cold, and rocky. A small cut formed on the heel of his right hand. Ike started to cry, tears juicing up and snot running down his nose. Brayden and Des' father stood up from his seat on the porch, took a few steps toward them and shouted,

Hey! Des and Brayden trotted back into their trailer. Mr. McCarthy followed, and the screen door slammed shut.

Last week, Ike saw Des in the hallway at school on the back of a shot-putter who had his elbows locked around her knees. She was laughing and burying her face between the guy's shoulder blades as he walked, bumping her hip, thigh and knee against the row of lockers. Ike kept his eyes on the mottos painted onto the cinderblock walls. *Where eagles learn to soar. Shoot for the moon. You may miss, but you will end up in the stars. Reflect, solve, create, grow, think. Rejoice!* The shot-putter's neck was thick, his eyes were wide-set and frank, and the lips that smiled when Des bumped her hips against the lockers were meaty and wet.

Six months ago, Ike's father told him, Give these to Mr. McCarthy. He gestured with a bunch of skirting panels when he said it. Their skirting is chewed up, he said.

Why?, Ike asked. It's their home.

Their home, our problem, his father said.

What do you mean we, Ike thought.

When Ike came by, Desiree was sitting on her porch with her father. These are for you, Ike said.

Tell Claude thanks, Mr. McCarthy said. His hair and beard were salt-and-pepper now and his gut had grown in the ten years since the tire swing.

Yes, sir, Ike said.

Des sat quietly beside her father, watching. Ike didn't look at her face for more than a split second, but what he saw made him itch.

Two days later, his father gave him a bunch of J-channel. He'll need these too, he said. Des was there when he brought them by that time, too.

You do well in school?, Mr. McCarthy asked.

I try, sir.

What sports you do?

Math and debate.

I wish my kids could be like that.

Des rolled her eyes, and Ike felt gooey inside.

***

A month later, Ike's father said, Screw McCarthy.

Are you sure there's nothing more I can't bring them?, Ike asked. He was surprised to find himself looking for excuses to go by their home. His father wrinkled his nose and snuffled. Beyond the entrance sign, a freighter's wake travelled up-river, toward lock number five. *On the way back, they will pass through Montreal, Quebec, Europe,* Ike thought. *Far from here. Anywhere but here.*

Yes, I am sure, his father said. His favors have expired.

What did he do?, Ike asked.

Hold this, his father said. More work, less talk.

When Ike delivers the eviction papers, he asks Des, Do you think we will get sky junk?

I hope so, she says.

Now she has her knees at a ninety-degree angle pressed together, swinging from side to side as her feet remain on the floor.

Where's Brayden?, Ike asks.

Louisiana.

What's in Louisiana?

She doesn't say anything. Instead, she stands up, takes his hand and opens the storm door and the main door. When they walk through the living room, *Gunsmoke* is playing on the TV, although the couch, the recliner, and the rest of the room are empty. An impeccably clean black-and-white cowboy with a white hat, a vest, a star, and a revolver stands in front of a bar with a pair of swinging doors at his six o'clock. An older man in a three-piece suit, a tie, a pocket watch, and a brimmed hat stands to his left. A blonde woman wearing lipstick and a poofy white dress stands between them. They all face the camera and speak, but the sound is turned down. Ike stops to watch and Des tugs his hand and leads him past the couch and the TV, to the first of the two small bedrooms off to the left of the corridor leading to the back of the trailer, opposite the washer and dryer.

When he hears the door click closed, Ike says, I've never seen so much girls' underwear. Bras, sweat pants, tee shirts cover the floor and the open drawers on the dresser and hang from the top layer of the bunk-bed.

Loser, Des says.

The room is dark. The lights are off and a navy-blue towel covers the window. When she faces him and rests her elbows on his shoulders and clasps her hands behind his head, he notices that she has to look up to meet his gaze. Her eyes are green with what looks like yellow flecks around the perimeter of the irises. He does not feel the peach fuzz on her upper lip when they kiss, but he hears a pop like the release of surface tension from the back of her throat when she opens her mouth into his. He did not expect that.

She is kind and patient as he fumbles. He did not expect that, either. So much dark and light, and warm all around. If he had time to think he would grin, but of course there is no time to think.

After they are done, Ike lies on his back and traces a heart with an arrow through it and the caption 'D and D 4Ever' written in blue ball point pen on the wooden slat above his head. *David? Dylan? Dumbass?*, Ike thinks. He traces a tattoo of a sunflower on the small of her back.

That tickles, she says, so he really tickles her under the armpits.

Hee, hee, hee, you moron, she says. You're going to have to leave soon. Kayla comes back from school now.

What is in Louisiana?, he asks.

Some pervert friend of my father's.

I'm sorry.

Not your fault, nerd-boy.

Ike would like to stay there forever. He thinks, T*o get through a minute, I have to get through a half-minute. To get through a half-minute, I have to get thru fifteen seconds. Can I take forever to come out onto the other side?* He traces the second D again and thinks, *Donovan? Dipshit?*

When he served Tin Hat Guy with his thirty-day notice, Tin Hat Guy told Ike, It's going to happen Friday. Wait and see. Everything will be blown away. Ike said, My father told me to give you this. No pay, no stay. That's the policy.

I don't have to pay it, Tin Hat Guy said. The President says I don't have to. The governor says I don't have to. You want to bring this in front of a judge? He'll say I don't have to.

Talk to my father, Ike said. I just hand out the notices. Tin Hat Guy grinned maniacally, his goatee disappearing into a fold in his neck. *Why are you smiling?*, Ike wanted to say. *You're not right. You're not even wrong.*

Wait until Friday, Tin Hat Guy said. Everything will be gone.

I thought you said it would be at Palmyra, Ike said.

Here, Palmyra—*everything* is going to be like, poof!

Ike thinks, *the McCarthys have thirty days to pay up or move out. Half of thirty is fifteen. Half fifteen, seven and a half.* You can spend a lifetime slicing it thinner. And a lifetime after that. *She didn't read the notice when I handed it to her*, he thinks, *but she's got to know what's in it.*

What's that?, Ike says. It felt like a thud—dull, soft—that made the trailer move just a hair.

It's a freighter, Des says. They carry cement and bump against the locks.

I never heard that, Ike says.

Because you never take your nose out of your fucking book.

You hear what Tin Hat Guy said?, Ike asks.

You don't know the half of it, Des says. He told us he has a rich uncle who is going to die. He said money will become worthless and the Koreans will invade.

Does he hear voices?, Ike asks.

Only the little green men.

I feel sorry for his wife. She seems pretty normal.

You don't hear them yelling at each other because you're in the big house.

Don't make it sound like a plantation, Ike thinks.

Maybe she should tie him up, he says.

Maybe he'd like that, Des says.

Heh.

Maybe he's rich.

Maybe he won the Nobel Prize.

Maybe he's Jimmy Hoffa.

Maybe he's CIA.

Maybe he's Witness Protection.

Maybe he makes his money from sperm banks.

Does he lose interest after he makes a deposit?

Maybe he's beaming thoughts into your head.

Thoughts like, fuck me?

I like it.

The afternoon sun streams through the cracks in the towel Des and Kayla have taped over the window. Ike is on his side, supporting his left hand and head on his left elbow. His other hand is on Des' shoulder blade.

Who's the pervert?, Ike asks.

We call him Uncle Hank. His wife made pecan pie for us.

You mean Pee-can.

No, I mean Puh-kahn.

What about him?

He came into my room when everyone else was asleep and you know.

I do not, Ike thinks. *That's why I'm asking.* Did he do this? Ike asks. He grabs a butt-cheek and pinches.

Stop! It's not funny.

Does it make you not want to, you know, now?

No.

Did it hurt?

He told me my father would be mad if he found out.

Is that true?

Yes.

Did your father find out?

Nope.

Do other people know?

Yes.

Who?

None of your beeswax.

Ike gets up from the bed, walks to the window, lifts the bottom of the towel that covers it. There are no cars or pedestrians on the streets. The folding chair on the porch of the trailer owned by Chriss Ferro, the mayor of the park, is empty. It could be the *Twilight Zone* episode where the town is enclosed in a force field. It could also be late afternoon in a mid-sized mobile home park in an upstate town that has seen better days. He notices that the McCarthy's lawn needs to be mowed and there are a few gaps in the neighbor's skirting.

He returns to the bed.

Now Des lies on her back and his hand sits on her stomach, inert. He kisses her neck and she says, Mm. He kisses her stomach, below the divot made by her navel, and she says, declaratively, Mm. Then she says, You need to go.

If I keep telling you stories, he says, will you let me stay all night?

No, Nerdball.

Old Vergil is sick.

I saw him mowing Theresa's lawn yesterday.

Those shades make him look like a mean old bastard. Did he yell at you when you ran across his lot when you were a kid?

Oh, yeah. Me, Brayden, and Kayla. We used to put cinder blocks on his steps, so that he would trip on them when he walked out in the morning. He told your father about that. And your father told mine. We also used to shoot water blasters into his windows in the summer. He loved that.

I'll bet he did.

He chased us with a baseball bat once, but he was kidding.

He has a weapon collection, you know.

He'd never hurt a fly.

He'd hurt a deer.

Vergil never yelled at *me*.

Of course not, boss-boy.

She surprises him by laying her head on his chest. He feels an erection coming on. You know, Vergil wasn't always a mean old guy, he says.

Oh, no?

Nope.

He was the best-looking and richest guy in the park. Of course, it was not a mobile home park then. It was a hunter-gatherer community.

Oh, jesus.

And before that, he was a spermatozoon.

A spermata-*what*?

Vergil Gagnon riding his tractor among hundreds of thousands of spermatozoa, wearing those wrap-around shades racing to the egg. He was the meanest bastard among all of them, and the fastest. He raced and elbowed the rest out of the way. That's why he's here now.

You gotta go, Nerdolator. I'm serious.

Ike would sell his right to his father's share in the park for another half-hour here. He'd move into a crappy single-wide and eat tuna fish for the rest of his days. He'd do wind sprints. He would swim the Saint Lawrence. Outside are shot-putters, eviction procedures, and a guy who wears a hat made of tin foil. Here, it's just him and Des.

Let's wait for space junk, he says. Let's wait for the end of the world.

No, she says. *Go!*

She raises herself on her elbow and gives his ribs a push. Oof!, he says. He rolls off the bed, pulls on his grunts, tee shirt, and jeans. When he adjusts his dick, it seems more substantial than it did this morning, but that might be just his imagination. All but a pie-slice of light is blocked by the blue towel over the window. The rest of the room is almost completely dark. Des lies on her back with her fingers locked behind her head watching him as he dresses, neither smiling, frowning nor talking. *Remember,* he thinks, *you won't come this way again.* When he steps out onto her porch, the storm door slams behind him. The river, or a river, is where it has always has been. The sun is occluded by what looks like clouds and there is a horizontal orange glow to the south and the west. It is quiet enough for him to feel his nostrils move when he breathes. It is the time of day after end-of-school but before end-of-work when nobody is on the streets or working in their gardens. It is neither hot nor cold. It might, or might not, be the end of the world. It is certainly a different world.

KNOCKING THE READER OFF BALANCE

A Conversation with John Kaufmann

James McNulty: John! Welcome to the pages of *Driftwood*! I'm excited to publish this formally daring piece, and I'm curious how readers will respond to it.

John Kaufmann: Hey, whaddya know—I am curious about the same thing!

JM: Most of the COVID stories that enter our submission queues struggle to incorporate current events in a nuanced or surprising way, but I think "Shrapnel" was an exception to this, both because of the specificity of the housing setting & the naïve voice of the narrator. Why do you think it's so difficult for many writers to write about current events, and in what ways did you struggle to write about these topics when drafting "Shrapnel"?

JK: That is an interesting question that I have not considered. Other than journalism and topical comedy, most writing about current events, I submit, can suffer from being too close to the material. I think of a writer as a puppeteer. The narrative voice is the puppet and the writer is the guy pulling the strings. If the puppeteer feels too strongly about, say, Brexit or the Republican primary, you can end up with a puppeteer who is making faces behind the puppet's back. That's not a good look—it is better to let the narrative voice do its work, without kibbitzing.

I did write one story during the pandemic about an owner of a mobile home park who goes crazy because of pandemic-era regulations. That one was not entirely about current events—park owners have been driven crazy by their business since the reign of John Paleologos—but it was turbo-charged by them. I think that it suffered from what I describe above.

JM: Why do you think it works in "Shrapnel"? Were you "far enough away" from the current events when you wrote it? Personally, I think the specificity of the back-and-forth, particularly small but important references like J-channel, make the setting feel lived-in and precise.

JK: I don't think that Shrapnel is about current events. It is about timeless problems—sex, the end of the world, the distance between people who are close, class, property ownership, contractual rights, oedipal struggles, memory, and perception.

If it had been about, say, the law passed by the New York State legislature in 2019, or Pandemic-era restrictions, that would have been too close to the bone for me to write about without being snarky.

JM: One of the story's primary preoccupations is cross-class relationships; Ike and Des' relationship doesn't seem to be on a steady path by the end. What do you make of the cross-class relationship difficulties, and how does this change, if at all, when the couple enters adulthood?

JK: The story is taken from a novel that is looking for a publisher. That is one of the main preoccupations of the novel. I would not phrase the issue so much as class as much as business. The issue is not that Ike has read about, say, the Byzantine Empire or taken a class in statistics and Des hasn't. That is just a difference in upbringing. Instead, it is that they have a business relationship that is reductionistic. To a renter, a living space is home—it is the place where, when you have to go there, they have to take you in. To an owner, the same dwelling unit is an entry on a balance sheet. These two views of the elephant are incommensurable with each other. That conundrum is baked into private ownership of rental property. I wanted to explore what would happen if two people confronted this barrier that stands between them with their clothes off. I think that what happens is that the clothes come off—but the barrier remains.

It is interesting that you end your question with "when the couple enters adulthood." In the novel, the Ike character grows up around the park, then leaves and returns when he is in his thirties to run the park when his father dies. The relationship with Des is strained when they are teenagers for the reasons described above, but this is exacerbated when they meet again because of the baggage (kids, exes, habits) that people accumulate after a certain age.

JM: What's the novel titled, and what's your elevator pitch for it as a whole?

JK: Leisure Living. Wall Street trader inherits mobile home park where he grew up, gets sucked back in, shenanigans ensue.

JM: What's your longer pitch? We're out of the elevator and eating lunch instead.

JK: It is a story about a trader who grew up in a mobile home park that his father developed in Ogdensburg, NY, on the bank of the Saint Lawrence. When his father dies, he has to move back from Manhattan to take care of the park. After he returns, he runs into Des, a woman he knew when she and he were in their teens. Conflict comes in the form of Des' ex, the state, rotting infrastructure, and a predatory investment fund that is buying up mobile home parks in the Northeast and squeezing mom-and-pops like Joe, the protagonist, out of business.

My sister says that salad is an excuse to eat salad dressing. I think that plot is to fiction what lettuce is to salad. The book is a meditation on time, memory, place, political power, economic inequality, housing, option pricing, and double-entry bookkeeping. A shitty mobile home park in Ogdensburg is as good a lens to view those things through as any.

The book was also a way for me to create a narrative voice that I enjoyed speaking through. Where else could I have an excuse to write about the last days of Socrates and the proper way to pitch a septic pipe?

JM: The story opens with background about a US satellite mission being scrubbed, and the resulting chaos that entails. Although this opening could be read in several ways, this editor read the space junk as a parallel for the impoverished tenants of Leisure Living, who are also abandoned by the government. "If you want a nanny, move to Canada." Does this reading at all match up to your own?

JK: I read it as setting the action on the lip of a volcano. The idea was for the physical danger to make the action more entertaining. But, yes, I agree that the space junk could be read as a marker of the breakdown of the social fabric that started with Reagan and has left us with opioids, the gig economy, and Trump.

JM: If you don't mind, could you expand on that a bit?

JK: Much of the social fabric that was put in place by the New Deal was undone by the small-government policies of the Reagan administration and Chicago school economics. Government used to be seen as a way for people to cooperate to do social good. Now people like to say, "The scariest thing in the world is when a man from the government comes and says, 'I am here to help.'" The social contract between government, citizens, employers, and workers has broken down. In 1970, the average CEO of a publicly-traded company in the US earned 23x that of a typical worker. In 2020, that number was 350x. People used to have defined-benefit pensions and jobs where they could expect to spend their careers, if they wanted. That has been replaced by an atavistic gig-type economy. This has led to depths of despair among the most vulnerable segment of the population. Many of those people live in mobile home parks.

What started with the Reagan administration wasn't 'creative destruction.' It was *destruction.* We are paying the price for it now in the fraying of the social fabric, medieval-levels of social inequality, and support for a demagogue who says that 'only he can solve our problems' by the segment of the population most hurt by the Reagan revolution. You expect that in Venezuela or Depression-era Germany, but not here. You could read the space junk in the story as a marker for that.

So, on second thought, maybe the story is about current events—but it deals with them metaphorically.

JM: The initial draft of the story swaps back-and-forth between speakers mid-paragraph, rather than breaking for a new paragraph with each speaker; without my prompting, you opted during revision to include line breaks "to make it easier on the reader." The initial effect produced a sort of dense, more frantic quality to the prose—the reader isn't allowed to take as big a breath between speakers—which mimicked the chaotic age & situation of the protagonist. Of course, paragraph breaks are also conventionally used for clarity's sake. Do you worry about the sacrifice of clarity in favor of the benefits this style brings? What, formally-speaking, can you do to mitigate clarity struggles on behalf of the reader—as I assume your intention isn't to confuse & confusion is only a negative byproduct.

JK: That is something I have been struggling with for a while. I *want* to knock the reader off balance a little. It seems to me that writing should be a depiction of consciousness. Consciousness is confusing. If you do not reproduce the confusion, the writing is flat. When I was a tax lawyer, clients wouldn't come to me and say, 'I received a nonperiodic payment on a notional principal contract,' or, 'I received a return of basis and capital gain.' *No!* They would say, 'I received a slug of money. How should I tax-account for it?' It was my job to make sense out of the bramble-bush. We do the same thing when we interpret light hitting our retina, or sound hitting our tympanum. I try to trust the reader to be able to replicate the process of sorting sense data.

How I can do that and still make enough sense to not piss off readers is a different matter. I don't like quotation marks because they ring-fence speech. Speech is not ring-fenced in real life—it is just sense data. For a while, I used en dashes before lines of dialogue. That works okay in long sequences of snappy dialogue, but not so much in other contexts. I tried mushing everything together with no paragraph breaks, as with the first draft of this, but that was *too* confusing. Now, I use a mix of paragraph breaks and dialogue tags ('he said,' 'she said,' e.g.). That seems to work better than anything else I have tried, but I am still experimenting.

JM: Another story in this issue had a similar concern. I like what you say here about consciousness being innately confusing; I think *Finnegan's Wake*, and other books like it, take that viewpoint well. And yes, so many writers have experimented with dialogue delivery; I tend to think anything can work depending on the tone you're going for—and what the story calls for. Have other writers informed your thoughts on punctuating dialogue? What other writers have most influenced this excerpt?

JK: I look forward to reading that story. For dialogue, I look to Beckett, Kevin Barry, and Roddy Doyle. The Irish are good talkers. They also, incidentally, seem to connect with stories about manufactured housing communities. Something about substance abuse, rural poverty, and despair. For interiority and suppleness of voice, Barry, again. For musings on memory and perception, Borges and Seferis. For deadpan, Kafka and Mel Brooks. One of the last two once said, "Tragedy is a redneck walking down a country road. His truck doesn't run, he is broke, his wife has left him, he has cancer, he is incontinent and impotent, his daughter is knocked up, and his son has overdosed. Comedy is the same guy falls into a manhole'. How can you top that?

JM: You mentioned earlier that you worked as a "tax lawyer." How has that career informed your writing?

JK: Law school made my writing much clearer. The first thing they taught us was to remove all the adverbs and two-thirds of the adjectives. A clinical instructor told me, "Write as if your audience is stupid. Keep it simple." The professor who addressed our first-year moot court class was a florid litigator and a media hog. He told us, "Get to the point quickly. There is a place in life for foreplay—but not in legal writing!" Effectively, he meant, 'Hook your audience.'

The process of writing articles for tax technical journals is very different from writing literary fiction and CNF. Every sentence that states a legal rule has to be footnoted and every footnote has to be checked and formatted. It is torturous. But submitting work for publication is a snap. Not many people write about, say, the characterization of payments under Section 1234A, or tax accounting for nonperiodic payments on notional principal contracts—but everyone wants to write about their mother. Supply and demand favors authors in one case and not the other.

JM: I tend to ask young writers to "write as if the reader is smarter than you," because otherwise there's a lot of hand-holding, explaining, and exposition. But of course, that's fiction and not legal writing, which should often be written in simpler, less intentionally misleading, verbiage. When you write fiction, which approach do you take? How much do you consider the reader when you write?

JK: I believe the clinical instructor really meant, 'tailor your message to your audience.' In that case, the audience was corrections officers.

I do not think that he meant that corrections officers are 'stupid,' but they are not all humanities-educated, and they tend to be tired and busy with a hundred things other than reading complaints in disciplinary proceedings. If you want to get through to them, you need to make your message clear and easy to read. In other types of legal writing, it is fine to be turgid, because your reader is obligated to read what you write. Judges get paid to do that—but you can't fire a judge.

A reader of literary fiction is different from a reader of, say, a legal brief, because a fiction reader signs up to engage in a game. The writer pitches balls to the reader and the reader, so long as she enjoys the game, catches the balls. In fiction, it is okay to ask your writers to fill in some blanks. That is part of the game. That said, it is one thing to expect your reader to do some work and quite another to expect her to work through boring prose. If you do that, she will pick up her phone and open TikTok. You can challenge her, but you can't bore her.

JM: Do other media influence you at all?

JK: I watch a lot of Netflix—too much, really. It crowds out reading. Recently, I have enjoyed *Succession, The Morning Show, Bad Sisters, Reservation Dogs, The Bear*, and *Slow Horses*. I look to TV for guidance about dialogue and story-building.

I am not a musician, but I do listen to music when I drive to the parks. James McMurtry is as powerful a poet as I have heard or read. I am now re-reading *Lonesome Dove*, written by his father. I am impressed at how closely Larry McMurtry's narrative voice rhymes with that of his son.

I think visually and regret that I never studied art. One of my sons is a talented visual artist, as well as a musician and a good writer. As a tax lawyer, I was not great at calling up legal minutia and I had a shitty bedside manner with clients and bosses—but I was great at drawing diagrams of complex instruments and deals.

JM: What else are you working on now?

JK: I am writing a cli-fi road novel. It is the first time I have written about something that is about neither manufactured housing communities nor me. It is *work*—this time, I have to make things up.

MY GRANDMOTHER'S AFFAIR WITH THE SAN ANDREAS FAULT

Sakae Manning

Note: Italicized copy is from the United States Geological Survey

> my mother is / from japan / islands set within / a ring of fire / a land of earthquakes and volcanoes / ground slipping and mountains erupting

The San Andreas is the "master" fault of an intricate fault network that cuts through rocks of the California coastal region. The entire San Andreas fault system is more than 800 miles long and extends to depths of at least 10 miles within the Earth.

When she arrives to California's Central Valley, my grandmother is swollen from earlobes to ankles with child. Deep ravines cross both shoulders. Calloused and scarred hands, a heart given to bouts of racing and jerking, and eyes swallowed into sockets from squinting into full sun, evidence of an uncertain, laboring life. Three generations chased by settlers who call them flatheads, steal their last cow, lynch an ancestor. They travel in bumps and starts to where oranges litter sidewalks for the taking, and sardines on saltines fill griping bellies. Dust Bowl grit lives in their lungs, so Oklahoma is always home no matter where they go. "We'd forgot what a blue sky looks like," Grandmother describes first seeing California, "and we put stock in its promise of good luck."

> my mother says women learn / from their own mothers / to shift their lives for family / unspoken dreams grinding / between clenched teeth / husbands holding a foot on their necks / are after-shocks used to bury scraps of hope

Almost any road cut in the zone shows a myriad of small fractures, fault gouge (pulverized rock), and a few solid pieces of rock.

For as long as my mind holds memory, every summer and fall, we gather, one large family, in the Sierra Nevada. My five aunties tell stories under a sky quilt knotted in stars, a patchwork of constellations. They speak of those gone too soon including my grandmother's baby, the one born without breath, and tsk long sad noises, each one adding her voice, until they become a murmuring chorus. Some click tongues behind teeth or on the roof of mouths. Crickets pause. Night birds go still. I memorize their words, adding wood to the fire they encircle, fetching tea, dumping a capful of whiskey and honey in mugs to warm knitted bones, and swat mosquitos until flames lick strong.

In the distance, quiet laughter, as young uncles and boy cousins leave, easily navigating narrow deer trails under moonless nights. They invite me to join, because I am the best at spotting deer and snakes balled up in warm boulders. They say I'm unlike other females, because I do not hold a woman's scent. I can cross slimy, moss-covered fallen logs to find a dropped trail, climb a tree to sit for hours, and hold watch before signaling with a tap against the trunk. This time, I choose to stay with the aunties. The elder uncles and my grandfather huddle around a wood stove in the shed playing checkers, warming up with brown liquor, whittling, chewing or smoking tobacco, and planning hunting trips. Every so often, from the blackness, a screen door squeaks and slams. The aunties laugh at their men, their small bladders, before returning to their own story.

The baby whose name is unspoken is the first buried in this quivering, foreign ground. "He came out frowned up," says auntie who married an icy-eyed white man. She shakes her head with the slow regret someone who has lived much loss understands. "His eyes and nose squeezed shut," says Baptist auntie who was there. She blows into her steamy mug, "I reckon the town stunk." Someone notices me. All eyes shift in my direction, "Your grandmother is brave." They agree in different ways, "She kept going with her head up," one says low from somewhere in the shadows. Heavy smoker auntie, tobacco defining the gaps in her teeth, wheezes before coughing, "She shoulda never had to work the fields in the first damn place."

The elder aunties, cheeks flushing, recall the meeting, as if my grandmother and the San Andreas shared a secret on that day. My grandmother once again heavily pregnant. This one might make it if she could hang on through the fig harvest. Oldest auntie recollects, "Well, the big ol' San Andreas was bothered by those government men tearin' up the mountainside, forcing water from one river to another, making lakes where none were meant to be."

Second oldest auntie spits through a gap, "Y'all already know." Another wad flashes past my head, sizzling when it lands in the fire, "The government don't hold a speck of respect for Indians, and none for the land."

"Provoking nature," oldest cousin says, face shimmering firelight, an edge in her college-educated voice. Her nipples round and prickly, reminding me of wild blackberries, poke at the United Farm Workers t-shirt she's been wearing since the heat of the day. She scoots closer to her mother, who drapes a quilt over her shoulders. I stoke the fire. Its reflection in their faces are mirrors of the women who came before us. Each has my great-grandmother's tall ears with fat lobes, her cheekbones, sharp and broad, and oldest cousin's eyebrows are wide like her mother's.

They tell of how the San Andreas is apt to shiver, rumbling all the way up and down California, cracking dams, collapsing mines, and generally, tearing up settlers' best laid plans. Second oldest auntie points to the sky, "You know what they say?" She grimaces, "God don't like ugly." Somewhere from around the fire, smoker auntie's deep voice utters, "The Creator." A log crackles, firelight rising before settling with her words. I add more wood, shift the embers with a long branch, and sit back on my haunches.

> my mother describes earthquakes / as life / in japan /
> americans are babies / real threats are tsunamis / bombs
> blowing families into ash

The San Andreas fault forms a continuous narrow break in the Earth's crust that extends from northern California southward to Cajon Pass near San Bernardino.

The trees sway, dipping way left, before dipping way right, dropping and bursting figs to waste. The aunties say during all the shaking, a freight train, at least ten miles away, shrieks one of those long death cries as it derails. Dogs howl. My grandmother stands up straight, arching to stretch out the ache. She is smiling broadly, holding her back, belly swollen and hanging from this young one's readiness. She wipes her brow with the sleeve of Pawpaw's old denim shirt, twirls some loose hair around a stained, thick finger, and pats her belly, feeling a rolling and a tiny foot pushing from inside her.

After the ground stops banging and sliding, it continues to shudder in bursts. The aunties laugh describing the farmer sputtering, "Good God almighty, damn that San Andreas fault." Flies and ants already feasting on the figs' innards. He punches himself in the chest, claiming the crop a total loss. Some say he let loose of some tears. Oldest auntie measures her words, "What he surely said was, 'get our Okie flathead asses off his land.'"

That season, all the aunties and uncles got new leather shoes paid for by money my grandmother earns selling whole preserved figs, fig jam, dried figs, fig tarts, and fig loaves. My father is born, and there is enough left to buy him a good blanket and real diapers.

> my mother grows tired of struggling / every year / with my defiance / longs for summer / when she will drop me off in the mountains / my grandmother and aunties already busy / putting up jam and quilting / she thanks them for teaching me / wears an outside face / a lying face

The fault zone is marked by distinctive landforms that include long straight escarpments, narrow ridges, and small undrained ponds formed by the settling of small blocks within the zone. Many stream channels characteristically jog sharply to the right where they cross the fault.

My grandmother keeps books neatly stacked on the maple sideboard, so she can study her love, the great San Andreas Fault. It is why she has a public library card. There is a ritual in how she bakes fresh cornbread for us, mixes up molasses and butter, and reads outloud, while I sit, legs curled up under me, eating until all that is left are crumbs, sucking the final sweetness from my fingers. Scientific facts. After-shocks. Richter scales. A strike-slip fault. Destruction of entire blocks designed by university-educated engineers. She reads through a round magnifying glass, nose pushed up into squinting eyes. I ask questions to draw out the evening.

There is an awe in her voice, a shifting in her hips, and I wonder if Pawpaw knows what's going on after I find a piece of paper where she has written "San Andreas Fault" in cursive and also printed in all caps. Line after line until there isn't any room left on the page. There are hearts doodled around the border, snow-capped mountain ranges, and flowers with curly stems, vines reaching beyond the margins, a wedding bouquet erupting, blooming until it takes over an entire page. My fingers trace my grandmother's commitment, left by the ballpoint pen, pressing until it puckers and pierces thick writing paper.

> my mother survives a world war / an atomic bomb / a
> disowning / by her own family / i am her undoing / my
> life / has shaken up / every part of her life / she says I
> am a regret / a living ghost

Blocks on opposite sides of the San Andreas fault move horizontally. If a person stood on one side of the fault and looked across it, the block on the opposite side would appear to have moved to the right. Geologists refer to this type of fault displacement as right-lateral strike-slip.

Grandmother sighs, closing the latest book, with a final pat of her heavy forefinger, carefully tucking the magnifying glass into her sewing basket, saying the San Andreas has woman energy, moving ground with a hard wind and a shove coming from above and from below—sometimes a jerk, and other times, a roll, depending on the great one's mood. Tapping a boars' head brush on her thigh, she unwinds the olive oil cap from the tin. I sit on the floor, between her legs, while she runs the brush down my hair, and describes an earthquake as buttery biscuit—flakey, nearly crisp, slippery beneath bare feet. "Always use your toes to hang on," she says, massaging oil into my scalp.

> my mother leads a life of suspicion / believes everyone is against her / she knows / in the mountains / my ponytail turns into braids / my skin darkens like a farmer / boiled potatoes and grits / replace gohan / I wear my boy cousins hand-me-downs / swim naked in creeks

During the 1906 earthquake in the San Francisco region, roads, fences, and rows of trees and bushes that crossed the fault were offset several yards, and the road across the head of Tomales Bay was offset almost 21 feet, the maximum offset recorded.

In the summer of my thirteenth year, all the grands come to the mountains where the elders live, way off the highway, in two single-wides, one a great-uncle's and one my grandparents', set on a couple of acres, unmapped and unnamed. We are here to help clear the land for fire season, start the harvest, dry seed, hunt, fish, and stay out of flatlander trouble. My hair has grown nearly to my tailbone. My grandmother's eyes greet me, admiringly, before she says the deer fat and olive oil have done their job. My mother cringes, peering up at the broad oak shading us, checking her own headscarf, and tells me to keep my hair in a ponytail before I get ticks or lice. She keeps her small hand on my back, tightly pinching my shirt before pushing me towards my grandmother. I turn to hug her, but my mother's arms are already crossed, as if she is cold, and she's stepping back towards the idling car. She scans the faces looking back at her, all my aunties and my grandmother. Her jaw rigid. Her body in flight. It is then I realize beyond language, I am the fault slipping between my mother and my grandmother.

my mother grins / sometimes she rubs her face with both hands / to keep from laughing / tells me this story / again and again / when she was a girl / her father / shoved her oldest sister's head / the talk back sister / the one she compares me to / in a bucket of well water / holds it under until she nearly drowns / again and again / a reminder for me to know my place

In the process of breaking or "faulting," vibrations are set up that are the earthquakes. Some of the vibrations are of very low frequency, with many seconds between waves, whereas other vibrations are of high enough frequency to be in the audible range.

One early summer morning, when freshly baked bread warms the trailer, the sun barely blinking over the Sierras, lunch is already packed in waxed paper and jars, a jug of sweet tea, another with spring water. Grandmother declares at thirteen, I'm old enough for a special trip. We are going to meet up with the San Andreas, "for a date." Cousins scatter, some take off into the woods, fishing poles, 22s, and rucksacks on their backs, and oldest cousin, who is in her moon time, jumps up from eating last night's cornbread to milk goats.

I'm ready, wearing a too long Boy Scout windbreaker, once belonging to oldest male cousin, over a t-shirt and jeans cuffed high to keep me from tripping. I run barefoot, a shoe in each hand, to the faded truck. She's carrying a wooden fruit crate. I'm sitting shotgun, shoving my feet into sneakers, a stack of Reader's Digest in a paper bag for just in case. Holes blossom where my big and little toe push out on each side. "You're in the growing year," Grandmother observes, "'spect you'll soon smell different, grow hair 'tween your legs, and you'll bleed like we do."

After a couple of turns, the ignition starts, and we set out slow down the long, rutted, dirt-packed road to a paved highway. Church songs hum from her throat. Grandmother has her hair braided and twisted into one of Pawpaw's red kerchiefs. She leans into the wheel, hitting the gas a couple of times before shifting gears, and squints into the oncoming day's brightness. The hem of her calico day dress flaps in the wind, showing more naked thigh, a woman who has worked fields and walked miles thigh. Muscular, strong, with veins so near her skin, I wonder, *is this what will happen to my thighs when I become a woman?* I squeeze my legs tightly together, thinking this is how I can stop myself from ever bleeding, from ever becoming a woman.

> my mother uses long bladed sewing shears / to slice open / my diary lock / learns i love both a boy and a girl / am content barefoot / naked / alone / in my room or / out in a field filled with yellow / lots of yellow light / in the air / dancing in rhythm with long grass / she strips me / of my clothes / leaves me locked / in my dark room

In an earthquake, people may note first a sharp thud, or blast-like shock, that marks the arrival of the P wave.

Driving to meet the San Andreas takes us on many highways until one transition opens up to a multi-lane freeway. That's when my grandmother pushes it. The truck roars, and we are flying, me hanging onto the seat edge, the window handle, the door, anything, because she's laughing now. Hooting and hollering, her eyes flickering amber, to brown, to amber again, in bright mid-morning light as we travel over bridges, through underpasses, and past tall trees waving us onwards. Clouds rimmed in hazy blues stretch long and wide forming an aisle on either side of wide, paved lanes. Crows circle in the distance, wings cutting razor thin lines in a sky calling for constant admiration.

> my mother tells warning stories / sends sea ghosts / kami wrapped in a leering uwabami / a drunken serpent / swimming out / from the dark closet / fish bones / the bones of defiant girls / hollow and dry / rattle from beneath my bed

A few seconds later, they may feel a swaying or rolling motion that marks the arrival of the S wave.

"You ain't like us," she shouts over the rushing air. It's too hot to roll the windows up, so I move closer to hear better. "Now, listen here, that's nothin' to feel some way about," she glances at me and back to the highway. Her mouth trembles ever so slightly before she presses her lips to her nose, like she's studying a new quilting pattern. Soon, the truck abruptly pulls over onto the highway's shoulder, "but I do reckon it's on account of the San Andreas." Gravel snipes at the windshield and leaves a thick dusting on the truck. She secures the screechy hand brake, "You fer sure wouldn't a been here if not for her mercy." She yanks off the kerchief, tying it around her neck. Her braid falls, shades of all the disappointment and joy ever lived, and rests on her back. Checking the rearview, my grandmother applies Vaseline to her lips, rubs the rest into her hands and elbows, before perching a floppy sunhat on her head.

She hands me two jugs and carries the box herself, as if it weighs nothing. "Come, 'fore the day gets too far ahead of us," she directs, marching off in her nursing shoes towards a vast open field where a few cows graze far up on rolling hills. She calls them orthotics, but my oldest cousin says she kept them from her job as a rest home LVN when they lived in Vallejo. Two lace-up, polished white reminders from when she still believed there was time for a future. I tuck a couple Reader's Digest issues into the back of my jeans.

It is a short walk, but one I suspect she's done many times, to a large overgrown ravine reaching as far as we can see in either direction. I moan, "This is just a dried creek bed." My cousin's jeans are sticking to my legs; sweat trickles down my back. "No, sugar," she spreads a large quilt smack in the middle of the flattest part, "this is the fault; the place where lives are changed, sometimes ended, where power is brewin' just under our feet."

> my mother reminds me / in japan / mothers abandoned / baby girls / on the edge of / dirt roads littered with / before war lives / pearl-faced girls / wailing / hungry / wanting

Local geologic conditions strongly influence the intensity of an earthquake. Commonly, sites on soft ground or alluvium have intensities 2 to 3 units higher than sites on bedrock.

We sit, soaking in the sun, on ground cradling us in its warmth, eating government cheese on heavily buttered homemade bread. Not a human, even if they had binoculars, could see us, down in the split earth, up to our ears in swaying deer grass and golden wildflowers. My grandmother's sunhat brim occasionally flips up to show her eyes deep in thought, as if she is in conversation with someone.

She wipes butter from the corners of her mouth, sucks the shiny dribbling off her finger. I like this grandmother. She's lost her religion. Pawpaw's voice left on the mountain. The bulgy-eyed pastor's voice left at the pulpit. She says no one owns me but me, "No babies. No man. You'll do just fine." She wipes her hands, offering me pickled okra from a mayonnaise jar, "You're one of us but also one with the San Andreas," and squinches her face up when I pull my lips back to take a teeth-only bite. The vinegar coating my throat until I chase it with sweet tea. "Go on now, swallow," she orders in her quiet way, "good for the constitution."

> my mother says i am the cause of / our family bachi / the clothes i wear / makes people think / i am a certain kind of girl / my big mouth / my selfish mind / my confidence / will cause my family to fall into failure

The earthquake of January 9, 1857, in Southern California apparently was about the same magnitude as the San Francisco earthquake of 1906. An account of the 1857 earthquake describes a sheep corral cut by the fault that was changed from a circle to an "S"-shape—movement clearly representative of right-lateral strike-slip.

We pee together under the wide and dense canopy of a lone oak. She hikes up the worn cotton dress, pulls her underwear down around her ankles, and squats back against the broad trunk before relieving herself. Her eyes close, a couple of ants dance a zig-zag across her foot, and she breathes deeply. It is a long time before she rises. I pee quickly and pull up my cousin's jeans. Acorns drop at my feet. When she finishes, my grandmother pats the oak's trunk, leans in, and whispers something. She leads me to a wet, spongy area, and digs with her hands. Suddenly, water begins to gurgle, then bubble like a low running drinking fountain. She brushes soil and grass away before collecting cool water in cupped hands, rinsing her face and neck. We return to study clouds from within the San Andreas' soft belly, a red-tail hawk circles high, slow and lazy, lulling us into a nap on the quilt.

> my mother is overwhelmed by a need to / save face / to manipulate truth / form a porcelain daughter who transcends / the one with crooked bangs / the daughter who / translates america for her

Geologic studies show that over the past 1,400 to 1,500 years large earthquakes have occurred at about 150-year intervals on the Southern San Andreas fault.

The earth moves, a heaving, heavy kind of breath, underneath me. My grandmother says that's normal. "The ground is family," my grandmother whispers, "She carries the weight of our struggle." I put my hand on the ground but only feel warm dirt. "She's welcoming you," grandmother pats the ground, "Say hello." She turns on her side, legs folded up, resting as if on a satin covered bed, like in the movies with Elizabeth Taylor, "See how we're here, in the arms of the San Andreas?" Her voice grows louder until she is nearly yelling, "This is how folks ought to honor power, because with one big breath, all of this," she rolls onto her back, reaching her thick, farmer, mid-wife, field plowing arms, high above her head, swinging them all around, and releases a big breath, "All of this is nothing." Grandmother says the San Andreas reminds us we're no bigger than a speck of day dust. She smiles mischievously, holding a shoe up to the sky, "She can change the tide, where a river spits into the sea." She rubs at a mark on her shoe, "show a man he ain't in control of this here ground."

> my mother says sex is / saved for marriage / i tell her i'll never marry / she blinks / presses her eyes tight / as if she is about to blow out birthday cake candles / tells me her one wish is / she could go back to japan

Along the Earth's plate boundaries, such as the San Andreas fault, segments exist where no large earthquakes have occurred for long intervals of time.

The San Andreas embraces my grandmother's hips, wide and soft, resting on their crusty edge, adoring her thick thighs, the kind that swish when she wears stockings, savoring her body's warmth. "It must be lonely," I say, "to not be seen until you shake things up." My grandmother focuses on something in the distance. Her mind is faraway, deep underground. The heat between the two is strong now, unlike any she has shared with Pawpaw, who I've never seen kiss nor hug her, not even when she reads the Farmer's Almanac out-loud or teaches him how to write his name in cursive until every angle and dot look just like hers.

> my mother believes / she is american / because of her american name / judy / after judy garland / i remind her / she is as issei as the day she stepped off the freight liner in san francisco / the gold paved streets / the ruby slippers / are an illusion

As the last large earthquake on the Southern San Andreas occurred in 1857, that section of the fault is considered a likely location for an earthquake within the next few decades.

Using her fingers, my grandmother brushes her hair until it is wild, fluttering in a sudden breeze. She reaches over and unbraids my hair, telling me to do what she does, and I do, running my fingers through, collecting loose strands. She winds our hair together into a tight bundle before placing it in a small hole she has dug. She drops dried herbs from her garden, pours some liquor onto the mixture, sprinkles a little tobacco, and lights it with a match. A quick "poof" rises and falls into the earth, simmering, crackling until it is soot. My Grandmother seals the hole with soil and tamps it with her hands. "Plant yourself where you belong," she says, slowly nodding at the hole, "your roots will grow with purpose." There is sweetness, filling my head, floating between my eyes, a sigh from the ground all around us. A vibration, slowly rises and falls from beneath my feet. My breath matches the rhythm. I curl my toes into the ground and slowly rock side-to-side with the deer grass, crows diving and dodging above, clouds fading into faint streaks in the distance.

INHERITED MEMORY WITH FRESH EYES

A Conversation with Sakae Manning

Claire Agnes: Thank you for taking the time to speak with me, and for sharing this piece with *Driftwood Press*. "My Grandmother's Affair with the San Andreas Fault" is a narrative as specific and memorable as its title, yet it explores thematics so universal one could mistake them for the whispers of the universe itself. The reader experiences this narrative through the braiding of the narrator's voice, passages of informational text, and poems pertaining to the figure of the narrator's mother. Of these three threads, which came first to this story, or to you?

Sakae Manning: The story about the grandmother and narrator having a picnic on the SAF came first from a journal entry, but it needed movement. I took a braiding workshop through Lidia Yuknavitch's Corporeal Writing. I was fascinated by the opportunities in opening up a story's space to breathe and for the reader's personal interpretation. This is more in alignment with how stories are told in my family, jumping from place, to time, to voice, and how different people weigh in on a story. Prior to this piece, I tried to write in a traditional short story format, but Ingrid Rojas Contreras changed my approach when she said to write from the place of your ancestors and culture, to tell the stories the way you know them. That changed everything. I'm definitely into hybrid writing now that I don't restrict myself to a traditional form.

CA: Were the styles currently ascribed to each voice apparent from early drafts onward, or did the particular rhythms and forms of each voice find you in later iterations of this piece?

SM: In most stories, the voices come first from handwritten words left in the margins of beloved books or in letters or cards I have saved for decades. This is even before questions about what I'm writing. In this case, I questioned what the picnic on the SAF meant. Why take me there?

I used to translate Japanese to English for my mother, as well as translating her English into what Americans could understand. I learned early on that many Americans are unable to listen clearly when it comes to English spoken outside the region in which they live. My ear for how people speak comes from a lifetime of riding public transportation, living in multilingual communities, and loving every moment when friends and family seamlessly switch between languages, or witnessing how their dialect gets side-eyed in public spaces. How the characters speak are based on real people. Their voices are integral to who they are, especially how they express themselves, so that came organically, early on. What they say, for the most part, is fictionalized.

CA: Despite the presence of a first-person narrator, this story appears to share narrative ownership, volleying the emotive life of the narrator (and therefore, the reader along with them) between the palpable momentum of the grandmother and the, as one editor put it, "cold staccato" of the mother. To whom do you ascribe ownership of this narrative, and why?

SM: This is a great question, because if I go back to how a story is told in my family, no one person owns the narrative. There may be someone who ties the story together, but the person speaking owns their lived part of the story. Someone may tell it slightly differently, or say, "You're windier than a West Texas windmill," in response, which brings laughter and doubt to the teller's version. My mother and grandmother could tell the exact same story but end up on polar opposite sides of what was said and what was an intentional slight. I attribute this to intergenerational differences, language disconnect, as well as my mother's resentment of living in a household headed by her mother-in-law.

In this story, the characters do not see the similarities between their lives. Both are formally uneducated, without their own financial means to survive, and reliant on a patriarchal construct where racism, misogyny, and classism are normalized. Both migrate to survive, leaving more behind than what they have ahead of them, are surviving their own traumas, and have tucked away unrealized dreams. Their intentions for the young narrator come from a place of love and fear. The grandmother sees hope in this young one. The mother upholds the patriarchy and what has been ingrained in her, because conforming means surviving.

CA: This piece speaks of the San Andreas Fault with such intimacy. Where did the interest in this specific setting originate?

SM: Everything for this story began with that picnic on the SAF with my grandmother. It frames each part of the family's journey. Living with breathing ground is something both the grandmother and mother have in common. In some ways, they both deal with earthquakes in an organic manner. They don't fight nature's ways. It is completely the antithesis of the colonizing approach of controlling and shaping nature and people into what invading countries and religions did in the US, using religion and exploration to steal ground and natural resources. The SAF represents a larger-than-life legend that puts fear in the hearts of all who believe they can control the stolen ground by disrespecting the very people who are caretakers and revere its power and gifts.

CA: Readers of this story experience the collisions of inheritance, of culture, and of trauma throughout the piece, a friction that is beautifully reflected in the informative passages pertaining to the San Andreas Fault that punctuate the narrative. We do, however, avoid true eruption—the earth does not quake and the dueling forces and faces that inhabit the narrative narrowly escape collision. Could you speak to the decision to avoid this expected climax of conflicts?

SM: It was really clear from the first draft that I didn't want to write a disaster story or one with a typical earthquake storyline. Instead, I wanted to draw the parallel to nature, how time isn't measured in minutes or years, but in its own force and rhythm. When I consider families exploding into violence, I realize most families live in some type of conflict. I wonder, if people could recognize all of the things happening in the present that could destroy their families, would they try and fix them, build a repair kit for sexually abused young ones, a survival kit for racial microaggressions, a guide for cheating spouses, and anything to quell mistrust and fear of the government?

For this family, who are connected to the ground and all that grows and lives on it, there is a clear ability to see how to care for others, but not for themselves. They have lived in this trauma until it is normalized in their DNA. There are outlets, like alcohol, avoidance, and conflict aversion, but hardly anyone confronts each other—not even the mother and grandmother. Ultimately, if pressure is released on a small scale, the big one is avoided, just like a real earthquake.

In general, I find this is how humans navigate living on the SAF. We disregard nature's behavior. We know the big one is imminent, because the evidence demonstrates how the earth lives and breathes, dormant volcanoes erupting and tectonic plates pushing against each other, resulting in massive earthquakes; yet, we live as if it won't happen in our time. Families are like this, too. They overlook signs, deeply held secrets and destructive behavior, so it may take many generations before the big one comes. In the meantime, pressure continues to force faults and fissures into the family. It doesn't mean it's all bad. Remember, the big one also brings gifts—like truth and transformation.

CA: I am curious what other means of research you employ in order to better inform your work. Is site-specific research a feature of your writing process? At what point in your drafting process do you typically begin outside research?

SM: When I'm writing, I'm reading, whether it is news feeds that lead into deep internet dives or some fact shared with me in a coffee shop conversation. For this story, I pinched a journal entry about my grandmother taking me on a picnic to the San Andreas Fault. She really did have this reverence and love for nature's power. I somehow got lucky, and it was just the two of us. I read books specifically about the SAF; in particular, *A Field Guide to the San Andreas Fault* (David K. Lynch). That book inspired me to visit key spots where the SAF has made a significant impact including Hollister, where the SAF is believed to originate. My Oldest, who has a strong history background, and I took off on a research road trip. I do this after the story stalls, when I feel it needs texture, usually after a few drafts. Visiting locations where stories are set is essential to my work, because every sense is influenced by ground and place. This holds true for places that have been erased, too, like Sacramento's Japantown post-WW2, or the land where my grandparents once had a farm.

CA: During the editing process, you mentioned having visited the San Andreas Fault as a means of research for this piece. How did experiencing the setting firsthand change, challenge, or otherwise alter the work?

SM: Journeying up into Central California, the coastline, and into specific towns, like Hollister, where my Oldest and I spent considerable time looking at fault displacement, refreshed my memories of the SAF and the stories my grandmother told. I felt a convergence of memories with fresh eyes. We drove to the Sierra Nevadas, where snow was still on the ground in April, because I wanted to introduce my Oldest to his ancestor. The most incredible thing happened on what started as a sunny day. We couldn't locate her grave right away. After a long search, many tears (by me), we found it with the help of a city worker who just happened to take lunch in the cemetery. As soon as I set eyes on my grandmother's headstone, it began to lightly snow. That emotion is captured in notes for this story. Most of what I write requires me to see, touch, and smell the places I write about. They aren't settings as much as characters, because my inherent belief system, having a Shinto issei mother and having indigenous ancestors who taught us without telling us what they were teaching, is that nature isn't to be reckoned with, nor is it to be formed. Nature is living and breathing. I've intentionally moved towards decolonizing my belief system about, for instance, how to manage forests, how cities are built, and why everyone in California has lawns that are inherently destructive to the ecosystem.

CA: This story challenges the reader's perceptions of self, inheritance, and the natural world as it explores the complexities of identity and the limits of our ownership over our own. What aspects of selfhood challenged you as the author during the writing process? Were there urges that needed to be ignored for the development of the story, or was some exploration and excision of the self required in order to put this narrative on the page?

SM: I learned through editing with you, Claire! I was holding back, keeping the very secrets or thoughts I deemed unimportant to myself. The questions posed during editing ultimately gave me a "my bad," kinda moment, because I realized I'm as guilty as my foremothers in trying to hold on too tightly because of fear and that damn unresolved intergenerational trauma.

I constantly remind myself that my writing is done to record memory, to honor ancestors, and in order for our experiences as bi- and multi-racial people to be seen. Intersectionality is paramount to drawing empathy and humanity into our own lives even while people, our own included, are conditioned to categorize. "What are you?" is a question posed to me my entire life, and it is expected for us to break down our background into fractions. Then, there's the response, "Oh, you don't look Indian," or "You don't look Japanese," or "I thought you were Mexican." For biracial and multiracial people, especially two spirit and LGBTQIA+ people, this becomes more complex and, at times when it comes from our own communities, can be confounding and frustrating. This story is my attempt at blending the young narrator into their own person despite attempts to compartmentalize their identity.

CA: I'm very grateful and humbled to have had a part in the shape of this story. I'm also very struck by the juxtaposition you mention here, the conflict between the duty to record ancestral memory and the desire to shape the narrator into an individual identity. Can you speak more to this tension? Does the story of the individual ever overtake the narrative weight of inherited memory, in this piece and/or others?

SM: Because we have our ancestors' DNA and their experiences imprinted upon our memories, whether we can recall them or not, the two are inextricably tied. I recognize in order to be my authentic self, I have to recognize all parts of my family's journey. That's where the difficulty comes into play, because some things are too unspeakable. I'm still wrestling with this in storytelling, and it manifests in how the protagonist sometimes keeps secrets, which you called out in your edits. Ultimately, how the individual processes the inherited memory, with fresh eyes, is how the story demonstrates transformation.

CA: The unpacking of what we have inherited from our families and communities is simultaneously one of the most cathartic and cataclysmic aspects of storytelling from an autofictive perspective. Is this piece a part of a larger collection? If so, are other identities braided into this same narrator's identity?

SM: I have a collection building around these fictionalized stories with essays acting as interstitials. The essays are themed around taking my sons on land visits to follow their ancestors' journeys from Oklahoma to California and from Hiroshima to California. It is becoming a hybrid project that combines both families.

CA: Thank you again for taking the time to speak with me, and for submitting this piece to *Driftwood Press*. Where else might we find your work? Are any other creative projects in the works?

SM: My work has been published by *The Tahoma Literary Review, Blood Orange Review, Carve Magazine*, and in *Making Waves: An Anthology of Writings By and About Asian American Women*, edited by Asian Women United of California, (*Beacon Press*). Most of it may be accessed online.

I'm really excited to be invited to work on my first performance piece, which will be performed live in June. That's pretty frightening, since I'm a writer, not a performer, but I made this year the year of "yes."

CA: A performance piece sounds like quite an exciting new challenge! When and where in the world might our readers find your stage? Are there any other details you are at liberty to share?

SM: It will be at the Victory Theater in Los Angeles, but may also be viewed via live-stream. The producers do these performances to sustain the theater, so there is a nominal charge of $10. Producers invite two fiction writers, two poets, and two non-fiction writers to write/perform pieces inspired by published works. Alice Walker's *The Color Purple* is what we've been assigned to use as our inspiration. The performance is on June 2nd, so by the time this anthology releases, it will be accessible on Youtube.

CA: Congratulations and the best of luck on this new creative endeavor! Thank you again for inviting our readers and myself into your process and for sharing these pages with *Driftwood Press.*

EFANYBODY
NOCKONES
DEOBDONA
ACEMISTO
EODANDE
ILEHUMKNO

UPON LEARNING MY ANCESTORS WERE GEECHEE FREED SLAVES AND OWNED AN ISLAND OFF LOUISIANA

Khalisa Rae

the South

says *nigga* and we know that means a string
something thin to tin-can us back to jim crow, clothesline
the minute we try to jump ship. say *boy, girl* and we know
that be manila, something thick and braided, the banana bread—
we'd hang ourselves on. you never can escape your mother
tongue. the first language we ever learned here was how
to be invisible. how to keep our heads down, tip
our hat and accept the slur, grit our teeth
at the cow-tipped comment oozing from his chapped
lips at the counter. to sip slow at the colored-only
fountain. we learned to tuck *Jambalaya* under our tongue,
hide oxtail, *gumbo* between our teeth, toothpick
it out when they weren't looking. twist our mouths
to rinse the sand from this speech. *Duh, him, da cry out, so'*
save for the yam, they whipped and called sweet.
sweet baby b'dout no home. *weh ya frum, chil?*
thank the gulf, I finally know how to answer.
my people are geechee women—from salt and rice,
sticky, black be the way we say grace, my home,
be the ocean—drowned us now we lay our head,
in it. my home be the island, land-locked to keep
you out, *less you want us ta' harvest, 'ya too.* my people
from gullah– where water don't bury, it brings ya' back to life.

KHALISA RAE

In Conversation

Sara Moore Wagner: First, I want to congratulate you on this win. All our editors unanimously upvoted your poem. We were immediately drawn into the story and continued readings revealed the close attention to craft. Could you tell us a bit about where this poem started for you?

Khalisa Rae: Absolutely! This poem was born from a deep sense of connection to the South juxtaposed with a very contentious, fraught relationship with water-locked Southern spaces, their symbolism, and weight. I was commissioned last year to write and think more deeply about my Southern roots and the timing could not have been more perfect. Sometime last year I began to get more curious about my Southern ancestors on both my maternal and paternal side.The prompt for the piece was, "Tell us about your hidden lineage or a forgotten people." For me, that begins with the mystery of my paternal ancestors that I know so little about, besides that they were freed slaves that bought an island off the coast of Louisiana and settled there. That mystery sparked curiosity and imagination. After doing research, I had to get inside the voice and mind of my ancestors—stepping in their skin to see what I believe they saw, heard, and experienced. The poetic images start with the idea of a braid. I wanted you to see and feel the many things that can be braided: a rope, hair, a noose, a word. That hybridity is an acknowledgement of harm, an exploration of identity, and a homage to the resilience and beauty of my heritage.

SMW: I'm so drawn to your line breaks in this poem, how every individual line has power. How do you approach line breaks?

KR: Thank you for noticing. I tried really hard to ensure that each line was crafted with intention, aiming to convey depth and resonance in every word of my piece. When approaching line breaks, I strive to create a rhythmic flow that mirrors the cadence of storytelling passed down through generations.

For me, line breaks are a tool to emphasize moments of significance, to create pauses that invite reflection, and to guide the reader through the emotional landscape of the poem. I often consider the natural breath and pacing of speech, allowing the breaks to enhance the overall rhythm and musicality of the verse. Most importantly, in this piece, I wanted end words/phrases to tell a story of their own. For each last word on the line to strike, shock, or perplex the reader—conveying some emotion that thrusts you into the moment of the poem.

Furthermore, I pay close attention to the visual aspect of the poem on the page, considering how line breaks can shape the reader's interpretation and engagement with the text. By strategically breaking lines, I aim to draw attention to key images, ideas, or emotions, inviting the reader to linger and savor each moment.

Ultimately, my approach to line breaks is guided by a desire to evoke an immersive experience for the reader, inviting them to journey alongside me through the layers of meaning and memory embedded within the poem.

SMW: There's also such sound in the individual words. It's incantatory! Does sound come naturally to you, as a poet? How important is sound to this poem?

KR: As a poet that follows in the Black griot tradition and a trained performer, sound is indeed a natural and integral aspect of my creative process. I often find myself drawn to the musicality of language, seeking to weave a symphony of sounds that resonate with the emotions and themes of the poem.

In this particular piece, sound plays a pivotal role in conveying the essence of my Louisiana Geechee/Creole heritage. The rhythm and cadence of the words evoke the heartbeat of the culture, echoing the melodies of Creole music and the lively chatter of family gatherings. Through carefully chosen words and phrases, I aim to evoke a sensory experience that immerses the reader in the sights, sounds, and flavors of my heritage.

Moreover, sound serves as a vehicle for oral tradition, paying homage to the storytelling traditions passed down through generations. The incantatory quality of the poem's sound invites the reader to participate in this tradition, engaging not only with the meaning of the words but also with the sonic tapestry they create.

Overall, sound is deeply important to this poem, as it infuses the language with layers of meaning, emotion, and cultural resonance. It is through the interplay of sound and sense that the poem comes alive, inviting the reader on a journey of discovery. I want the sound to wrench and twist the reader in this piece.

SMW: Is there anything you would like our readers to know and understand about Geechee freed slaves, historically or personally?

KR: It's crucial for readers to understand the historical and personal significance of Geechee freed slaves in the context of Southern history.

Historically, Geechee freed slaves were part of a distinct community that emerged in the Lowcountry regions of South Carolina and Georgia. Descendants of enslaved Africans who gained freedom either through manumission or escape, Geechee communities developed their own unique culture, language (referred to as Gullah), traditions, and way of life. They preserved elements of African culture, blending them with influences from Native American and European settlers, resulting in a rich cultural tapestry that continues to thrive today.

Personal understanding of Geechee freed slaves is equally important to me. The descendants faced immense challenges and isolation. Despite the harsh conditions of slavery, Gullah people maintained strong ties to their African roots, and kept that spirit alive through music, storytelling, foodways, and religious practices. This is a testament to their remarkable resilience, creativity, and perseverance in the face of adversity. Their stories illuminate the power of communal connection and its ability to sustain individuals through generations.

Furthermore, it's essential to recognize the ongoing contributions of Geechee communities to American culture and society. Gullah food is woven into our favorite dishes like gumbo, jambalaya, hoppin' john, crab stew, cornbread, and more. Their music, cuisine, art, and language have left an indelible mark on the cultural landscape of the South and beyond, enriching the tapestry of diversity in our nation.

SMW: How can readers learn more about this history, if they aren't familiar?

KR: I encourage people to watch the Netflix series *High on the Hog.* It is a personal favorite because it delves into the profound influence of Creole cuisine and culture on American foodways, highlighting its significance in shaping the culinary landscape of the United States. It explores how Creole cuisine, originating from Louisiana and influenced by a blend of African, European, Native American, and Caribbean culinary traditions, occupies a central role in the series as it explores the intersection of culture, history, and identity.

There are also numerous books, scholarly articles, and academic resources that delve into the history, culture, and experiences of Geechee communities. Readers can explore titles such as *Geechee: The First Free Africans in America* by Jacquetta M. Few and *The Gullah: Rice, Slavery, and the Sierra Leone-American Connection* by Joseph A. Opala and Cynthia Schmidt.

I'd recommend documentaries and immersive experiences that can deepen understanding and appreciation of Geechee Creole history. Titles like *Gullah, Geechee: Evolution of a People* and *Daughters of the Dust* offer insights into the culture, traditions, and struggles of Geechee/Creole communities.

Visit the Gullah Festival in Beaufort, South Carolina, and the Penn Center Heritage Days Celebration on St. Helena Island, South Carolina. Juneteenth Celebrations: These events provide opportunities to honor Geechee ancestors and reflect on the ongoing struggle for freedom and equality.

SMW: Does this poem connect to a larger project for you? If so, we'd love to hear about it!

KR: This poem is the brink of a burgeoning book project that seeks to unearth and illuminate the untold stories of my lineage stemming from Mississippi, Alabama, and Louisiana. Growing up, discussions about our Geechee/Creole lineage were sparse, shrouded in a mysterious silence. It was as if there were chapters of our family history locked away, waiting to be discovered and shared.

This silence sparked a desire to excavate the buried narratives, to honor the voices and experiences that had been marginalized or overlooked. My exploration into this hidden aspect of my identity became not only a personal journey but also a literary endeavor to reclaim and celebrate the richness of my heritage.

In this project, I aim to delve into the untold stories of my Southern heritage, shining a light on the complexities, beauty, and resilience of Geechee/Creole culture. Through a blend of personal reflection, historical research, and storytelling, the book seeks to honor the voices and experiences of my ancestors while also examining the intersections of identity, memory, and belonging.

Each chapter of the book will offer a glimpse into exploring family traditions, community rituals, Southern foodways, and the legacy of resilience in the face of adversity on both sides. By weaving together personal narrative with historical context and cultural analysis, I hope to create a multi-dimensional portrait of my heritage that resonates with readers and fosters a deeper understanding and appreciation for the richness of Southern culture.

Ultimately, this book project is not only a creative endeavor but also a deeply personal journey of self-discovery and connection to my roots that lie in both the swamplands of Louisiana and Mississippi. I believe there's resilience and truth in water, and I'm excited to explore how that informs my identity.

NIGHT SKY II

Steven Pan

Leaves dried by the last season's
    sun, veins fixed into soil. Counting
the days kept in orbit, the last winter

as this far away. Every night,
    closer than where last left, distance
relative to the next spate of rain

over an ocean: how heavy water lies,
    in dawn's fist full of light. Like rain
did you only learn to stop

here? Miles and miles passed,
    one gas station in town. Wind chimes
by a window, a boat adrift in fathoms

of open field. The last wave broken
    over cottonwood, rise of summer's
breath, picking the last year's weeds

circling the steel frame of a swing
    swaying by itself in the breeze. Months
into a season, a season into a past

folded like an envelope. Rusted mailbox
    tilting over bruised soil, name painted
over the bolster, just to see it

right there. Watching the lamppost from the porch
    shape the asphalt for no one. A road mirrored
by the horizon, two reflections

diverging into a night sky. How long to pass
    a juncture between North and nowhere, alive
and still alone. How many years until

an unmarked letter arrives
    from the next lifetime, asking
as all letters once did: how far

you've made it? The stirring of everything
    moving onwards in the night, guiding
a hand the way it guided a dream

to the next day. The feeling of spring's
    roundness in the earth underneath you
while you stood there and waited.

All the things that make leaving
    seem real. Filling up the tank one last time,
listening to the wind chimes ask

where the years went, before
    driving into another evening.

STEVEN PAN

In Conversation

Sara Moore Wagner: I was immediately drawn to your striking images in this poem, how the images stand alone. Where do your images come from? Do you have a different method for each poem you write?

Steven Pan: In writing in general, I see the individual elements as steps towards a destination. To some truth or clarity or understanding. Imagery in poetry determines if it's light or dark at the end, if the journey is easy or treacherous. I find the images take shape as I get a better grasp of the poem itself, becoming more defined and concrete the further I go along like walking towards a painting. The images are chosen for the way they sound and the inherent feeling they convey. In this poem, all the things I've seen or haven't seen that convey a sense of lostness, and the paradoxical feeling of any direction still being a possibility. I often fill in the details retrospectively after I reach the end. In a way, I guess that's how memory and consciousness work as well, and poetry is an extension of both.

SMW: This form feels so organic (in the Levertov sense). What is your process with structuring a poem? Is it something that comes later, in revision, for instance?

SP: My favorite aspect of poetry is the way in which it both constructs and deconstruct language. Without changing any words, variation in forms can completely alter the reading the poem. Sometimes, I begin a poem with an understanding of the structure, and sometimes I experiment a lot with form after my first draft. In those cases, I will eventually settle on a structure with a tempo and cadence that feels most natural. In many ways, poetry is like music, and involves conveying something in a way that sounds 'right' to you.

SMW: This poem is the second in a series, but it stands alone. How many "Night Sky" poems have you written? Could you tell us about how you see poems in a series, their ability to create meaning individually vs. in conversation?

SP: Right now, I have written four. I'm not sure how many I will end up with in the series. Each poem is meant to capture one night over the course of the speaker's life—so for that reason, each poem stands on its own the way a quantity of time remains fixed in place and eventually becomes part of the past. But just as any understanding of the present or future is shaped by what came before, the goal of "Night Sky" is for the poems to also be in dialogue with one another. To me, reading poems in a complete series feels like a 20,000 ft. view, to be able to see something in its entirety.

FOR VERA

Marina Kraiskaya

We begin again, intracultural.
Rephrase each second question,
make little corrections,
go on.

A kind of white magic, the quiet
we sow here. I mail it with my passport
via USPS. Circling and circling the
125 stores of Las Americas, I turn
in a black Honda Civic at midnight,
bringing flowers for the migrants
who know only my name. Our custom.
I cover fresh bread – immutable,
folded – with cloth.

Your long hair, little sister.
For a rough half an hour, I imagine
having a brother. Then he's gone
for New York. I let them all be
my symbols for speech
and for faith in rehearsal.
Their earth is split open
and they hardly sleep.

They walked last winter for miles through a flurry of white,
hitting the deep brown of the chestnuts – rows of them
saved by arborists before the war. Now, there
is more than could ever be checked
for signs of survival.

I take them to dinner overlooking the ocean.
I make space in the house.

When I say *windbreaker*, they picture
a sword. If *southwest*, then
they think of Odessa. I leave Texas
out of it – would rather not break
these literal spells. She arranges
her minimal shots of equivalent
edges. Her own dark sleeves.
Familiar windows in concrete,
grey on grey with no first or last floor.
A chipped crystal whiskey glass.
Curled-up cat. Close sky
of immeasurable mist.

Clean and disposable days.
When together we slow to a roar
along the American River,
we picture the water as neither
pure nor polluted, its deep green
not thorn-heavy nor sweet.
Any gold rests below melting snow,
yellow iris and emerald bloom. Maybe
it tumbles in soft push toward escapeway.

MARINA KRAISKAYA

In Conversation

Sara Moore Wagner: I'm often intrigued by the choice to title a poem for a person whom the audience may not know. In this poem, Vera feels like a sort of other and mirror for the speaker. Could you tell us a little about who "Vera" is in your life?

Marina Kraiskaya: Vera is a young woman—one of many Ukrainian citizens who traveled to the U.S.-Mexico border as Russian aggression continued on with no end in sight. Even though we didn't know each other, we connected online. I picked her up (and others) in my car and helped out a little bit before they moved on to establish new lives and careers in other cities, like my mother did when I was a child. I am happy to have offered a friendly face, and I am so impressed by Ukrainians' bravery, tenacity, and optimism. Vera is also the name of my great-grandmother, an amazing woman.

SMW: I am drawn to the often-conflicting images in this, how they leave a sort of swirling hazy picture of immigration and home. How did these images come to you, in this poem?

MK: "Swirling" seems so right. My immigrant identity is half-removed and becoming only more barbed with complexity, bewilderment, guilt, insult, not-enoughness, loneliness, gratitude. I can't decide if it is claimed in community to more relief, or only more pain. But it is definitely better catalogued or exalted in poetry. The grey haze of slice-of-post-Soviet-life polaroids and the murky rush of the American River in Sacramento are beloved vessels I need—forms that I am not in. But at the edges of.

SMW: The other thing I love about this poem is the way the speaker grapples with interpretation. Words like *windbreaker* and *southwest* are transformed by the audience. This makes me think about the actual power of language, especially if there is a barrier. What is your view on what can be communicated in a poem?

MK: Thank you! I am hoping that the callout to focus on specific words can recreate the way language "barriers" can bring people closer to one another as they speak. As frequent travelers know, dissecting what someone else is saying in a language you're unfamiliar with, and all the bumps in the road toward mutual assumption, leads to such interesting and strange and fun places. You learn about yourself, and others. It's good for art to shake an audience out of the comfortable U.S.-centric seat.

MEMORIAL ME, BRAZORIA, TX

Karen Sherk Chio

in memory of Aunt Chris

By the river

We butterfly and sniffles, tears toward the river, a jungle greening the far bank. Sweat small back and pool, the river water brown, snaky. Distant train rumble, horn announcement. Grey skying against grey tree mossing. Voices patter, break, water-eye our cheeks. We marvel as wings beat, settling butterflies a surprise, feet light, perching on hands, shoulders, hair. See there? Goodbye Aunt alights with wings too fragile to pet. Then beer, down-the-river-gin, laughter barrel river-wide, jalapeño poppers. We celebrate, swat mosquitoes. Wish.

In the rental

Blades ceiling fan the roofline cavern. Only boy cousin sleeping off beer headache. Walls slick serial portraits of killers, Texas clichés. Gathering cousins girl around resin bottle-capped tabletop, finger spoons plastic, banana pudding sopped. Glee rises to ceiling height. Boy cousin pleasants a-grumble. Gathering cousins' *remember when?* raindrops off asphalt, big summer droplets ricochet, fast spread, puddle. Neighborhood dog paws the door, claws skeletal, sits in soupy evening, concrete ribs, cicadas saw. Central Airbnb, wine sweat. Glass condensed water, river in a wavy dark. Cousins nod and secret.

On morning walk

Day-break humidity chest-heavy, wet. No shoulder, curb, asphalt crumbles to sand. Cowboy hat goats livestock feed, animals gather, chirp, surround stoop. Trailers empty, floodwater-nipped, siding curling, Harvey soaked. Grass high, green. Homes cinder block stacked, precarious. Yard stove, dead car, pooless float. Moss from trees unwrapped bandages. Black-eyed Susans weed, lick ankles. Animal scent breeze, sky flat-land heavy, cloudless. Alone on this road, each step, grief.

At diner lunch

Red plaids table cloth, sweet tea potato, bean casserole, chicken fried. Cowboy hat corner-shriveling listens, recommends Butterfinger pie. Father-who-lost-a-sister side-eyes. Father-who-lost-a-sister happy mother's day us. Father-who-lost-a-sister, Texan with boots, a transplant. Father-who-lost-a-sister says, sister you a new one. Cole slaw runs. Walls bare fading paint, laughter bubbles loud. Sister lost, sister found. Twangless, we say *thank you.*

KAREN SHERK CHIO

In Conversation

Sara Moore Wagner: The sound in this poem is so lush. Do you have a method you use while writing or revising that focuses on sound and/or form?

Karen Sherk Chio: Thank you for your kind words. Sound and rhythm are important to me when I write. I read and re-read (and re-read) my poetry over and over in my head. If in my reading, a word, phrase, or sound does not flow, I'll revise it until it does. I workshopped this poem in one of my MFA classes for which I was required to audio record myself reading it. I am sure that extra step helped me refine the sonics.

SMW: Did you have an original goal in mind for this poem? Did that transform?

KSC: The aim of this poem, which revealed itself only as I drafted, was to capture the bewilderment of grief, family, and the feeling of belonging to people (my boisterous paternal family in Texas) but not place (I've lived most of my life in New England). I tried to push and bend language in ways I might not normally use it, creating a sense of disorientation while still conveying meaning.

SMW: This poem is such an interesting take on the elegy! The juxtaposition of the images presents a clear sensory portrait. Can you tell us a little about your aunt, and why this might be a fitting elegy?

KSC: My dad is the oldest of five, and Aunt Chris was his youngest sibling, eleven years his junior. She was my favorite aunt. She was artistic with a wry sense of humor and a down-to-earth practicality that made her easy to talk to. She took kind care of those around her. I have visceral memories of her warmth, voice, and laugh. I've been told I look like her; we have a similar gap-toothed smile.

Aunt Chris' memorial was the first time the family had gathered in a number of years. She would have loved all of us together again. After the ceremony, we laughed loudly, played down-the-river-gin, and ate her favorite foods. I will always reflect on that experience with a wish that she could have been there.

SMILING KITCHEN

Russell Zintel

We counted its pots & pans & forgot how else to use them.

It was a clown house inside the house,
& it breathed fire inward. This was strategic.

What didn't get counted?
The rush of air when the last guest left, or child.
Some of the smiles, which were painted.

I kept my mind on outside, on what the weather might've been.
Young-old winter. Beating hearts summer.

A substance evaporated from all the upturned lip corners,
Something like wax & got sucked up into the hoods.
Its benediction defied gravity.

The floor wasn't lava.
The fires were controlled by forces we comprehended
When the grease slick ignited,
& the pots & pans clanged as they counted us, too.
We found ourselves dancing
To go along with our expressions.

& in the end, if nighttime was the end,
The painted smiles looked green in the moonlight.
Exposed, they leaned into it,
Smiling harder from underneath.

RUSSELL ZINTEL

In Conversation

Sara Moore Wagner: I love the surrealness of this poem. It feels like domestic fabulism! Where does your instinct for surrealism come from? Do you have any influences you would recommend?

Russell Zintel: I'm grateful for your good feelings about this poem's weirdness. I've always enjoyed reading and writing surrealist poems, and I think part of their beauty is you never knew you needed them, yet their language and elusive message seems so resonant and indispensable, once codified on the page. As a pre-adolescent, I read science fiction novels that were above my reading level, but I was always enamored with the dreamlike state they still guided me into, despite that I might not have understood the larger implications of what was going on, or even all the words I was reading. I almost look at writing surrealist poems this way: engaging compellingly and effectively with forces you don't entirely understand. A few years later, I discovered Calvino's *Invisible Cities* and *If On a Winter's Night a Traveler* at an impressionable age.

Some of my more recent influences are Elizabeth Willis, Marosa di Giorgio, Roberto Bolaño, and Diane Seuss. While not a surrealist poet, I will list Samuel Delany, particularly his novel *Dhalgren*, as another substantial influence.

SMW: This is both about a place (the kitchen) and not. How do you see the relationship between speaker and place in this poem? It feels experimental and so interesting!

RZ: There's certainly a mixed sense of ordinariness and the surreal in operating in kitchens, whether it be at home or, for me, professionally in a restaurant, and the poem tries to portray a few angles of this brackish mentality. On the one hand, cooking food is a regular activity, and the kitchen is a familiar, often central part of the house. It's also an arena wherein almost anything that could happen in life can play out, if the conditions are right. Some days, it's no effort at all to think a little bit more than usual about a particular animal's life, the waste or pollution or anguish that propelled its path to my table, or even whether or not vegetables are sentient. Overall, there's a lot of slippage in this part of the house. In this light, the kitchen, usually so rife with literal language and thinking, seems like a place that could well be rediscovered through surreal language and imagery.

SMW: Your title is deceptively simplistic, in a delightful way! How do you approach titles?

RZ: Thank you! For me, titles are a matter of feeling, but there is more logic behind them than I probably give myself credit for. In this case, I wanted a simplistic seeming title that was, in reality, doing a fair amount of work. You have the possibility of a kitchen that smiles, or a kitchen wherein smiling takes place. There is the sardonic/ironic interpretation of the action of smiling, or its figurative meaning, and then there's accepting its intentions as perfectly sincere. I'm also fond of titles that are apt and uncomplicated, quaint you might say, that don't add or subtract or complicate anything in the poem, almost as if they're there to be egoless and stand watch. Long titles are fun, too, particularly some of the ones found in Diane Seuss's *Wolf Lake, White Gown Blown Open*. Overall, I am not such a fan of titles that do the majority of the work in a poem, though I remain open to and respectful of this approach.

SPOKEN ELEPHANTS

Adia Micah Muhammad

There is only one way to eat an elephant: a bite at a time.
—Desmond Tutu

Fuck Desmond Tutu—eat elephants headfirst. Flambé the trunk, pluck the eyes,
crush the tusks to powder. And what you cannot stomach, save. A jar of golden eyes.

Uninvited, I arrive: the elephant in the room. Someone sputters, laughs; someone
else offers me, weakly, a drink. We leave for the kitchen. Behind us is a story told in eyes.

"Well, an elephant never forgets," he snips, and I wonder if he's calling me fat,
or old, or wise. The worst memories are remembered through another's knowing eyes.

The office white elephant exchange is a flurry of jolly thefts. Bigger isn't always better.
I take from the pile. Through a rip in the wrapping paper, I meet Mr. Potato Head's eyes.

In Mecca, a Muhammad is born in the Year of the Elephant. In Persia, a fire that raged
a thousand years is snuffed. His mother says it burns to hold him, to gaze into those molten
eyes.

ADIA MICAH MUHAMMAD
In Conversation

Sara Moore Wagner: Your first line and your epigraph are instantly engaging. Do you have any advice about using epigraphs?

Adia Micah Muhammad: An approach I borrowed/stole from my creative writing professor was to use the beginning of a piece to ground the reader as quickly as possible. The first place we look for context in a poem is the title ("Spoken Elephants" is a poem about phrases involving elephants, done and done), but there's also the risk of giving too much exposition before the poem has even started. I like that the epigraph here is used to elaborate on the title and sets up the first line to be even punchier without further explanation.

SMW: I am so drawn to your examination of the ways we use the word "elephant" (elephant in the room, white elephant, a comment on weight, etc). So much is held in one word/creature! Can you tell us more about how you see the word functioning in this poem?

AMM: I love elephants! And perhaps even more, I love to take figurative language at face value. The reason we're encouraged to cut idioms from poems is due to laziness, using a common phrase instead of a fresh image. Even though these are all phrases that have been so spoken to death that we no longer envision them, the interest comes from the contrasting qualities we can get out of the same animal. Elephants are simultaneously big, wise, awkward, ugly, and beautiful. Seemingly, what matters more than what they are is how we use them.

SMW: Your final image is extraordinarily powerful. How do you approach endings?

AMM: Endings are the hardest part for most writers, and I'm no exception. Though I'm more accustomed to free verse, the structure of the ghazal really helped guide the last image. Since it's customary for the poet to include their name in the final couplet, and I found the birth of "a (Adia) Muhammad" to be a bit coy while also upping the stakes dramatically. We go from cussing out a theologian to the birth of a prophet in less than ten lines. My latest approach, then, is experimenting with forms that push me, and trying to convincingly shift the tone, if not the topic, from the beginning of the piece.

THE FLAT CIRCLE (V)

Beth Gordon

God was waiting in the river of lava. Clinging to the four-post bed. Pirate-souled. My painted feet a tipping point from ballerina to rescued dog. Always in the wrong car at the wrong time. Yield signs at roundabouts: the beginning of violence & heartbreak. My face in the soupy current. Am I the reflection or source? Bare-legged, teetering, hungry. Those yellow triangles like so many hollow wildflowers trapped in the mouths of lovers. Prairie mice. Perfect hawks.

BETH GORDON

In Conversation

Sara Moore Wagner: That first sentence is so instantly engaging. How did you come to that as an entry point?

Beth Gordon: First, just let me say thanks for deciding to publish this poem—many of the other *Flat Circle* poems were picked up by other journals but not this one, and I honestly think it's because of its strangeness. As far as the opening line—it came about as two pieces of a puzzle which is a common way I think about my poems. The first piece was the memory of playing pirates with my brother on our parents' four-post bed and pretending that the floor was lava. The second piece of the puzzle is related to thinking about God as both a creator and a destroyer.

SMW: This poem unfolds from that beginning to the striking end in such a strange and intentional way. The images leap from one to the other and make sense without extra explanatory language. Does this come naturally, or do these things come in with revision, for you?

BG: I'm a fairly relentless editor of my own work, but I also trust when something is working and doesn't require a lot of revisions. Some of my favorite pieces were written in an almost trance-like state and this is one of those. Hard to explain but I can look at this poem and know that I wrote it without clear memories of writing it—it's like I go somewhere else.

SMW: This is part of a phenomenal larger sequence and collection. Tell our readers more about it! How does this fit in with the whole of the "Flat Circle"?

BG: The collection is an exploration of tragic loss and the aftermath of loss. After not writing poetry for many years, I started writing again in 2014 following the death of my seven-month-old granddaughter, Daisy. I used writing as a way to process my grief and I was also attracted to movies and TV shows that explored some of what I was already experiencing, specifically "time displacement," which is a very common symptom following an unexpected loss. The problem for me was/is that it never went away. It's been almost eleven years since Daisy died and I still struggle to process time in the way I used to, i.e. "linear." The first season of *True Detective* is where I got the idea of the "flat circle" and the movie *Arrival* also touches on a lot of the same themes. I think this poem captures the surreal nature of death and grief—and I hope that its "weirdness" is also why it makes complete sense.

I SELDOM REMEMBER

Luisa Caycedo-Kimura

mamá

papá's lap

the stereo

placido

colombian fire-glazed black clay jars

white flowers

geraniums

drawn graphite

papá's baritone

sinatra john denver

mamá's

own key

own beat own road

i seldom remember

brighton beach caviar

she and he

kissing

her arm his shoulder

her thigh his hand

LUISA CAYCEDO-KIMURA

In Conversation

Sara Moore Wagner: This poem feels, in form, like trying to pull words through memory. Tell us a bit about how you came upon this form.

Luisa Caycedo-Kimura: When I started writing poems about childhood, I mostly wrote about abuse and domestic violence. But even in abusive homes, there are peaceful, and even happy, moments. For this poem, I forced myself to remember some. Because these forced memories came to me fragmented, I wanted the form of the poem to reflect that fragmentation and that struggle.

SMW: There's a blending of music (John Denver, Sinatra, your parents' voices) here. How important is music to you, in your life and in your work?

LCK: Music of all kinds, from classical, to folk, to popular, was ever-present in my childhood home. Ibagué, the city where I was born, is known as The Musical Capital of Colombia because of the emphasis placed on musical education, and my father was a formally trained vocalist with a beautiful baritone voice. My mother couldn't carry a tune, but she loved music and sang all the time. So, although I'm not a musician, I absorbed that music from an early age. It became a part of me. It helped me through periods of deep depression, and now helps me feel in communion with my parents who are dead. With respect to my writing, while I don't usually write about music, I have always been aware of language's musicality. I remember, even as early as elementary school, I often chose words in my writing based on sound, especially the way they sounded together in a sentence. As Robert Pinsky, with whom I had the honor of studying in grad school, says, "a sentence is like a tune," and "we sing to one another all day." I look for musicality, not only in my own work, but in the work I read.

SMW: The ending feels tender, but there's a hint of swirling danger. Was that an important juxtaposition for you? That duality feels like an important theme to this.

LCK: Thank you for noticing that. It is important because, in an abusive relationship, even in happy moments, there is always the risk that something will trigger the abuser (in this case, my father). That tension never seems to go away.

Hank, the nights might find me at parties, despite my running the other way. There is the good light but the people, the people all over the place,

downstairs apartments, upstairs, in the ballroom around the corner, the new lofts by the train. My scope is so limited, Hank,

my body unable to make more than a mite's assumption about the size of this environment, this long crawl

of entrances, escapes. Hank, I spend hours inside a doorframe, just waiting for the host to blink or turn the other direction,

for an excuse to leave or an excuse to be seen, the offer of a fried or stuffed something, a toast, a reason to stay, to believe.

Bootcut, Hank. Bourbonous and waiting to pitch horseshoes, I picture you back home, circumnavigating society in a similar way,

like a coyote drawn to campfire out of their scrubland wastes. What temperature must we reach, what palm offer,

how predator, how prey, how long does the party have to be sleeping for me to retire back into the dark?

C. HENRY SMITH
In Conversation

Sara Moore Wagner: First, I love how this and your chapbook are centered around poems directly addressed to "Hank." Could you tell us a little about Hank?

C. Henry Smith: Thanks for saying so, and yes, absolutely. The "Hank" in these poems really began as an anonymous addressee. Just a nice sound, an easy refrain. The exercise that started this series had the speaker calling out, reaching toward something over and over in the verse, and initially it just felt good writing to someone, falling back into their name anytime I needed it, and the form—epistolary, apostrophic, whatever—stayed fertile ground from the single poem, to a version with eight sections for a long time, to a dozen, then twenty-one, up to twenty-seven briefly, and now twenty-four finally.

Hank has, I think, become aligned with the central ideas of this piece: separation, longing, the challenge of loving a complicated homeplace, living the past and present simultaneously. Once the work expanded, Hank became clearer and clearer: someone receiving these postcards back home, perhaps as a childhood friend, a spiritual sympathizer, or a mirror version of the speaker themself. Creating this character made it easy for me (but not me) to write to myself (but not myself) and dig into things I might not have without the comfort of an addressee, a nonjudgemental ear. If nothing else, it made for a fun exercise. You should try it!

SMW: Do you consider this poem to be epistolary? What is most appealing to you about direct address or the epistolary form?

CHS: I think so, yes. In my MFA we took a class on the epistolary form, focusing on the collaborative possibilities of the style (with models like "The Mothers" by Leila Chatti and Dorianne Laux or "Lace & Pyrite" by Ross Gay and Aimee Nezhukumatathil) as well as the intimacies it can create. This poem, though directed to a fictionalized version of the self rather than a real-world collaborator, really stole from that experience. The epistolary, to me, creates a safe space for telling secrets and a powerful space for conjuring things that one writer couldn't on their own. Then, it's a form that keeps giving back—the more you pour onto the addressee, the more they offer, troubling and inspiring new missives.

SMW: Tell us more about the line structure here. It feels like prose but is divided into distinct couplets. How did you think about the poetic line in this poem?

CHS: They used to be so short! Initially these little bursts of longing and story seemed to sit well in a briefer line. I usually rely (perhaps too much) on the energy of enjambment and quick turns in my writing; however, as I wrote more and more of these, I really fell into that sense of reaching—reaching across time, geography, and, eventually, the page. I began thinking about authors who use long lines (or those fold out poems you find in magazines that are stretching twice as far from the margins as others) and tried to see if I could write with enough energy to sustain the longer line. Eventually, it became like casting: letting go of the reel and seeing how far your momentum would carry the line across the water.

Right now, I see them as long lines that have to wrap back into themselves and thus indent on the line below. It would be fun to see this poem or another from the series printed on a broadside or some form that allowed the lines to stretch out and lay flat on top of each other, but for now, seeing them collapse and stack up seems to serve the work.

AM

Robert Laidler

We don't know what that man was thinking
or what he wasn't thinking. We heard the pop,

saw him fall, and the big black birds swarmed
within seconds. They made the sky darker

than it ever was before in the middle of morning.
September made it get dark early,

but the birds turned it into December. Heat
from the sun muffled the image of his body

laying in the brush. The colors of cattails
and red dirt started to meld together. We knew

we'd been staring. An older woman sprouted
out of the thicket and started to holler. She

looked at us in angry grief: *Why ain't y'all do*
nothing? We said we couldn't. We didn't know

how.

ROBERT LAIDLER

In Conversation

Sara Moore Wagner: This poem is extraordinarily powerful in the way it bears witness. Could you tell us a little about the story behind this poem?

Robert Laidler: Essentially, this poem, like the others in the longer sequence, is in the voice of a different (Southern based) individual/collective responding to either hearing, seeing, or hearing about a suicide that took place in the woods of Southern Alabama. The collective voice in this poem is more youthful, a group of teens, who were helpless in their witness, but accurate in their reporting.

SMW: I am so drawn to the first-person plural speaker. How did you come to that decision? What is the role of the first-person speaker in a poem, in general?

RL: Relative to the collective teen voice mentioned in the previous answer, the way news travels in the secluded south, which is the setting for the longer poetic sequence this poem is excerpted from, is via word of mouth, phone calls, and in passing conversation. I wanted this poem to read as conversant as possible, while still keeping a poetic undertone. Persona, to me, is one of the most powerful tools, and if I'm able to tell the story, paint the scene, or expand on a topic using a first-person speaker who is authentically separate from my own identity, I will do it, every single time. When we personify others, we have a responsibility to be "borrowed" by them, almost as if they are utilizing our poetic capabilities to tell a truth, a lie, or something in between without the concern of losing their individuality. In this entire poetic sequence, I took that responsibility seriously.

SMW: The birds in this poem are striking and atmospheric. The image carries so much in the way it transforms the scenery until the speaker's voice is interrupted by the woman. Did this structure happen naturally for you? How did you build this poem to its climax?

RL: I intentionally use black birds (an unspecified type of bird that can be turkey vultures, crows, etc.) when thinking of a looming darkness as a way to explore implausibility within the context of an absurd reality. In this poem, the implausibility is the death of the man and the echoes of everybody's different retellings of what happened to him; the sheer shock of him actually being gone, and the stark change from what people were doing before, and after. The weather reflects this, the birds reflect this, and even the beckoning of the older woman reflects this. Building this into the poem felt like a natural trajectory, and an overall rewarding one for the remaining poems in the sequence.

ANTS

Stefanie Kirby

Picture a grounded
apple, held firm
by earth. You, ants
in a line leading
to that apple. All of
the daughters I didn't have
join you, the daughters
I did, indistinguishable
in ant bodies that cover
the apple and gloss
its skin. No difference
between the bodies,
your ant bodies
lining the apple
in threads that pull
into horizons, that
shimmer like suns
or daughters.

STEFANIE KIRBY
In Conversation

Sara Moore Wagner: First, we are so excited to have published *Fruitful*! Could you tell our readers how this poem functions in the collection as a whole?

Stefanie Kirby: This poem originally emerged as the second half of a two-part poem written to a prompt on gravity. The first section, "Apples," appears much earlier in the collection. In it, daughters fall through the mother's body as apples. For me, "Ants" functions as a sort of counterpoint to "Apples"—the apple is grounded with the daughters migrating out of and away from the fruit as ants. These tiny, mobile bodies have more agency due to their ability to move, the sort of self-determination that the body of an apple lacks, I suppose. Despite generating these poem halves together, the piece ultimately felt too compact, and I placed this poem near the end of the collection to allow the two original sections to echo across the chapbook.

SMW: I love how the ants populate this poem. What drew you to ants as a metaphor?

SK: Years ago, I witnessed an entire colony of ants moving their eggs from a rotting log to a new location. They moved quickly, shuffling the pearly eggs along their sometimes erratic but always efficient lines. For me, the ants became representative of a shifting destination. I think I wanted to imbue the daughter figures in this piece with the ability to shift the narrative, to shift their futures away from the fallen fruit that will ultimately decay, and to move toward a new horizon instead.

SMW: As our most recent chapbook contest winner, what would your advice be to someone who is submitting to our contest (or other chapbook contests!)? Any thoughts on the submission journey?

SK: During a conversation with a journal editor recently, he mentioned the uptick in submissions the past couple of years. In that sense, getting a single poem accepted feels like quite the win; I think that's why getting the call from Carolyn Hembree about my chapbook having been selected for the Adrift Contest felt like winning the lottery! I get a bit overwhelmed thinking about that, the sheer odds poems face when they're sent out into the world. And yet, the parts of the process I have control over remain the writing and the sending out of that writing, so that's what I come back to at the end of the day.

UNTITLED

Melinda Freudenberger

tv light plays with BA-BEE from the shadows at the bottom of the door
i am peaking thru smashed to eye level / her feet flush with the floor
like two thin lips meeting in disappointment / one more dream to unravel
me : perched on a branch is a single blue bird / i had been LOOKING
for it all this time something like love : crouched and starved for it /
i am a / seed on gravel i am a virgin with no oil wrapped in steely yellow
light / in a dream i come to BA-BEE blue bird snapped between my
jaws / she touches my head / eases me all my right places / one high
pitched yelp from me and her feet flinch ! *WHAT DID I SAY* ! and like a
quick right turn like the feeling i got when BA-BEE locked the
door / a fraction of a second pacing over and over the same floor

SPRING

Geoff Anderson

I watched magnolias frost over magnolias I waited

all winter to see unsheathe pink swords from stubborn

holsters snow in April unforgiving and unforgiveable

four years in a row my son has never seen a color

besides brown a brown that ice pummels into fresh mulch

lanky blades of grass my mower eyes from the garage

not that my son cares his down jacket pockets full of

limp petals what does not fit he flings in the air

a game out of death he should be miserable

seeing all the blooms who never unlocked their cellar

doors after such slate months a season of clouds

that marbled as they spit flakes and drizzle at our faces

instead he is dancing as it rains dead confetti around us

a scoop of blossoms ready to leap from his hands

the same hands that pry open my fists until

I too am holding what was a flower and letting go

GEOFF ANDERSON

In Conversation

Sara Moore Wagner: I'm immediately drawn to the way this poem shirks convention in its double spacing and lack of punctuation. Tell us more about these stylistic choices.

Geoff Anderson: I find that by removing punctuation and giving more space around the lines to work, the lines in the poem breathe more freely and operate more independently while also being part of the whole. They also allow the momentum of the poem to flow without interruption, much like the moment they capture—we don't always know the significance in the exact moment we're in until it passes, and I find reading pieces structured like this capture a similar sentiment. We are almost forced to double back and re-experience what we experience.

SMW: Nature feels violent here, in the unsheathing, the blades, the dead petals. It also feels masculine. Is this poem trying to show the reader something about masculinity? About what the father passes on to the son?

GA: Masculinity wasn't an overt focus I had for the piece as much as the tension between how the speaker used to find himself in nature versus the current natural world he finds himself in. Having said that, the dynamic between a father and a son naturally carries with it undertones of masculine lineage and how it changes—what can a father pass on and what can't a father pass on. Conversely, what can a child pass on to a parent? Much like in a classroom, where the role of student and teacher is in constant flux, father and son are endlessly impacting how each encounters the world.

SMW: It also feels somewhat environmental. Would you consider this to be an ecopoem?

GA: The father-son relationship took center-stage when crafting the poem, but the backdrop of climate change is an undeniable element of the tension. Climate change implies a difference between past and present. Fatherhood is no different. Being able to weave both together in the moment allows the tensions of each to horribly and beautifully complement each other. In that sense, I think ecopoem is one label the piece would fit under.

NIGHT WELDER OF MOON ROCKS & GASX

Katie Dorfman

"Yale University takes no responsibility for the hundreds of fentanyl substitutions that took place at the Fertility Clinic; it blames the single nurse who was able to steal the fentanyl"(ABC News, 2021).

This whole time there was a shadow behind the glass
and I was wade-willowing

like a beetle on bark root. A broom that cuts through
panel like an ostrich feather in gray dark. We are

candle bars and crooked linen, grid
and bow and small circular night.

The window in my ceiling is paper-glass,
I have jumped into the next life and it is

a tongue on air extended in mayflower,
black. If I could find the center of a word,

would I bite it?
My future stares & grids

I gape (don't touch me)

with her (Please. I'm begging)
as we
(branch, extending)
Ma do we (ever)
stop bleeding?

We are gathered here today
(through and through, we are making the dead
deeper 'till)

we reach Yiddish, my grandmother's
womb fractals, melted caramel

(I can't recall her, I am ladeled).

If you put me in a vat of acid,
would language come out?

Futz n' nosh, klutz & schvitz.

The last time I knew myself was temple candles
conjuring sound I knew from back throat, my

keppie lollied dumb, the place you schlep
and laugh from. Laser sliced right

through doorstep like eight legged
creeks of ember moon. Was I always this

negligent, do I always forget, did
I never look-how the dark

makes all decorations, a
stomach breaks and fills

with liquid-gold,
20 egg-donors sob

without their fentanyl. Tachlis,
we could feel it all,

the scalpel reached pain

no prayer
could (dissolve).

AS IF THERE'S SOMETHING LEFT TO TASTE

Staci Halt

I licked the last of the jam from the bowl   the morning before
Johnny choked   on a blueberry at the orchard   How his baby lips blued
right under my chin   in the baby carrier   how I wrenched him free   to sweep
his throat   The blueberries   clanged   on their branches   like bells
A crowd appeared   from the rows of bushes   like crows alighting
around something dead   I snapped   *stay back*   until the vomit cleared
until Johnny's lungs   then mine   ballooned again   as we sat in relief
a sloppy pietá   the onlookers   beheld the limp baby

My oldest hissed her testimony   *Mom you always do this*   I waited for sirens
Someone always calls the police on mothers who snap who *always do something*
I heard sirens wail in the air   from then on   Every light is flashing
red-blue-red   Every morsel could be my last   on the outside
Not one   of the babies have died   yet   I am waiting
for the worst   to come   Maybe you feel it too   One day

you're eating jam   you find yourself   almost guilty   find yourself

half-buried   like some yieldy part of you was yanked   upwards

as if gravity is a lie   and the truth   is simple   is with

whatever   is on the other side   of that pulley

STACI HALT

In Conversation

Sara Moore Wagner: I love the slipperiness of this poem, how it even formally slips across the page, like jam. It has me thinking about identity in motherhood, how slippery that can be. Was this something you were thinking about?

Staci Halt: I like that that's how it feels reading it! The caesura I hope does the work of both propelling and halting momentum, stretching time. The poem's motor, at least when I initially wrote it, lay not so much about the slipperiness of identity in motherhood as much as the two essential terrors of motherhood: first, that you are a bad mother, and will somehow hurt your children, and second, that someone is going to think you are a bad mother, and take matters into their own hands, reporting to police or social services, which will hurt your children. The stakes couldn't be higher. This poem I think wrestles with fear, and what lies beyond it.

SMW: In this poem, when you pull in the "you," I, as a mother, felt that, the universal in the moment. What made you want to turn this poem outward?

SH: This is something that has happened in quite a few of my poems. A speaker of the poem exploring a narrative and then abruptly turns and invites the reader, or pulls them unwillingly perhaps, into the mess with her. I almost never intentionally do this, I feel like poems are sentient, and poems like this one, that move from first-person to second are somewhat desperate for something which can probably be distilled into: Please let me not be alone, see look, you're here now in the poem too. Motherhood is isolating and terrifying. Sit in this orchard with me with a not-breathing baby and wonder if the cops are coming, do you feel it?

SMW: Much has been said lately about poems on motherhood, with poets like Nancy Reddy pushing hard to amplify these voices. Do you have any poets you admire who are also doing the hard work of writing about motherhood? What do you wish the contemporary poetry world would understand about the subject?

SH: What a great question. I admit, I am trying to write the poems I haven't read yet. I've read of a lot "love my growing belly" poems, which are beautiful, but that was not my experience. I wanted to die my pregnancies were so terrible. There isn't a lot out there about that. It is salient to me that there is a rabid political movement successfully curbing women's access to abortion, and turned its attention to limiting access to birth control as well, because while I consider motherhood to be a massive privilege and a true joy, I grew up in an oppressively patriarchal religion that specifically taught me the only reason I am on this earth is to have children. For so many women, past and present, and the numbers are growing daily in states with abortion bans, motherhood requires holding two difficult truths at once: I didn't have a choice, *and* I love my kids beyond description. Writing in the churn of those truths is difficult. Society pedestalizes mothers while people in power are actively working to ensure it grows more dangerous and risky to be one. We need more poems about this, I think. I can't write them all, so join with me!

COUNTY FAIR AT NIGHT

Emilee Kinney

Horse heads poke out stall windows
like the deer we've mounted
on our walls. Dusty rafters house
a cathedral of manure sweat

and sweet feed, shake straw
on our shoulders, fill our hat brims
with sawdust as we stuff our bootcut
jeans into our boot tops and click

clack down the concrete aisle toward
a moonlit pasture. Someone's
truck is humming with a song about
strawberry wine and the crickets

are lowing in protest. We are an army
marching out to the dew-soaked field,
our skin slick, everything glowing.
Looking back, the barn lights

are a thin sliver slicing across
the field's crest. The men here
smell like oil and spearmint tobacco,
like whiskey and tree sap and they all want

to hold our bright-belted hips.
As much as small-town folks
can be, most of us are strangers.
I recognize the man that's pulled

me into his matchbox-frame,
from three aisles over in church,
he's wearing the same green flannel
with the left elbow burned, but

I don't know his name. We dance
for awhile: he tries to peck
my neck, my chest, when he dips me
to the tall grass, a baptism

in Queen Anne's lace.
His arm is tight around the small
of my back and I see his dark eyes
beneath the curled brim

of his camo ballcap like two
river stones pressed into his skull.
We dance until someone lights
a fire out of old napkins and their uncle's

moonshine on the front seat
of an abandoned pickup rotting
in the tree line. Smoke swells
in the cab like a bruise until

someone breaks the driver's window.
A blaze lashes out, snaps against
the dry bark. Thorn apple branches sizzle,
adorning the rising ash in rings.

EMILEE KINNEY

In Conversation

Sara Moore Wagner: This poem is so atmospheric! What advice do you have for establishing setting in a poem?

Emilee Kinney: For establishing a setting in a poem, my advice is to think about the minute details, the things you normally overlook, things only people who aren't from there seem to notice. Make those details front and center right away, so you can ground the reader regardless of whether this is a place they have never been or a place they are familiar with.

Growing up in rural Michigan, the 4H Fair was a lifestyle, an expectation of the summer. When I moved away and started sharing stories with people who grew up in cities or simply places without this ritual, I realized how unique and strange and beautiful it was. To really capture it for someone who has no reference for the experience, I needed to engage all of my readers' senses. For example, "Dusty rafters" are something you can see and smell, you can hear the cowgirl boots "click // clack down the concrete aisle," and you can feel the contrast between "sawdust [and] the dew-soaked field."

For a truly immersive experience, even once that grounding work is done in the beginning, I think it's important to keep introducing new sensations to the reader throughout the poem. Call on active images and specific details that enhance both the story of the poem and of the place the poem inhabits.

SMW: This poem feels so distinctly American and rural. Can you tell me more about where you come from and the place that inspired this poem?

EK: I'm from Kenockee, Michigan which is a rural farm town about twenty-five minutes away from Lake Huron. It has a typical small town feel where everyone knows each other (or at least, about each other), lots of farmland hosting corn, soybeans, wheat, and hay labored over by hard working families.

I grew up just down the road from the Goodells County Park which hosts the St. Clair County 4H Fair every summer. It is easily the biggest event in the area. 4H kids work year-round, preparing and training their animals. During the fair, there are barns full of horses, cows, rabbits, chickens, and more—each of them with a sign on their stall that tells a little bit about their story and the kid who loves/raised them. Lots of families camp out with their animals during fair week, so the fairground itself becomes a little community—a small town within a small town.

This poem, "County Fair at Night" is a blend of the Goodells County Park and the Sanilac County 4H Fair which is where I ended up competing with my horse the most. At the end of the Sanilac Fair, there was always a Teen Night when they'd play music and high school kids would dance under a pavilion. When the music ended there, the party often continued in a nearby field, away from parents and younger siblings. This was an exciting time for teenagers—fair week provided this empowering liminal space where we were responsible for ourselves and our animals. We had spent the week equally working together and competing against one another, sharing meals, tack, and tools—we felt like adults and usually ended the week trying to celebrate the way adults do.

What has always fascinated me about this space is the inherited ritual. Most of our parents had shown their animals when they were kids at the same fairgrounds, went out in the same field with their friends, caused the same mischief. One of them probably drove the now-rotting pickup and got it stuck in that tree line in the first place. Don't get me wrong, there have been plenty of changes over time—new stadium lights around the riding arenas and more food truck options—but after a long fair week, different generations trudge through the same wildflowers to find a clearing in the field and dance in the same shadows of thorn-apple trees. Out of all the things we pass down, this cycle feels most beautiful.

SMW: This poem feels like a dance. What's the best way to bring music into a poem?

EK: "County Fair at Night" has a physical dance within it that I wanted to be reflected in the language and pacing, so the reader could experience the dance along with the speaker—I'm glad it seems to have worked! For me, alliteration and internal rhyme make the most magic for a lyrical poem, but I was conscious of the line length for this poem as well. Visually, the lines are relatively the same, but looking at the meter, the longest lines are when energy in the poem is rising: "We are an army" and "a fire out of old napkins." Likewise, the shortest line is when the speaker is dipped into "Queen Anne's lace," an action that requires a physical pause and a moment I wanted to linger with the reader. I like to imagine poems having breath and with that breath, a rhythm that I can set language and images to, something that will ultimately pace a reader's breath in the same way a song gets stuck in their head. I don't know if it's the best way, but pairing alliteration and internal rhyme with the ebb and flow of breathing has been the most helpful way for me to bring music into a poem.

REMINDERS TO SELF

Danielle Harms

If Jupiter is a planet in the solar system,
we live in outer space too.

If I refer to mammals,
it's *we* not *them*.

If he calls for a mom,
he is looking for me.

If a trunk scars,
the tree is closing a wound.

If soap blooms on craft paper,
you have exhaled.

If someone asks who you are,
give them your name, not his.

DANIELLE HARMS

In Conversation

Sara Moore Wagner: I love this poem for the way it wrestles with the intense challenges and transformations of motherhood in such a small space. How do you go about condensing your poems? How was that choice made here?

Danielle Harms: The truth is I feel like a novice when it comes to poetry. Even though I've been writing poems for years, it's not my primary genre, and I often feel like I'm putting on a disguise and trying out what it feels to be a poet when I write in verse. It's a feeling I want to hold onto, because there's a freedom in approaching poetry as an amateur fan, trying out experiments and playing around with what the form can do. I don't feel the same sense of control that I do when writing an essay or short story, and I find myself turning to poetry when compelled to write about something that feels urgent but unresolved, and when I might have more questions than answers. In early parenthood I found a kind of shelter in poetry, partly because of its capacity for compression—it's a space that can hold that concentrated feeling of uncertainty, contingency, and ongoing novice-ness. Poetry doesn't demand resolution, and I think here I wanted to subvert my own impulse to endlessly overexplain, instead moving from one thing to the next with the clipped pace that resembles the way my child would often careen from one topic to the next as a toddler, exploring what he knew and how he knew it.

SMW: This poem also feels like a negation of the strong masculinity of Kipling's "If" poem, while keeping that hypothetical construct. Was this (or any other poem) something you were thinking of?

DH: Oh I wish I had been so intentional! I love poetry that engages with a lineage of poems and actively resisting or re-envisioning something. But really this poem sprang out of a moment when I surprised myself: someone asked for my name, and for some reason, I gave them my child's name. It took me a while to understand what had come out of my mouth, and I wanted to understand what had happened in my brain. Linguistically, it mirrored how those first years of parenting sometimes felt like a collapsing of the self. But I wasn't sure I believed that my verbal slip was some tidy indicator of my own suffusion of identity. Sometimes parenting feels like a big conditional if/then experiment, where you test out new conditions and observe the results: if I do this, then what? How about this? That's the kind of never-ending litany of questions my child will unfurl with me, and I found myself testing that in this poem. At one point I started each second line with "then," so the stanzas were if/then statements, but I ended up fracturing that because it implied too much clarity of cause and effect. I wanted it to be more muddled, in the ways we remain undecipherable to ourselves. I wasn't thinking about a specific poet, but I love the ways that the poet Claire Wahmanholm explores language, caretaking, and precarity in her work, like in "P." I have read and re-read Layli Long Soldier's poem "Left" from *WHEREAS*, and always find new meaning.

SMW: There is both an erasing of the speaker and a reclamation of the name happening that is so powerful. Could you speak a little about how the poetry world or art world sees a mother, or any motherhood poems which inspire you?

DH: I once heard an author tell a story in an interview about reading something related to motherhood, and the author was marveling that she had liked the work, because she normally found motherhood literature boring. My child was two months old at the time and I was furiously chopping carrots in my home, listening to that interview while my own baby slept on the kitchen counter. I felt ashamed because I resented the story and understood the sentiment—I too had casually dismissed motherhood tropes in a way I had to recognize and de-construct. Authors who explore gender and sexuality helped me in that process, both critical work and creative writing. How my writing self and this new caretaking self could co-exist felt like such a question early on, but less so now that my child is six-years-old and I've found models for how to bring my whole self to my work, and show up that way as a reader and fan of others. I am constantly returning to the work of the scholar Sara Ahmed. I love my friend Kate Partridge's collection *Thine*. I devoured your (Sara Moore Wagner)'s *Hillbilly Madonna*. Marianne Chan's *Leaving Biddle City* feels expansive and resonant. Maya Marshall's *All the Blood Involved in Love* is a seismic exploration of forms of mothering and care.

THE HEALER COUNTS BACKWARDS / ____ *1

Mackenzie Polonyi

INSTRUCTIONS: INCANT BY FILLING ALL BLANK SPACES WITH ONE HOMONYM PER INCANTATION. CONSIDER THE TWO READINGS OF EACH HOMONYM. CONSIDER HOW A VERB, LIKE A NOUN, IS AN ENTITY AND HOW A NOUN, LIKE A VERB, MOVES. REPEAT WITH RELEVANT-TO-YOU HOMONYMS AS NECESSARY. THE HOMONYMS ARE AKIN TO PSYCHIC WOUNDS.

Ten maggots in my _____ one drops out nine left
nine maggots in my _____ one drops out eight left
eight maggots in my _____ one drops out seven left
seven maggots in my _____ one drops out six left
six maggots in my _____ one drops out five left
five maggots in my _____ one drops out four left
four maggots in my _____ one drops out three left
three maggots in my _____ one drops out two left
two maggots in my _____ one drops out one left
one maggot in my _____ one drops out not a single scrap of grief left.

HOMONYMS

VÁR	*castle*	*wait*
SZÍV	*heart*	*suck/draw*
SZÉL	*wind*	*edge*
SÍR	*grave*	*cry*
PARADICSOM	*tomato*	*paradise*
NŐ	*woman*	*grow*
LÉP	*spleen*	*honeycomb*
FOG	*tooth*	*hold*
ÉR	*brooklet*	*vein*
ÉG	*sky*	*burn*
⋆ DOB	*drum*	*toss*
		(to throw to the daughter)
		(to waft a kiss)

[1] *After a Magyar folkloric curative incantation for healing wounds (Hungarian Folk Beliefs, Tekla Dömötör).*

REDUCED TO SHOES, A BLOUSE, AND A JAR

Joshua C. Gaines & Ben Clark

under two feet of dirt. Found some bone
fragments too, Ed tells me, my foot down
on the first stair. The sun through the kitchen
window falls on the stairs, reflects into the cellar,
creates a square of light on the dirt floor. At the edge
of the light you can see her bare toes, testing
the light, facing the stairs, waiting. I step back up,
turn away, ask Ed, What was in the jar?

Don't know, he says. Coulda been anything.
The label said, *Use For Consumption.*
I imagine dying like that.

Does she ever come upstairs, I ask.
No, she has to stay touching the dirt.

How do you know that's what keeps her
down there? I don't, he says, but just in case
we always kept those stairs clean.

JOSHUA C. GAINES

In Conversation

Sara Moore Wagner: I'm intrigued by the way this poem plays with narrative. There's a story here, but also it's more focused on a feeling of dread. It feels like history. How do you think a poem functions differently than, say, a short story?

Joshua C. Gaines: My poems have always leaned toward the narrative side, and in my head I do see them as tiny stories. I think the difference between the two for me is in what isn't said. Like Alfred Hitchcock (who was just amazing at this) breaking away to sound and suggestion, the space in poems allows an openness into the metaphorical and into the reader's thoughts. In a completely unfair generalization, poems tend to ask more questions and short stories tend to answer more questions. The "what is it" of poems is often open-ended, and that expanse at the end of a line is crazy exciting to me.

SMW: Is there anything you want our readers to know about the story underneath this poem? What inspired it?

JCG: This poem is from a collection of poems that is a ghost story, and a "history" of the farm of Art Farm in Nebraska. The entire collection was written with a fellow writer, and very dear friend, Ben Clark, who also writes mostly narrative poetry. So, when I say "my" in all this, I'm really talking about our amalgamation of voices that created these particular poems.

On the farm there are multiple structures in a constant state of renewal and decay. Throughout the summer people live and work there, rebuilding and creating. In the winter the weather takes over. The raccoons take over. The ghosts come back. Sometime in the early 2000s, what would become the Floating Barn was being moved from another farm on huge steel I-beams. When they reached an Art Farm field, the barn started to shift. Instead of risking further damage they stopped moving and built a trailer-high post foundation beneath the I-beams and reinforced the damaged areas. The building seemed to float there above the prairie, dropping shingles and wall sections until it finally collapsed in a 2018 winter storm.

Another structure is a farmhouse built around 1910, and I lived in that house with the mice and mosquitos and attic raccoons for two months. Tucked around the corner of the dilapidated kitchen is a door, and through the door is a staircase leading into darkness. Near sunset, when the sun is low, light through a cobwebbed window spills down the stairs and onto the dirt floor, and if you stare long enough you can almost see a shape waiting just out of the edge of the light. One day I was told, "We don't go down there."

SMW: I am drawn to the way you use spacing here, how that enhances the horror elements. What led you to choose extra spacing here?

JCG: We used them in two ways really. (And, to be fair, Ben typically found the best break for most lines.) Line breaks direct a possible end of a thought in a way standard sentence structure just doesn't allow, especially when that thought can stand alone and also be morphed by the continuation of the "sentence" in the following line. Ben and I often experiment with that same idea of sentence fluidity by writing contrapuntal poems. Those consist of two poems with an equal number of lines, side by side. Each of the poems work as their own poem, but if you read across from one poem to the next they form a new third poem that expands on the theme.

The other use was exactly as you said, enhancing horror elements. The blank space in the middle of a longer thought creates suspense, like ending a chapter on a cliffhanger. It also gives the briefest of moments where readers might guess what's coming before the next line shows them. Or in the absence of something concrete to look at, (when A. Hitchcock breaks away to sound and suggestion) we're given the terrifying space to picture ourselves looking up from the bottom of the stairs.

SMW: To me, this poem is about the ways women are kept down by history and false narratives. What would you like your readers to take away?

JCG: Oh, definitely this. What you see in this poem is beautiful. So, in the middle of writing this collection on the farm, the 2016 election happened. Aspects of that election worked its way into many of the pieces, some on purpose, and some not. It was one of those historical dividing lines, before/after, like background radiation after we tested atomic weapons. Nearly everything that has come after has, in some significant way, been marked by that day, including these poems.

EROSION

Audrey Towns

The river near our home claims the
soft parts of the land's body each year.

It burrows in
until the base of our beliefs breaks,
comes closer and closer
to dropping in its wet veins.

My father stacks the fallen trees
          starting to be swept away, to redirect the flow,

trees I sang under with my sisters
while the Roosevelt elk scattered
          through the thicket, the points of their
antlers branching like too close roadways,
so sure of their direction, and us

following their lead, rippling
like the rivers.

The paths are not so clear now.
The stacked moments, now
only timber.
They slow the pace,
but our lungs will fill and our
bodies will widen, diluted
with the city dams.

In the evenings, our family breaks
wood and cooks dinner
under a sky so bright that we wonder why
we even bother with the land. We dream

about dropping off the clouds
and into stellar drifts where winds carry
sails into a white freckled forever,

but the dark edges call us back
to the growing green ground, where if we squint
just right, the trees are as binding
as the stars,
like the bridge to Nana's kitchen
where sockeyes simmer

next to geoduck steam and heavy cream, unless
they slip through the season's cycles again,
their bassinet benthos bare
in the warming water.
But even the stars exhale
drips
of light that stain

soil with the same finish
that colors the rushing rivers
of our backyard, the savory

wild whites of inevitability

that seemed so distant

they couldn't possibly pass through
our eyes or our world
or our windows,
where the tinned salmon grounds
are rising, the rich

taste of traditions rushing out
to sea, the last of us
searching for higher ground,
sucking in the sea change,

forgetting how to ripple.

AUDREY TOWNS
In Conversation

Sara Moore Wagner: I really appreciate the pull back-and-forth between personal and environmental concerns here. It reminds me that the history of people is the history of the land. Is this something you were thinking about with this poem?

Audrey Towns: Yes, it is a recurring theme in much of my work. After all, the environment is not only shaped by us; it shapes us as well. My stepmother and brother's family own land near the Quinault Rainforest, where I've spent time engaging in the wonderful traditions they share. Many of these traditions involve the river. Recently, I returned and was shocked by how much of the river had eaten away at the land. River erosion has always been an issue, but seeing it so extreme evoked feelings of loss. I don't know their views on environmental issues, but when I researched river erosion and its impact on the area, including the Native American reservations, it inspired this poem.

SMW: How do environmental poems factor into your work in general? Are there poets who write ecopoetry you would recommend?

AT: Many of my poems explore themes of environmental concerns, human and nonhuman connections, and deconstructing the nature/culture binary. Even my simpler, more nostalgic poems attempt to address how we respond to these issues. In my more recent work, I've explored how information overload affects our ability and desire to act on environmental concerns. For ecopoetry, I recommend reading Jorie Graham, Juliana Spahr, and Di Brandt. However, I also suggest reading any poetry that encourages humans to engage with our environment and the nonhuman lives we share it with. As John Shoptaw writes, "...ecopoetry doesn't supplant nature poetry but enlarges it."

SMW: The ending of this poem is so striking. How do you know when to end a poem?

AT: Thank you for the compliment. Sometimes, I have an ending in mind before I even start a poem. Usually, though, I think of an ending about halfway through, and then it becomes a matter of working toward that conclusion. Occasionally, I realize I should have ended it a line or two earlier, but in this case, the ending came very naturally. I knew I wanted to contrast the idea of humans feeling like part of nature (rippling) with the sense of losing that connection (forgetting how to ripple). Using "ripple" as the comparison stemmed from the poem's central force—the river.

THE ORACLE OF SANTA MONICA PIER

Maranda Greenwood

1.

Sitting just beyond The Playland Arcade glowing that come-for-a-swim supernatural blue is Zoltar, that jewel-eyed turbaned charlatan who always strikes it right every time we meet. The first time we met here, he warned me that I would stand in the same spot time and time again, until I could recognize what I came for. His crystal ball blinks green, his mechanical hands wave over it. He commands me to listen closely, the speakers sizzle. I lean closer. The same message as last time—*Still standing in the same place I see.* The yellow ticket tears from the metal slot.

2.

You have been holding onto the idea of something or someone who no longer serves you at this time. Heed my advice dear one: as soon as you let go, the path reveals itself. This is my religion and Santa Monica Pier is my Church. This is where I come to put all the losses to rest. The not being able to make friends, the regret of not having said enough, the humiliation of having said too much. Spending too much time in the company of people who make you feel alone. How I held eye contact and convinced my grandmother it would be ok, when I knew it wouldn't. When does a white lie lose its light and become a shade of who you are?

3.

The crowd is a river split in half
and flowing in opposite
directions. All elbows and arms
like pinball flippers changing your course.
Everybody zig-zags, laughing
and camera clicking like neon
and nighttime and the
glitter in the shoreline
could escape them.
The Ferris Wheel bulbs
tint the ocean nebula colors.
Sea breeze pulls cotton
candy from sticky fingers,
someone wins the water
pistol race and there—

against the ocean rail, a street performer open-case plays her catalogue of B Side
heartbreaks. I stand at the center of it, the 105-year-old boards splintered and
uneven crunching beneath my thinning soles. I find the strength to keep going.

This place moves like the bridge
of a song. it makes you feel like
you're almost somewhere.

MARANDA GREENWOOD

In Conversation

Sara Moore Wagner: What's so interesting is that I was JUST at Santa Monica Pier before I read your poem, and I was struck by how completely you captured this weird place! What is your experience with Santa Monica pier?

Maranda Greenwood: Santa Monica had always been sort of a mythical place for me growing up. I'm from New England, where at least half the year is a frozen overcast that makes you wish you were anywhere but. Well, at least for me that's how it's always been. I grew up on TV shows that took place in California, and I gravitated toward beach movies. I wanted to live there because the environment feels like a reset. No matter what has gone on in your life, standing in 75 degrees in front of the ocean, specifically a place like Santa Monica, it feels hopeful. People gather at places like the pier because they are hopeful. When I finally went there for the first time, it was exactly what I thought it would be, a place that feels like a reset, where you put everything down.

SMW: I love how you capture the place, but the poem moves beyond snapshot into pure feeling. What advice do you have for capturing place in a poem?

MG: My process for capturing place starts with research. It's either a deep dive on the total history of a place or a specific event that happened there. Depends on what your project is. Then I pluck a piece of that history out that resonates with me, I tie that to how I feel about it, I kind of sew it to my own moment. Delivering lines with the weight of what came before you is powerful. This would have been impossible to write had I not actually gone there. I always recommend visiting the place and while you're there, run through the senses. I write heavy narrative; a snapshot isn't enough for me in any style of writing. If the place is the star, then what does it say? A snapshot can be beautiful but it's not alive, so make it move. The answer to making it move is why it moves you.

SMW: How should a poem approach place differently than something like a story or essay?

MG: I do the same research, location visits, and exercises for short stories, poems, essays, etc. This poem is a part of a series, the poem recurs with new advice throughout a longer storyline with the intent of feeling like an old friend showing up just in time to help you make decisions. I like linear projects, where all of the poems are telling one story. So, I like to map them out before I start. Place is always a character to me that represents more than just an image or snapshot. I can only answer this question for myself, there are no real rules in writing, it's whatever works for you and resonates with the reader. What works for me is story first, the gymnastics of creating the environment second, parlor tricks last.

SMW: Tell us about your sections. How do you make the choice to section a poem vs using stanza breaks?

MG: The story dictates the choice of section breaks. Time jumps, following another character and creating a sense of hyper-focus on a specific detail all warrant section breaks for me. This poem's format is a visual walk down the pier. I get two Zoltar tickets when I visit Santa Monica. The first ticket I apply to my life and upcoming choices, the second ticket I apply to my love life. So, sections 1 & 2 are formatted to look like Zoltar tickets. The italicized lines are directly from his speech before the ticket comes out and parts of what the tickets say. Section 3 is wandering the pier afterwards, and getting to show that movement in the lines was a fun way to amplify that feeling of walking through a carnival setting. At the end of the pier, there are staircases on your left and right that lead you to the end of the pier to look over the Pacific. Every year there is always a street performer here, whose song selection only ever seems to reinforce Zoltar's advice.

LIKE MAGIC

Kristin Gifford

She insisted there must be a deer—
picked at the blood crust on his red

flannel until she had white hairs, trekked
to the scene dusk after dusk, parting

thick curtains of mosquitos with faith
and flashlight, hoping to conjure

a foreleg, a torn and weeping
flank. Like the crumpled hull

of her husband, the ATV sagged, shocks
and exhaust blasted off on impact.

In the dim light of the garage, she wiped
the long-cooled engine with white

cloth, sniffed for singed fur, and when
her heel tripped the bottle behind the gas

can like a live wire, she hauled Jack
Daniels up by his neck, looked clear

through. Gentle, so gentle, she bedded
him back down in oil rags, returned to us

with light and cloven step.

KRISTIN GIFFORD
In Conversation

Sara Moore Wagner: I love how this poem starts in so much unsurety—is there a deer? Who is she? It's disorienting, but made me want to keep reading. How did you come about that as a first line?

Kristin Gifford: First lines are such a process for me and often emerge later during the revision process from within the body of the poem itself. I give myself permission in the drafting process to write a really bad, didactic first line to jump start the poem.

I originally had something more expository here, and the poem was more focused on the events of a four-wheeler accident, but in the midst of a conversation about this poem with a fellow poet, I said, "She insisted it was a deer"—and my friend said, "There it is! That's the first line!" Everything was revised around creating a central "she" character, and creating narrative tension around her.

SMW: This poem captures so perfectly the exact "magical" (or delusional) thinking a partner of an alcoholic or addict does. It hit me right in the chest. Would you like to speak a little about that (and how easy or hard that was to capture in a poem)?

KG: It's so painful how alcoholism poisons an entire family. When I pulled the "she" to the forefront of this poem, I could begin to isolate details that create the loneliness caused by alcoholism. The trauma of alcoholism isn't so much in the major, dramatic events that might occur (like a four-wheeler crash), but within a lifetime of keeping a family system of denial in place. There's a dark and costly magic involved in keeping a lie for this long.

The small details began to open up fairly easily as I imagined this "she," and all the small actions she would take to tend to both an injured spouse and to the illness, the delusion—by how she would interact with the shirt fabric, the place next to the road, the machine, and then the bottle. These concrete details helped me ground the poem and pull back the curtain on the "magic."

SMW: The turn at the end of the poem (she IS the deer, in a way!) is astonishing. I am drawn to how much is unsaid, but is still perfectly clear. What advice do you have for our readers about what to leave out?

KG: Image! Image! Image! Let the image land! I often figure out exactly what I want to express in an ending by writing out a whole paragraph about what I want the poem to express or by having a conversation with another poet. Don't be afraid to write a bunch of really bad/okayish/great endings before you feel the right one emerge. Lately, I've been challenging myself to end my drafts five different ways.

Here are a couple of the endings I tried for this very poem:

> When she found/the empty Jack Daniels behind the gas/tank in the garage, she set it down soft/so soft even the concrete could ignore.
>
> No one was there/to pull anything more from the wreckage.

Neither of those endings really evoked the illusion/delusion being created by the "she" in the poem. I sat with the image of the garage in the twilight and a ghostly deer appeared in my mind, walking towards a house. I knew that by hinting back to the missing deer, there was a way to capture the fragility of the situation and of the "she" herself. I also trusted that readers would use the mystery to draw their own conclusions about what this imagery meant to them.

THE WATER ITSELF

Sarah Dravec

As much as it might want as much as it might
push the truth is that the edge of the water
for all it wants for all it wishes to touch
will never be worse than the water itself
and once I get to the water itself
for all I want I am bereft I suck the air
hard between each of my teeth because I know
the feeling before it comes I know
how much it is going to hurt when I get
to the water itself how am I supposed to look
down into the pebbles down into the mud
dancing swirls as it is touched by the current
down into the roots where grass can
find a way to somehow break through both earth
and water and harder still to look into
the eyes of the fish who scatter as if
to know well enough to know to be afraid
all of this wanting just on the edge
of the water and how am I supposed to inch
closer how am I supposed to disrupt the surface
when it is clear enough to know what I am
and how am I supposed to go in

SARAH DRAVEC

In Conversation

Sara Moore Wagner: What first drew me to this poem is that the form is genius-level organic—the way the words "touch the edge," the lack of punctuation, it all feels like water. How did this form come to you?

Sarah Dravec: Prose poetry brings me tremendous comfort as a form. Sometimes, I gravitate to it more naturally than I do writing in lines because the paragraph feels more arbitrary to me, at least as I'm starting to write, so I can allow the draft to flow more naturally. I owe a lot to my teachers—Mary Biddinger and Robert Miltner especially come to mind here—for helping me understand that a prose poem is a poem in a box, and the box contains its own reality, however chaotic it may be. This makes a great deal of sense to me when I'm trying to organize details and feelings with an often confessional style. Prose feels like a home, which made it easier for me to approach this particular poem, which is from a series I call the *session poems*—those I wrote during the first couple years of therapy. I tend to prefer the way prose poems fall naturally within the margins, allowing that arbitrary nature to come through—but as I worked through revisions for this poem, forcing the margins felt important to give each word a fraction more space, and bring forward the fear that drives the poem, perhaps forcing the reader to read even a bit more slowly to stay in that feeling longer.

SMW: Do you have advice for our readers about finding a form?

SD: Allow yourself to experiment. If a poem doesn't feel quite right in lines, remove your line breaks and see how it reads as a prose poem. Perhaps try couplets or otherwise manipulate your stanzas, if you're working with stanzas rather than a long, uninterrupted scroll of line breaks. This is a difficult one for me, but you may also try to explore the space on the page and physically stretch the poem out in some way. Once you consider the form as important as the words, it can be very helpful to have two (or more) versions of a poem side by side—

even the act of giving yourself options to react to will make it easier to decide which is stronger.

SMW: I also love how this poem rests in uncertainty. There's so much wisdom in the unknowing. It defies those poems where the poet is pretending to be a prophet. This, I find, especially happens in masculine "nature" poems (i.e. those transcendentalists). Are you pushing against that tradition here?

SD: This interpretation means a lot to me—the kindness of seeing the uncertainty of the poem as its power. I'm grateful for that. I had mentioned that this poem came out of the process of going to therapy. That process was one of great uncertainty, so in truth, I set out to record that experience and understand the emotions as I tried to hold onto them. The metaphor of traveling through the forest came naturally, so I found myself examining the trees and looking into the water as if they could give me the answers I was looking for. That exploration was important in arriving at the understanding that I could only find the answers by looking inward.

SMW: Is there anything you can tell our readers about how to invite in uncertainty?

SD: I can tell you it is difficult, but worth it. Uncertainty means discomfort, which we may naturally want to avoid—but it also means opportunity, whether to learn, understand, or feel more deeply. My therapist would recommend being curious, and remind me that uncertainty as an emotion isn't good or bad—it just is. This is important to remember when exploring something new that gives you an uncertain feeling. When facing uncertainty, you're not weak. You're showing yourself what you can do.

HORSE TERCETS

Ezra Dan Feldman

Our fear of never kissing
was the fear of green lunch apples
left in their lockers.

We blew off exams to ride the high river,
almost twisted under
in our heat. We liked to believe

we'd gallop where we feared.
You were only you
when you were wanting I liked

to believe; I liked to forget my own tongue
writhed in reluctance
at its unreluctance.
                    But haven't

we cupped flames in other states
than agony? One doesn't always crack
a tooth on a kiss.

We learned a seed
that's hard to learn: it's flesh
most lovers want.

We rode a horse that ate an apple,
that shied at the river however we dangled the reins.

EZRA DAN FELDMAN

In Conversation

Sara Moore Wagner: Your lines move through sense in such an interesting way. They are so tight and visual and force the reader to see things differently, in a James Tate-like way. This poem is so weird and romantic and sensual! Tell us a little more about how you approach language and sentences in a poem.

Ezra Dan Feldman: I love sentences, probably more than I love lines or line-breaks. When I'm writing in verse, I try to put the line-breaks in the service of a sentence's rhythm and in the service of the poem's developing meanings and half-meanings. I think of verse as living on those half-meanings, the ideas a reader anticipates at the end of a line that might not actually show up in the language that follows. Prose has a harder time inviting those half-meanings in.

SMW: I love the title, the tercets and the breaking of the form feel like a horse being led. How did this form come to this poem? How and when do you decide to break a form?

EDF: My notebook draft of this poem isn't in tercets, but I put it into tercets in my first typed revision, even before I titled it. Tercets seemed to suit the subject matter, because the poem's "we" is a dyad, but the poem is full of objects that appear as thirds: the green apples, the high river, even the speaker's tongue.

But I didn't choose to break the form until my very last revision, when I decided that a closing tercet was too neat. I adore the closing tercet in a good sestina, which compresses the permuted end-words of the sestets, but in this poem of tercets, I wanted to underscore the incompleteness of the poem's wishes and wants.

SMW: This really is a love poem. Do you have any love poems you love? With so many centuries of love poems, what do you think a love poem should be doing now?

EDF: I like lush love poems and I like spare ones. The first spare one to come to mind was Rae Armantrout's "Distribution" (The New Yorker, September 24, 2018), which begins, "You think category / isn't sexy, isn't / sex. Seems you're wrong." But when I reread it, I'm not sure how to convince anyone else to see it as a love poem. The first lush one to come to mind is Edna St. Vincent Millay's "Love is Not All": I adore how the poem sets us up with a confession that the speaker might, under the right circumstances, trade love away, and then concludes with a negation transmuted by the pressure of the lines above into affirmation after all: "I do not think I would,"

Love poems don't have to do anything different today than they ever did, but the task is a tall one: to persuade readers that their language is the only language of love—and that fluency looks like *this*.

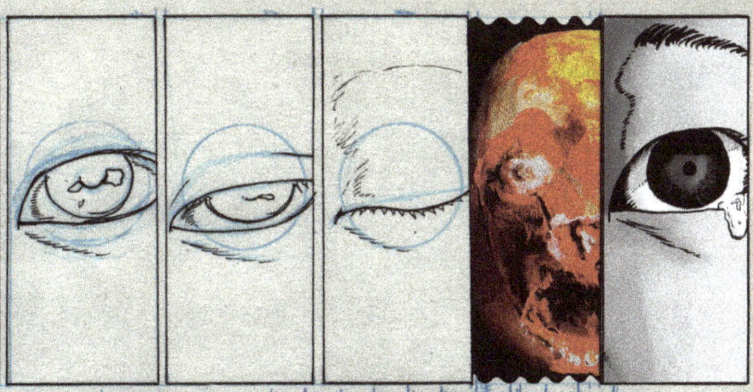

AUDIENCE PARTICIPATION

I NEED TO TELL YOU SOMETHING ABOUT HER – AND YOU'RE NOT GOING TO BELIEVE ME BUT YOU NEED TO TRY.
CAN YOU DO THAT FOR ME?
UH...
OKAY...
ANYTHING, DUDE.
I ALWAYS KNEW SHE WAS STRANGE.
WE ALL DID, RIGHT?
I JUST ASSUMED SHE WAS NEURODIVERGENT. MAYBE SHE WAS, BUT IT WASN'T THAT.
I JUST... NEVER FELT LIKE I COULD SEE HER IN HER ENTIRETY.
AND THEN ONE DAY I NOTICED SOMETHING...

SHE KISSED WITH HER EYES OPEN.
OKAY...
BUT, I MEAN- WE ALL DO THAT SOMETIMES.
HELL, YOU MUST HAVE HAD YOURS OPEN TO EVEN NOTICE.
I THOUGHT THAT TOO, BUT ONCE I NOTICED I COULDN'T STOP. SHE ONLY KISSED WITH THEM OPEN.
SO I ASKED HER ABOUT IT...
AND SHE SAID, AS IF IT WERE THE MOST NORMAL THING IN THE WORLD...
SO I CAN SEE YOUR FACE INSTEAD.
INSTEAD OF... WHAT?
EVERY TIME I CLOSE MY EYES...
I SEE A FACE.
IT'S BEEN THERE EVER SINCE I CAN REMEMBER.
LIKE...
IN YOUR MIND?

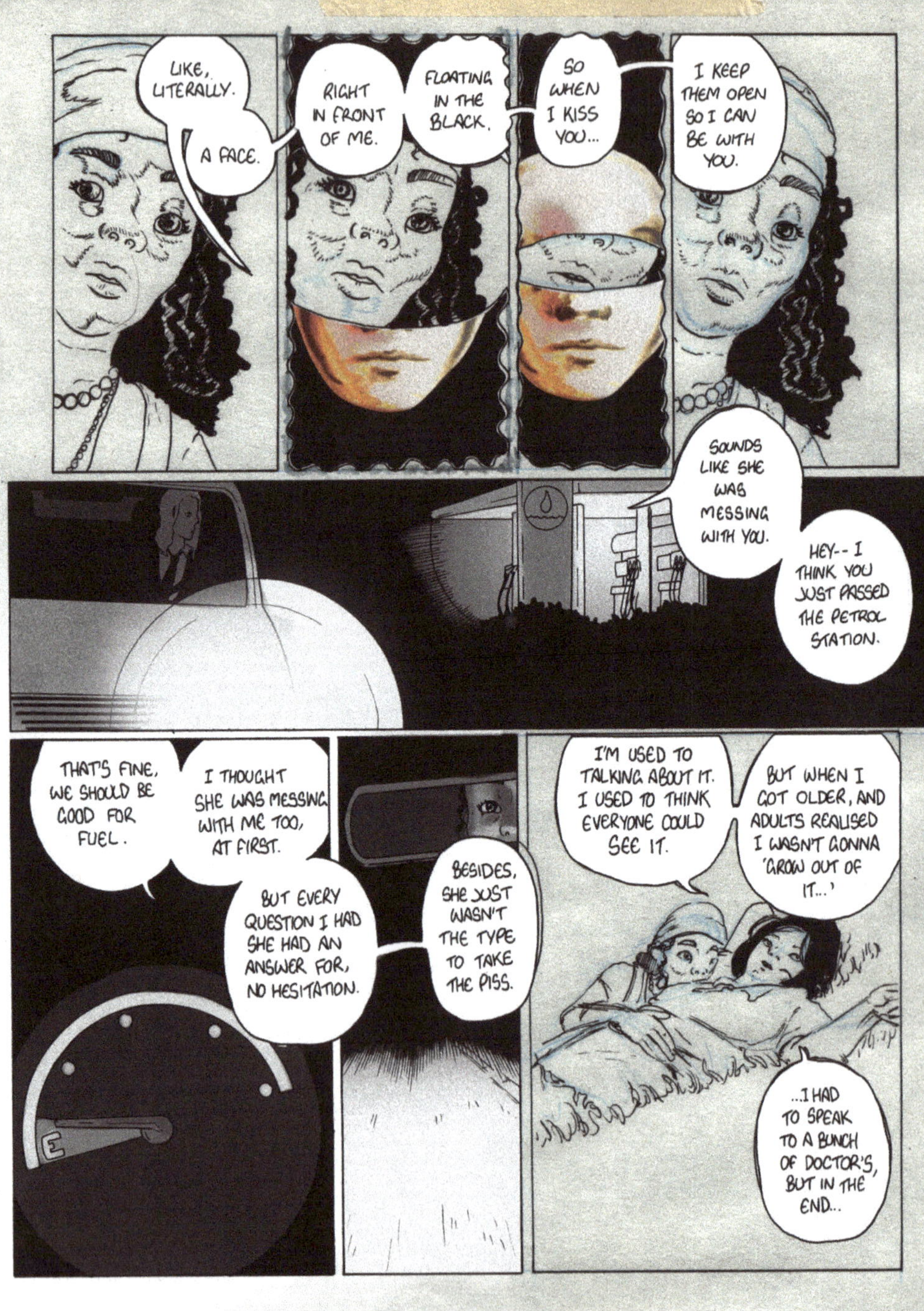
LIKE, LITERALLY.
A FACE.
RIGHT IN FRONT OF ME.
FLOATING IN THE BLACK.
SO WHEN I KISS YOU...
I KEEP THEM OPEN SO I CAN BE WITH YOU.
SOUNDS LIKE SHE WAS MESSING WITH YOU.
HEY-- I THINK YOU JUST PASSED THE PETROL STATION.
THAT'S FINE, WE SHOULD BE GOOD FOR FUEL.
I THOUGHT SHE WAS MESSING WITH ME TOO, AT FIRST.
BUT EVERY QUESTION I HAD SHE HAD AN ANSWER FOR, NO HESITATION.
BESIDES, SHE JUST WASN'T THE TYPE TO TAKE THE PISS.
I'M USED TO TALKING ABOUT IT. I USED TO THINK EVERYONE COULD SEE IT.
BUT WHEN I GOT OLDER, AND ADULTS REALISED I WASN'T GONNA 'GROW OUT OF IT...'
...I HAD TO SPEAK TO A BUNCH OF DOCTOR'S, BUT IN THE END...
E

SHE WASN'T SCHIZOPHRENIC OR SOMETHING?
SHE SAYS THE DOCTOR'S COULDN'T DECIDE ON A DIAGNOSIS.
AND AFTER A WEEK OF INTENSIVE GOOGLING, NEITHER COULD I. SURPRISE, SURPRISE.
TRUSTY GOOGLE.
WITH JUST A FEW CLICKS ANYONE CAN BE AN EXPERT.
HEY-- WHERE'S THE NEXT SERVICE STATION?
I TOLD YOU, WE'RE GOOD FOR FUEL.
IT'S NOT THAT...
I'M JUST GETTING KINDA HUNGRY.
OKAY.
...
SO... THE FACE, WHAT DOES IT LOOK LIKE?

KINDA BLAND.
LIKE A MILLION FACES BLURRED TOGETHER ...
...UNTIL IT LOOKS LIKE NO ONE.
WHAT'S IT DOING?
NOTHING.
IT SLEEPS DURING THE DAY.
BUT AT NIGHT...
IT TELLS ME STORIES.
WHAT KIND OF STORIES?
SOMETIMES SCARY, SOMETIMES FUNNY. SOMETIMES IT'S LIKE THE WORDS ARE FAMILIAR SOMEHOW, BUT THEY DON'T MAKE ANY SENSE...
THE FIRST STORY I CAN RECALL WAS ABOUT THIS PERSON LOST IN THE WOODS WITH THIS BLOODY KNIFE...
THEN THE KNIFE TURNS INTO A FROG...
AND IN ANOTHER, THERE'S THIS FLOATING VAMPIRIC HEAD.
OH! AND THERE'S THIS ONE I GET A LOT ABOUT THIS BOY— I THINK IT'S A BOY,— HE'S LOST IN THE WOODS TOO.
CAN YOU JUST... TALK TO IT?

I THINK IT KNOWS I'M THERE, BUT I CAN NEVER BE SURE.
IT'S ALMOST DARK...
WHEN DO THE STORIES START?

SO I WAITED WITH HER UNTIL THE SUN WENT DOWN COMPLETELY, AND ONCE IT HAD I ASKED HER TO TELL ME THE STORY.
ALONE.
ARE WE EVER TRULY ALONE?

IF A TREE FALLS AND NO ONES AROUND TO HEAR IT; DOES IT MAKE A SOUND? IF A LITTLE GIRL SCREAMS ALL ALONE, DOES SHE TOO NOT MAKE A SOUND?
THERE'S THIS GIRL... SHES ALL ALONE. THERE'S NO ELECTRICITY.
WE DISSOLVE IN FEAR, IT STRIPS OUR FLESHY EGO TO ITS BONES, LAYS BARE THE INADEQUACY OF OUR FRAIL FORM -- ARE YOU AFRAID?
SHE'S AFRAID.
WHAT IS THERE TO FEAR IN SOLITUDE, BUT THE SELF?
SHE THINKS SHE'S ALONE... BUT SHE'S NOT. SHE CAN'T SEE IT, BUT IT'S... THERE.
YOU CAN FLEE THE THINGS THAT GO BUMP IN THE NIGHT, BUT THERE'S ONLY ONE WAY TO ESCAPE THE TICKING OF YOUR MIND.
SHE'S GOING FOR THE STAIRS! SHE NEEDS TO GET TO HER ROOM BEFORE --
WE CLAW AGAINST THE DOOR, CLAMOURING TO GET OUT -- TO BE FREE OF INTERIORS. WE CRAVE THE BURNING OF THE SUN, TO WASH THE LONELY SHADOWS OFF OUR SKIN.
BUT THE STAIRS! THEY JUST KEEP GETTING LARGER. EACH STEP, IT DOUBLES AND DOUBLES. SHE --
WE HOWL FOR...
WAIT.
'WAIT.'
WHAT?
i'm still here

what do you want?

AND WE JUST SAT THERE LIKE THAT FOR A WHILE. I'D BARELY SEEN HER EMOTE BEFORE, BUT NOW...
...SHE WAS IN BITS. SHE JUST SAT THERE, EYES WIDE AND TEARS RUNNING DOWN HER CHEEKS.
EVERY TIME I THOUGHT SHE WAS OKAY, SHE'D BLINK...
...AND SCREAM.
WHAT... HAPPENED..?
...

AND THEN?
NOBODY KNOWS.
STOPPED ANSWERING HER PHONE.
STOPPED GOING TO WORK.
COMPLETELY CUT OFF CONTACT WITH EVERYONE.
SOMETIMES I WONDER IF SHE'S OKAY. I WONDER IF SHE STILL SEES THAT FACE.
BECAUSE I CAN STILL SEE HERS.
HEY WHAT ARE YOU—

PADRAIG CAMPBELL

In Conversation

James McNulty: Such a haunting comic! From the shifting art styles to the innovative paneling and beyond, there's so much to talk about here. Let's start at the beginning: how did you conceptualize this story?

Padraig Campbell: The basic premise for "Audience Participation" has been percolating in the back of my mind for about a decade, but every time I tried to figure out how to execute it I kept bumping into the same issue; I was telling and not showing. Eventually I figured maybe there was a way to show through telling. The comic is basically 90% talking heads and exposition—a narrative cardinal sin. I wanted to see if I could lay enough clues within the medium itself to signify that the exposition was hiding the character's true feelings and motivations, and get the reader to wonder about the relationship between truth and fiction.

JM: Talk to me about the drafting process. When did you decide to draw in multiple styles here? The flashback is more sketched, the frontstory looks more digitally drawn, and the face is in color. There's so much attention paid here to the craft decisions here; the pages even fluctuate between a paper background and a plain white one.

PC: I think sometimes it takes a writer or an artist a while to figure out what they're trying to communicate with a piece, but once you do the creative decisions really fall into place. There's three layers to the narrative, and so the presentation helps not only to differentiate these layers but allow them to inform each other. Do we trust the Driver's recollection less because it appears sketchy and unfinished? Or is there a greater degree of truth because it's so 'raw'? The character of the Face is made to look a lot more physically tangible than its cartoony co-stars, drawing attention to how simplified and overly designed they are.

JM: Can you also share with us what tools you used?

PC: I always draw and ink my comics by hand; if I could constantly undo and redo every line I would never finish anything. The grey tones are of course digital, and the face is a combination of ink wash drawings digitally overlaid over manipulated photographs of a real sculpture. I always sculpt my characters' heads so I have a reference to work from.

JM: I thought of Junji Ito and Connor Stechschulte while reading this. Which artists inspired "Audience Participation" most?

PC: I'm flattered my work would even momentarily make you think of two far superior artists.

I really love the 'strange' when it comes to storytelling, but especially when the strange speaks to something very human. I think the best example of this is something like David Lynch and Mark Frost's *Twin Peaks*, the way it has such an emphatically human core but it's hidden within something that seems so alien and other.

In a similar vein, I guess Gary Spencer Millidge's phenomenal self-published comic *Strangehaven* was something of an inspiration. Not just for the reasons above but because of the way in which it was made. Millidge seamlessly blends photographs and illustration at points, and he switches up the style of the comic a couple of times. It really got me thinking about how a small decision to change the presentation can really alter your perception of the same piece.

I also can't deny the influence Charles Burns has had on me, his work is so beautiful and brimming with this hauntingly uncanny aesthetic. I wish I was half the draughtsman he is.

JM: What does this comic mean to you personally?

PC: For me it's all about telling stories. I think the separation of truth from fiction isn't as black and white as people think; fiction always comes from a point of truth.

JM: How would you describe your aesthetic?

PC: That's pretty tough because I still don't know if I have a consistent aesthetic. I love to work in black and white but have recently started experimenting more with colour. My work used to be very crosshatch-heavy, but I'm slowly easing up on the lines as I get more confident.

I'd love to be confident enough that every comic attempts something vastly different. I really love Liam Cobb's work for that.

JM: When did you create "Audience Participation"?

PC: I started this piece at the end of January 2024, after about a month of complete creative inactivity. I work a full-time job with long days and low pay and was feeling pretty crappy overall. Naturally over the Christmas period my free time was devoted to family and friends, so I was unable to pick up a pencil for a lot longer than usual and so I was struggling to get back into the groove. I think "Audience Participation" was key in reigniting my comics work. It's a comic where I've really tried to make the most of its medium. I wanted to make something that could only work as a comic, something that got my brain working.

JM: When creating a comic, what are your biggest visual goals? What do you like to emphasize?

PC: I'm a big believer that any story or artwork should fully utilise its medium. If a comic could work just as well (or better) as a short story, or a play, or a film, then I don't believe you can justify making it the way you have. Of course you can adapt it to suit another medium, but the original must justify its medium. Like with my other work, I've tried to make the visuals of "Audience Participation" really demonstrate that this is something that can only work as a comic. The visuals here are essential in deriving any meaning from the story.

JM: What inspired this comic? Tell us more about the origins of its creation and whether any aspects of it were inspired by real life.

PC: The very basic idea for the premise—this disembodied face the Ex sees when she closes her eyes—was inspired by a trailer for an incredibly obscure film. The film is called *EGG*; it's by Yukihiko Tsutsumi, and from the trailer I could discern it was about this woman who sees an egg every time she closes her eyes, but one day it hatches and a monster emerges. The premise was so bonkers to me and really inspired a lot of ideas going forward. Because the film is so obscure I couldn't find any details about the plot, let alone watch it. I spent years and years imagining where that idea could go. When I finally saw the film just last year, I remember being very surprised; it's a lot more comedic than I thought it would be and didn't go where my ideas had taken it.

Thematically, "Audience Participation" is about stories. It's kind of inspired by people who will tell you these absolutely insane stories and pass them off as truth. I've never wanted to write these people's accounts off, even if you know they're not true in a literal sense. These people are still trying to communicate something to you, you've just got to work a little harder to figure out what.

JM: Tell us a little more about the drafting process. What was the hardest part of crafting this comic?

PC: With this piece I started with a script; it's something I don't always do—especially for shorter works. With comics, scripts can be handy, but you run the risk of putting the script first when you come to drawing it. A script is a blueprint more than anything and will always need to be adapted to better suit its medium. For me that was the hardest part. You can be really set on the pacing of dialogue or the build-up to a certain line but you can't be precious about anything when adapting that. It's a comic first and foremost, and whilst it's very dialogue heavy it'd be silly to have the pictures play second fiddle just for the sake of preserving some dialogue I was pleased with.

JM: How do you outline or draft your comics?

PC: Depending on what kind of story I'm telling I might start with a script, but it really depends. If it's very thematically or dialogue heavy I definitely will, just to figure things out. Otherwise I'll start with idea generation. I come up with most of my ideas daydreaming, but I won't do anything with them until they've gestated long enough to become a story.

I start by thumbnailing the pages; thumbnails are like these very crude diagrams for panel layout and composition. They're so crude sometimes I'll look at them later on completely mystified as to what I was trying to draw. Once I'm happy I'll start with the pencils. I do these full-sized because I'll lightbox it for the inks. This is where the magic really happens. Working full-size, you'll realise that some compositions become too cramped—or perhaps you've got more space than you realise—and you'll end up ignoring your thumbnails because you've figured out a better use of space.

Because the pencils are so messy, I then essentially trace the drawings using a lightbox. Inking is the last chance I take to change things; even at this stage you can figure out more interesting ways to present the images or depict the characters. Once I've scanned the inked pages I try to only correct smudges or really terrible linework, I don't draw digitally because I know I'd spend hours and hours undoing and redoing a single line and I don't have the time for that. I will colour and tone comics digitally though, as it allows for greater experimentation.

JM: Transitioning from creating artwork to fully-fledged comics can often feel daunting for artists. Do you have any tips for aspiring comic writers? What were things you wish you would have known when you were starting out?

PC: You have to learn to work a lot differently. Stand-alone artworks have to stand out, but with comics there's a little more room to hide because the images are designed to be looked over for as long as it takes the reader to draw the necessary information to move onto the next panels. Single artworks are designed to be poured over and analysed. I'm not saying you should be a hack when it comes to comics—craft is so important—but you need to learn when to let a drawing go and move onto the next.

Benji Nate once said that a page of comics only needs to have one good panel, and I think that can be a helpful way of looking at things. If you're proud of one panel then you can tell yourself the page is fine.

I think that's a pretty good piece of advice. Your catalogue of work will show your growth. If you're not happy with something, then work at it by all means, but just know that the next thing will always be better than what you're working on now, so it's okay to let something go even if you know it could be better.

JM: What piece of comic-making advice has helped you?

PC: I can't remember where I heard this piece of advice, but it's so important to work on shorter stuff before you tackle anything big. I wrote this off for a really long time. I was working on a graphic novel for about two and a half years but recently decided to scrap it and start again. It was only once I took some time off from it to work on some shorter pieces that my growth as an artist began to accelerate. Shorter pieces allow for greater exploration and experimentation which is so important for an artist. I've been making comics since my teens, but so much of it was unfinished; I thought that just because I've been drawing comics for so long I was ready to do a graphic novel. You need to make stuff you can finish to learn all the lessons that piece can teach you.

My graphic novel isn't going anywhere; the ideas have only grown stronger because of my shorter works. I know that when I finally restart that project I will be in a better place to do it justice.

JM: If you had to narrow it down, who would you say are your three biggest influences?

PC: Junji Ito was a massive source of inspiration growing up; my sister had the *Dark Horse Museum of Terror* series and *Uzumaki*, and I remember being awestruck by his work. I loved just how out there all his ideas were, and how intricate the line work was. I remember just being blown away by how simple yet intricate it was. How could a pen and ink drawing be so rich? I wish *Viz* had been churning out his back catalogue then like they're doing now.

More recently I've been really taken in by Hayashi Seiichi. I was first introduced to him by *Breakdown Press*'s *Red Red Rock*; at first I was really turned off by it, but the more I read, the more I fell in love. Hayashi's work is, simply put, poetry in pictures. If you think that comics can't be art, then you haven't read any Hayashi Seiichi. I don't think any of his translated work is still in print besides *Red Colored Elegy*, which I genuinely think is a crime.

Thomas Ott's comics I find incredibly exciting. He really is the master of short, self-contained narratives, and he does it without any dialogue or captions. His work is always so twisted, they always make me feel like I'm privy to something I shouldn't be. His style is also so uniquely his; I'd love to try my hand at scratchboard in the future.

JM: Where can our readers find more of your work? Have you been published before?

PC: I've got an Instagram, you can find me at 'upwards.incursion'. If you want to keep up with what I'm working on that's the best way to do it. I've only self-published before, twice actually. Both had extremely low print runs and only my most recent effort sold out. I'm pretty shy about publishing my comics, but I'm getting better at that. I'm working on a pretty lengthy collection right now, so if you want to know when it's ready definitely follow me on the 'gram.

JM: What are your own artistic goals for the future? Simply, what do you want to do next?

PC: So I'm working on an anthology right now; it's called *Upwards Incursion*. The comics are all very spooky and strange, a bit like "Audience Participation"—but also very different. They're all set in the grip of a summer heatwave and depict a plethora of characters finding themselves in a variety of unnatural scenarios.

Once I've wrapped on that, I'm going to reignite my graphic novel project. I was working on it for two and a half years before I scrapped it. It's a very personal story for me, and whilst I'm a firm believer in seeing things through and finishing them even if you don't think your skill set is where you'd like it to be, this project is my one exception. It's a ghost story and a family drama. It's probably the darkest thing I've ever worked on, and when it's finished I think it'll probably be the best thing I ever make.

JM: What drew you to *Driftwood Press*?

PC: What initially put me on to *Driftwood Press* was Ryan Holmberg. He posted an open call for the press on his Instagram story. Holmberg has never associated his name with anything short of great, so for me this was a pretty resounding endorsement.

NIGHT
TRAIN

22
SUPE

so
what did the psychic say?
hmmm
well
PSYCHIC

oh cool. That persons going to the psychic
mind your own buisness
I'm just curious
...
y'know what they say..
...about what happ
there
NYOOOM

he stopped moving
don't look
hey
what
what're you doing?
sitting
why
I'm tired
I mean
just thinking
but I'm getting up now

he's crying
Don't look
what did the psychic say?
oh
nothing

JADE MAR

In Conversation

James McNulty: From page one, it's clear that this story will play with perspectives; the cafeteria image in particular really gives a sort of off-kilter, almost fish-eye perspective that I think flags very early the incoming surrealism in this story. How do you typically make decisions on perspectives?

Jade Mar: I decide on which perspective to use for each panel based on...

1. How I see the story playing out in my mind.
2. Using a composition that will compliment the panel's intended mood.
3. By using film shot techniques such as establishing shot, medium, close up, etc.

My starting point is generally figuring out a way to establish a location that feels lived-in. When I was in high school, my friends and I would waste countless hours after school in McDonalds or various other establishments which encourage teenage loitering. The more specific an environment feels to me, the easier I am able to reiterate it through drawing. I want a reader to be able to hear peripheral conversations, overwhelmed employees yelling out orders, or the clattering of plastic utensils. If I do my job effectively, a suspension of disbelief is conveyed and you can feel like a ghost in a room eavesdropping on mundane conversation (with a touch of magic).

James McNulty: Despite its short length, there's plenty of innovative paneling happening here. I was particularly enthralled by the page featuring the psychic, which paces the surreal event perfectly. What does the drafting process look like for you, and how do you decide on paneling?

Jade Mar: The pages depicting the psychic were the meat of what I wanted to convey in this story. I tried to use depicted perspective in the panels as a way of creating visual metaphors on perspective.

The story is narrated through a third person omniscient perspective which creates tension between how we can imagine the protagonist must see. While the figure looks at a road only seeing tall grass, we, as the omniscient, may view the beginning, middle, and end of a journey.

James McNulty: What materials did you use to craft this?

Jade Mar: Sumi ink, micron 0.05 (I like thin pens), a pencil, and lots of patience.

James McNulty: On a personal level, what does this comic mean to you?

Jade Mar: I made this comic two or three years ago when I had just moved to New York and was starting a new school. I've never been the most talkative person and was incredibly frustrated with myself for not being able to effectively communicate in class. Years before this I had gone through numerous stressors and was trying to acclimate to the new environment. My therapist at the time would often say I would oscillate between past and present. This was my cathartic diary entry driven by a desire to communicate telepathically. I would think if only I could communicate instantaneously, life would be better. Talking takes too much time and patience.

James McNulty: This comic felt like a mash up of many phenomenal cartoonists, which came together to craft a surreal style all your own. Taiyo Matsumoto & Freddy Carrasco's linework, Connor Stechschulte's horror, Mat Brinkman's heavy markers & character models; I'd be curious if you've read any of these cartoonists. What artists or works of art most inspired this comic?

Jade Mar: The only asset my family has is our comic book collection. Growing up my dad would tell me about the extensive lore within the DC or Marvel universes. I loved hearing the stories and mythology and always wanted to invent my own. From the moment I started reading until now, I have devoured any comic book I could. In elementary school, I would go to the library religiously and read any manga they had.

Also I've studied painting for the last ten years and Martin Wong is one of my favorites! The environments within his images feel like perpetual dusk.

Dave McKean was an especially influential comic artist for me (along with anyone else putting stuff out during Vertigo's golden age). I adore how he pushes the boundaries of comic art by making every panel different and constantly switching his mediums, especially in *Arkham Asylum*. Bill Sienkiewicz too.

Also, I love any shojo manga as long as it's not complete trash. Actually, I take that back. I love shojo trash too—but not shonen.

James McNulty: What are you working on next?

Jade Mar: I just put out the first issue of an ongoing series called *Welcome to the Butterfly Effect*. It's available on the *Domino Books* website. I'm also making a short film.

Comics by Johnny Damm
With text by Theodore Roosevelt

This Park...
is the property of Uncle Sam
and therefore of all of us.

I don't go so far as to think
that the only good Indian is the dead Indian,
but I believe
nine out of every ten are.

[This Park] must be kept

for the benefit and enjoyment of

all of us all.

It is of incalculable importance

that America, Australia, and Siberia

pass out of the hands of their red,

black and yellow

aboriginal owners and become

the heritage of the dominant world races.

[T]his park
is to be preserved
as a beautiful natural playground.

Lower Falls from Artist Point.
Grand Cañon of the Yellowstone

Historic Entrance to Mammoth Cave, Ky.
9A-H2396

CRYSTAL
CHAPEL

Text by Theodore Roosevelt, taken from a 1903 speech at the ceremonial “Laying of the Cornerstone of the Gateway to Yellowstone National Park,” an 1886 speech, and the 1889 book *The Winning of the West*.

JOHNNY DAMM

In Conversation

James McNulty: Let's open by talking about the genre: collage comics! This isn't a very popular genre, so I'm curious who you took inspiration from & why you were drawn to this genre in particular.

Johnny Damm: Sure, thanks for the question. There's a long history of collage in U.S. comics. Probably most famously, Jack Kirby sporadically incorporated collage into his Marvel and DC comics—combining superheroes with magazine cut-ups to create these trippy pop landscapes that I love. I'd also point to the artist Jess, who in the 1950s, collaged old Dick Tracy comics into a new comic strip he called *Tricky Cad*, alongside other great collage work. Siglio put out a collection of Jess's work that I highly recommend.

As to why I began making comics this way, I suppose it simply started with looking for a visual approach that I could be satisfied with. Like most comic fans, when I pick up a comic book or graphic novel, I make an immediate snap judgement based on the art. I'm probably not going to read any text if I'm not first compelled in some way by the physical appearance of the page. So when I began to make comics, I first experimented with collage because I was looking for a visual style that would cause me to stop and read if I came across it at a comic store.

But the other crucial element, I guess, is that I also came to comics from a poetics background, and I've always been particularly drawn to constraint-based work—setting rigid rules for how a piece is made as part of the process. So I typically start a project by choosing what elements I want to make the comics out of. The choice of collage elements are my constraint. In the case of this comic, I started out with a simple idea: I wanted to make horror comics out postcards.

JM: The text in this is a part of the collage as well. Can you delve into the quoted speech here?

JD: To answer that, I think I should probably go back to why I was drawn to postcards in the first place. I started making these postcard comics—what I later called *tourism horror comics*—during the lock-down phase of the first Covid wave, when we were first confronting mass death and having a humans-as-contagion moment. Travel was impossible. So, there was something about the old-fashioned tradition of sending postcards while on vacation that felt a bit sinister to me. Not to mention, there'd recently been news coverage of people breaking into Joshua Tree National Park and trashing it, tearing out Joshua trees with ATVs and things like that.

So I had these old postcards I'd gotten from a family's estate sale, and I discovered that most of the cards came from visits to national or state parks. The largest set of postcards was from Yellowstone National Park. So, I looked into the history of Yellowstone, and this brought me to Theodore Roosevelt, who is widely known as the U.S.'s "conservation president."

Underlying Roosevelt's notion of land conservation and, sadly, underlying the U.S. parks system is settler colonialism. A transfer of stolen indigenous land, around 86 million acres, forms the foundation of our national forest system, and much of this transformation of indigenous land into so-called "public land" was spearheaded by Roosevelt. His notion of conservation ties directly into the larger colonial project, and the quotes I use in this comic demonstrate, I think, the psychology and the horror underlying the U.S. parks system and the ongoing legacy of settler colonialism.

JM: You've added panel breaks on some of the pages, which I think sufficiently helps the collage images feel more like a comic. How did you decide where to place these panel borders?

JD: I have a very convoluted method of making comics. I scan old comic pages—in this case, I was using a comic book from the 1940s called *Planet Comics*—and then I print out these pages on my printer. With an x-acto knife, I cut out everything inside the panels. So what I'm left with is a page layout or grid, with all the panels empty. Then, using collage, I fill back in the panels. In this case, the rule I set for myself was that every page would be filled from a single postcard and elements (hands, in this case) taken from old horror comics.

In some cases, it worked best to use a single full-page panel for the layout. Other times, I was able to break up the postcard landscape using smaller panels. This was mainly determined by what worked best visually.

JM: This comic is part of a longer collection of collage comics, right? You mentioned your *tourism horror comics.* Please tell us about the longer collection. Is it similarly political in its thematic messaging?

JD: They are all made from old postcards which had belonged to a single family before I bought them at an estate sale. Unlike the ones here, the first comics I made from the postcards used the writing on the back of the cards. I took the quick, jotted notes between family members and made them into a particularly creepy series of horror comics which I called "Hello Betty." A chunk of that series was published by *The Offing* some years back.

The project as a whole, I think, serves to unsettle our ideas about tourism and that includes our relationship to parks and nature. That sounds pretty grim, I realize, but I also hope the comics might be a little funny.

JM: Where can our readers find more of your work? What are you working on next?

JD: I've published two full-length graphic novels, *The Science of Things Familiar* and *Failure Biographies,* which can be found at or requested from your local bookstore or library. More recently, I've been publishing minicomics, and I'm working on the third issue of an ongoing comic book series titled, *"I'm a Cop": Real-Life Horror Comics*. The series uses statements from U.S. police leaders to explore the horrors of policing. Hopefully, these comics are available at your local comic store, but in any case, I invite folks to find me on the internet.

CONTRIBUTORS

Charlie Watts, after an accidental career as an HR and communications consultant, returned to fiction writing in 2013. Since then, he's been fortunate to have stories appear in *The Chicago Quarterly Review, The Petigrew Review, Narrative*, and *CRAFT*, among others. His story, "Arrangements," won the 2015 Raymond Carver Short Story Award and was performed in a recent episode of the radio program, *Selected Shorts*. This spring, he walked 1,924 miles of the Appalachian Trail primarily as an excuse to visit coffee shops.

Danielle Barr is a full-time stay-at-home mom and sometime-writer. She is currently querying her first novel and lives in rural Appalachia with her husband and four young children.

Phoebe Phelps is a writer and professor based in Brooklyn, NY. She is working her way through watching all of the films of Robert de Niro.

Aziza Kasumov grew up in Ludwigshafen am Rhein, Germany, but has spent the past ten years of her life in the US, first in Los Angeles, then in New York. She studied international relations and journalism at the University of Southern California and worked as a reporter for news organizations on both sides of the Atlantic, including the *Financial Times* and *Frankfurter Allgemeine Zeitung*. She holds an MFA in fiction writing from Columbia University.

R. Hunter Whitworth lives in North Carolina with his wife and daughter, where he teaches and coaches JV Football. He holds an MFA from the University of Alaska Anchorage. His fiction has appeared, among other places, in *The Threepenny Review, Chicago Quarterly Review, The Saturday Evening Post*, and the *Cincinnati Review* as the winner of the Robert and Adele Schiff award for Fiction.

John Kaufmann is an attorney and mobile home park owner who lives in Southern New York State. His writing has been published in *Off Assignment, Pleiades, Channel Magazine, Ep;phany, The Journal of the Taxation of Financial Products, The Journal of Taxation of Investments*, and *Tax Notes.*

Sakae Manning, a Choctaw/Nisei two-spirit, centers storytelling on alliances and intersectionality amongst BIWOC communities. Their work lives in *The Tahoma Literary Review* (Pushcart nod), *Carve Magazine, Dryland Lit, Gathering, A WWS Anthology,* and *Blood Orange Review*. Manning is committed to creating inclusive and intersectional spaces for BIPOC and underrepresented writers. They facilitated strategy and implementation for the most recent Altadena Co-Poet Laureates and have co-produced events amplifying BIPOC LGBTQIA+ writers for AWP Seattle and LAMBDA Lit. As writer-in-residence at The Annenberg Community Beach House, they developed programs and community spaces for BIWOC writers. Manning is an AWP Writer-to-Writer Program alum, an Anaphora fellow, and serves on the board for the non-profit Women Who Submit.

Khalisa Rae is an award-winning author, activist, and storyteller. As a queer rights advocate and community builder, she seeks to uplift Black queer voices. She is the author of the poetry collection, *Ghost in a Black Girl's Throat* and the sold-out play production, *Seven Deadly Sins of Being a Woman.* An accomplished performer, journalist, and playwright, her writing has been featured in countless literary journals and magazines, including *Pinch, Salt Hill, Autumn House, Rumpus, Hypertext, PANK, Autumn House, Jezebel, Blavity,* and *NBC-BLK.* Her impactful work has received a Appalachian Arts and Entertainment Award, a Gwendolyn Brooks Prize, and multiple Pushcart nominations, among others. She is the founder of *Think in Ink Literary Collective,* and a co-founder of the Griot and Grey Owl Black Southern Writers Conference. Khalisa Rae's YA novel in verse, *Unlearning Eden,* is forthcoming.

Steven Pan is a first-generation immigrant currently residing in New York. His work is featured or is forthcoming in *The Southern Humanities Review, Poetry Northwest, The South Carolina Review, The National Poetry Review* and elsewhere. He is a former Fulbright Scholar.

Marina Kraiskaya is a Ukrainian-American writer and editor of the journal *Bicoastal Review.* She recently won the Markham Poetry Prize and *The Letter Review* Nonfiction Prize. Find her poetry and nonfiction in *Poetry International, The Rumpus, Southeast Review, Mississippi Review, The Los Angeles Review, Zone 3, The Shore, EcoTheo, Deep Wild, Petrichor, Leavings*, and more. She lives by the sea in San Diego.

Karen Sherk Chio (she/her) is an MFA candidate in poetry at the University of New Orleans, an associate poetry editor for *Bayou Magazine*, a full-time public health worker, a parent, and a spouse. Her work has been published by *Salamander, CALYX Journal, great weather for MEDIA, Thimble Literary Magazine,* and *SmokeLong Quarterly*, among others.

Russell Zintel lives in the Catskills with KT, his beloved wife, and their cat. He works as a chef, specializing in pasta. His poems have appeared or are forthcoming in *decomP, San Antonio Review, Pangyrus, Sledgehammer, Jupiter Review*, and more.

Adia Micah Muhammad is a writer and former English teacher from Clarksville, TN. Now pursuing an MFA at the University of Michigan, they are the winner of *The Pinch*'s 2022 Literary Award for Poetry as judged by Phillip B. Williams as well as a Pushcart Prize winner. They've received support from SAFTA's 2024 summer residency, and have work published or forthcoming in *HAD, fifth wheel press, Glass Mountain*, and elsewhere.

Beth Gordon is a poet, mother, and grandmother currently living in Asheville, North Carolina. She is the author of several chapbooks including *The Water Cycle* (*Variant Literature*), *How to Keep Things Alive* (*Split Rock Press*), and *Crone* (*Louisiana Literature*). Beth is Managing Editor of *Feral: A Journal of Poetry and Art*, Assistant Editor of *Animal Heart Press,* and Grandma of *Femme Salve Books.*

Luisa Caycedo-Kimura is a Colombian-born writer, translator, and educator. Her debut full-length poetry collection was selected as a winner of the Hillary Tham Capital Collection prize and is forthcoming by *The Word Works* in Spring 2025. Other honors include a Connecticut Office of the Arts Emerging Recognition Award, a John K. Walsh Residency Fellowship at the Anderson Center, an Adrienne Reiner Hochstadt Fellowship at Ragdale, and a Robert Pinsky Global Fellowship in Poetry. A three-time Pushcart Prize nominee and Best of the Net nominee, her poems appear or are forthcoming in *Four Way Review, Denver Quarterly, The Cincinnati Review, Shenandoah, Rattle, Mid-American Review, RHINO*, and elsewhere. She is an Editor of *Slapering Hol Press.*

C. Henry Smith is a poet from West Texas. He is the author of the chapbooks *Warren* (*Ghost City Press*) and *Twenty-Four Covers of a House on Fire* (forthcoming, *Finishing Line Press*), and his Pushcart and Best of the Net nominated work has appeared in *Colorado Review, DMQ Review, Psaltery & Lyre, LIT,* and others. He received his MFA at Oregon State University and is grateful for past residencies through Spring Creek Project and Chicago Art Department.

Robert Laidler is an assistant professor at Wayne State University in Detroit, Michigan, a graduate of the University of Michigan's Helen Zell Writing Program, and the author of a poetic libretto, *The Fallen Petals of Nameless Flowers*, which premiered at Chamber Music Detroit in 2022. Most recently he was a finalist for The 2023 National Poetry Series, and the Adrift Chapbook Contest. His poems can be found in *Missouri Review, Ilanot, Driftwood, Oxford*, and elsewhere.

Stefanie Kirby is the author of *Fruitful* (*Driftwood Press*, 2024), winner of the Adrift Chapbook Contest, and *Remainder*, forthcoming from *Bull City Press.* Her poetry has been included in *Best of the Net* and appears in *West Branch, phoebe, The Massachusetts Review, The Maine Review, The Cincinnati Review,* and elsewhere. She lives along Colorado's Front Range with her family.

Melinda Freudenberger graduated from The New School with their MFA in Poetry in 2020. Their work has appeared most recently in *Anomaly, Always Crashing magazine, Spectra Poets*, and *the New Delta Review.* They live in Brooklyn, NY.

Geoff Anderson is the founder of *diVERSES* dedicated to guiding poets towards creative and financial freedom. He is a Cave Canem and Callaloo fellow with work in journals like *Ninth Letter, Tar River,* and *Indiana Review.*

Katie Dorfman is a senior at the University of Michigan, studying Psychology and Creative Writing & Literature. Her work focuses on tracing familial pain through religion, food, family, and the body.

Staci Halt writes and teaches near Boston. Her work has appeared or is forthcoming in *Rattle, Salamander Magazine, The Los Angeles Review, Abraxas Review,* and others. She is a mom to six rad humans and a slew of doting cats.

Emilee Kinney hails from the small farm-town of Kenockee, Michigan, near one of the Great Lakes: Lake Huron. She received her MFA in poetry at SIU Carbondale and is currently pursuing her PhD at the University of Southern Mississippi. Her work has been published in *Passages North, West Trestle Review, Cider Press Review, SWWIM* and elsewhere.

Danielle Harms has been published in *Conjunctions, New Letters, Fourth Genre*, and *American Literary Review.* She is an Assistant Teaching Professor at Marquette University and holds a PhD from UW-Milwaukee. Her writing was listed at *Notable* in the *2023 Best American Essays*, she is the winner of an AWP Intro-Journals Award, and she was a staff scholar at the Bread Loaf Writers Conference.

Mackenzie Polonyi is a Pushcart-Prize-nominated Hungarian-American poet and the author of *POST-VOLCANIC FOLK TALES*, a winner of The National Poetry Series 2023, forthcoming by *Akashic Books* 2024. Her published work may be found or is forthcoming in *Barrelhouse Magazine, Crab Creek Review, Palette Poetry, Hayden's Ferry Review, Tupelo Press, Quarterly West,* where she was a finalist for their 2022 Poetry Contest, and elsewhere; furthermore, she was *A Public Space* 2023 Writing Fellowship finalist. Mackenzie is a Cornell University 2022 MFA Poetry Graduate, Lecturer, and 2021 Robert Chasen Memorial Poetry Prize winner.

Joshua C. Gaines ditched a promising military career to write books, run a profitless press, and build blanket forts with his daughter. He earned his writing MFA from The School of the Art Institute of Chicago and was a writer in residence at Art Farm Nebraska where he and his dear friend, and fellow poet, Ben Clark wrote their unpublished book, *After the Floating Barn.*

Joshua's work has been published by the U.K.'s *Dark Mountain, The Mayo Review,* and *Hobart*, and he is a current member of Chuck Palahniuk's writing workshop. He lives joyfully with his wife Anna, his daughter Lorien, and his basset hound Crumpet in Portland, Oregon where it rains way less than everyone pretends it does. This year his favorite flowers were zinnias.

Ben Clark currently lives in Minnesota and works as a city bus operator and editor for *Muzzle Magazine*. He is the author of two poetry collections: *if you turn around I will turn around* and *Reasons to Leave the Slaughter*.

Audrey Towns, a literature and composition instructor in the heart of Fort Worth, Texas, explores intersections of environmental, social, and political concerns. Her work is interested in the spaces between deconstructing binaries like human/nonhuman and culture/nature. She has published, or is forthcoming, in *Spellbinder Quarterly Literary and Arts Magazine, Black Fox Literary Magazine, The Amphibian Literary and Art Journal, Eunoia Review, Willawaw Journal, Cathexis Northwest Press,* and *Beyond Words Literary Journal,* among others.

Maranda Greenwood holds an MFA in Poetry from Arcadia University. Her work can be found in *Cathexis Northwest, White Stag, Sun Dog Literature, Crab Fat,* and other journals and anthologies. She was a recent prize winner of Vermont Poetry Society Poetry Contest. In her free time she collects Zoltar tickets.

Kristin Gifford is a writer living in Minneapolis. She taught English for a decade in public school and is working on her first collection of poetry.

Sarah Dravec is a graduate of the NEOMFA. Her chapbook, *I do not feel a mountain between my breasts,* was a finalist for *Driftwood Press*'s 2020 Adrift Chapbook Contest. She has been awarded a University and College Poetry Prize from the Academy of American Poets, and her work has appeared in *Bone Bouquet, Gold Wake Live, jubilat,* and others. Sarah lives in Northeast Ohio with her wife.

Ezra Dan Feldman teaches Science and Technology Studies and English at Williams College. He is the author of *Habitat of Stones* (*Tebot Bach*), and his poems have appeared in *RHINO, Crazyhorse, PANK, DIAGRAM,* and *Ger-*

trude, among other journals. His current projects include a book of sci-fi poetry (*On What Sun*) and several picture books for children.

Padraig Campbell is an artist and writer from the UK. He began drawing at a very young age, when he and his mother would produce sprawling fantasy landscapes on rolls of wallpaper. He started making comics in his early teens, alone in his bedroom instead of going to parties with his friends. Despite making comics since his teen years the majority of his work has never seen the light of day, having only self-published on two occasions, with extremely limited print runs. His work is frequently centred around themes of creation, identity, and queerness. He currently lives in Devon with his fiancé and their cat, Fergus.

Jade Mar is an artist. San Francisco Art Institute, Diego Rivera Gallery featured Jade Mar's work in the past.

Johnny Damm's current comic series, *"I'm a Cop": Real-Life Horror Comics*, has been featured in *The Washington Post, Boing Boing*, and *In These Times* and named in *The Comics Journal*'s best comics of the year in 2022 and 2023. Damm is also the author of the acclaimed graphic novels *Failure Biographies* and *The Science of Things Familiar*, both published by *The Operating System.* His comics, prose, and visual poetry have appeared in *Guernica, Poetry, The Offing*, and elsewhere. He lives in Santa Cruz, California.

Ío Wuerich is an Argentinian illustrator who lives in Spain. Ío loves plants, cats, and watches cartoons all day. They also like to draw with ink, watercolors, and gouache, and loves making small digital animations.

MORE TITLES FROM

DRIFTWOOD PRESS

poetry, fiction, & comics

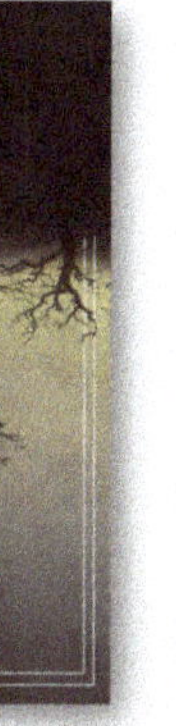

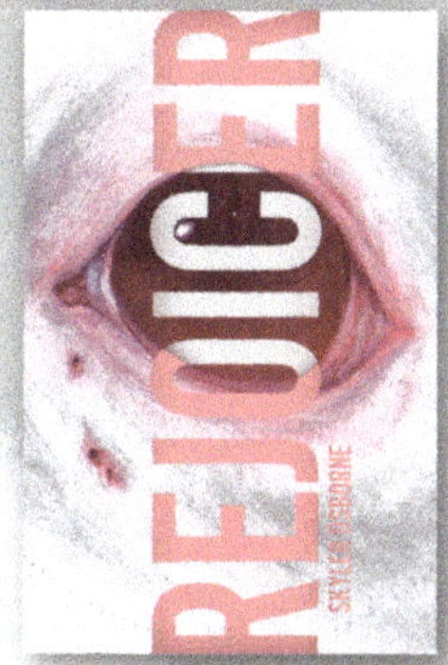

www.ingramcontent.com/pod-product-compliance
Lightning Source LLC
Chambersburg PA
CBHW050440200726
48295CB00024B/744

* 9 7 8 1 9 4 9 0 6 5 3 6 7 *